Cinderella
AND THE
DUKE

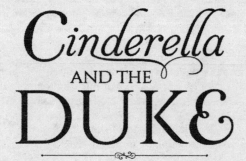

LYDIA DRAKE

Entangled Publishing, LLC
644 Shrewsbury Commons Ave., STE 181
Shrewsbury, PA 17361
Visit our website at www.entangledpublishing.com.

Amara is an imprint of Entangled Publishing, LLC.

Edited by Lydia Sharp and Liz Pelletier
Cover art and design by Bree Archer
Photography by Shirley Green
Stock art by PinkyWinky/shutterstock
Interior design by Toni Kerr

Print ISBN 978-1-64937-314-4
ebook ISBN 978-1-64937-315-1

Manufactured in the United States of America

First Edition January 2023

AMARA

For Rebecca, who stood by me through the darkest parts of my story.

CHAPTER ONE

Julia knelt upon the floor, making the final adjustments to her ball gown. She took the last pin from her mouth and stood, surveying her work with pride.

"There," she said. "You couldn't find better on Bond Street."

Her mother's gown might have been old, but elegant simplicity made it timeless. It was a periwinkle satin with delicate lace trim edging the sleeves and neckline. Julia was a few inches taller than her dear mamma had been, and a bit fuller in the bust, but she was a talented seamstress. After all, spinsters needed something to occupy their time. She'd spent the last week completing all the necessary alterations.

"I don't know why we couldn't get your gown fitted at Mrs. Maxwell's." Julia's stepsister, Susannah, entered the room with a book in hand. She shook her head, copper ringlets bouncing. "Mamma ordered my entire season's wardrobe from there."

"Ah, but your mother hopes you'll make a good match your debut year." Julia fluffed the bottom of her dress. "Whereas if she could force me to attend a ball without a stitch of clothing on, she'd be only too happy."

"Mamma wouldn't do that," Susannah said half-heartedly.

"No indeed." Julia lifted an eyebrow. "Even at my advanced age, wearing nothing in public might secure me a proposal or two."

"Julia!" Susannah laughed, sitting beside her on the sofa. "You can be quite scandalous."

"A touch of scandal is good for the blood." Julia took up an old pair of slippers that had also belonged to her mother. She slid a foot into one, hoping it would fit. Constance, her stepmother, would never dream of purchasing new ball slippers for Julia. "We must conserve our resources," she'd say with a fluttering handkerchief. "For dear Susannah's dowry." Meanwhile, Susannah's dowry was among the most substantial in London society. To put a dent in it, one would need to buy eighty pairs of solid gold shoes and half of Gloucestershire.

"Maybe if tonight goes well, Mamma would allow you to chaperone me at future events," Susannah said. Julia wrapped her stepsister in a quick embrace. Her father had married Constance when Julia was thirteen and Susannah four. After his death a mere year later, Susannah had been the best possible comfort. Having her as family was worth being tied to Constance. Mostly.

"Darling, if Constance weren't currently laid up with a chest cold, there'd be no question of my chaperoning you. While we're in London, she'll probably lock me in an attic trunk and allow me out only for small tea breaks."

Susannah sighed, but she couldn't deny the truth. Julia put on the other slipper, stood, and walked back and forth across the room a few times. Her shoes fit beautifully. Julia beamed—until the right heel wobbled. *Damn*. If only she were a talented amateur cobbler as well.

But if being allowed out in society meant wearing bricks, she'd gamely clop her way around the Weatherfords' Mayfair ballroom tonight. Julia had missed the past ten London Seasons, forced to stay behind in Kent.

"The only reason Constance allowed me to come to town for your first Season was because I'm quite in the prime of spinsterhood." Julia appreciated how the sunlight winked on the beaded toes of her slippers. Her mother's taste had been excellent. The thought gave Julia a quiet pang; if only she could remember her. "She knows you'll be the center of attention, and rightly so. Meanwhile, it's less likely I'll secure an offer of marriage than that someone will mistake me for a coat rack."

"Julia!"

"Well, I am quite tall, darling." Julia sighed as she took the slippers off. In a perfect world, her heels would be steady. But in a perfect world, her father would still be alive and dear Constance would have been fired out of a cannon long ago. "Tonight could be my first and last chance."

"To find love?" Susannah asked.

Julia's smile rarely faltered, and she fought against the impulse. "Love is asking far too much. But a distinguished widower with three thousand a year and one or two amusing jokes should be possible."

Despite being twenty-seven, perfectly ancient

in her stepmother's opinion, Julia still possessed a full head of golden hair, and eyes that had been described as cornflower blue. She had one nice dimple, a full lower lip, and an easy way with words and smiles. All she required now was a single opportunity to turn a man's head.

"You'll find the perfect match tonight." Susannah got up and embraced Julia. "A true prince."

"Or a slightly used duke. One must be sensible, after all."

Julia sighed when she heard the tinkling of a bell somewhere upstairs, and the tromping of obedient feet. The parlor door opened and Mrs. Stanley, the housekeeper, entered with an apologetic look.

"Beg pardon, Miss Julia. Her ladyship would like to see you."

"Does she require someone to pour her tea? Fluff her pillow?" Julia winked at Susannah. "Fan her with ostrich feathers?"

"Julia." Susannah stifled a giggle.

"Found a religion in her name and serve as high priestess?"

"I believe it's time for her medicine," Mrs. Stanley replied.

"So predictable when one is sick. I expected more originality." Julia left the other women and climbed the stairs, noting her father's portrait on the way. She blew a quick kiss to him as she passed down the hall to her stepmother's bedchamber.

Julia knocked and entered. The curtains were

half drawn, leaving the room in semi-darkness. Constance lay tucked beneath quilts, pillows fluffed behind her back. She wore a lace nightcap, and a small selection of ladies' magazines nested at the foot of her bed. A half-eaten box of marzipan fruit sat directly beside her. From the way she reclined against the cushions, eyes fluttering shut, one might've thought her afflicted with consumption or a rare tropical disease. She'd always been dramatic about infirmity. One time she'd developed a hangnail and summoned the doctor in a panic.

"Julia?" she croaked. "Are you there?"

"No, I left, but I'll return in a moment," Julia said.

Constance coughed.

"Humor is a bad quality in a woman. Come." She pointed at a bottle upon her bedside table. "Tend to me."

Tend to me. Words Julia had heard over and over since her early adolescence. She obeyed, taking up the bottle and a spoon, and sat beside Constance on the bed. Julia poured a dark, syrupy liquid and gave it to her stepmother. Lady Beaumont, as Constance became when she married Julia's father, had not been born to privilege. By all accounts she'd come from humble origins before marrying her first husband, a wealthy merchant, and then wedding a less-than-wealthy baronet after said merchant's death. Julia admired the pluck and resourcefulness Constance must have possessed to make such a climb.

Unfortunately, upon entering the aristocracy

Constance took the worst of their snobbish traits to heart. She looked down upon servants and tradespeople and performed the most fluttering, histrionic sorts of helplessness.

Julia's stepmother wanted a companion and nursemaid for the remainder of her life. Susannah would marry, and Julia would stay at home and tend to her. It had been Constance's design since Julia's father last drew breath. It was not, however, Julia's design. Indeed, she'd sketched an altogether different set of plans.

"Well, girl," Constance said after Julia handed her a glass of water. "I pray you are not wearing *that* to the Weatherford ball this evening."

"No, dear stepmother." Julia smiled sweetly. "I'd intended on sackcloth and ashes. They say it's the height of fashion this season."

Constance *hmph*ed. "I hope you won't joke in such a tasteless manner tonight. I don't want poor Susannah's chances crushed by a stray comment. The gentlemen may think madness runs in the family."

"I will loudly remind everyone I meet that Susannah and I don't share blood."

"Very well." Constance sounded mollified. She frowned again, as she did often. "Mrs. Stanley says you asked to have the pearls brought out."

"*My* pearls, you mean?" Julia had to be careful now. "The ones my mother left me?"

"I'm afraid they are out of the question," Constance said. "They are far too valuable to be worn at such a crowded event."

No, it's because they might look becoming upon

me, and then some man might notice. Julia had known Constance far too long. Her stepmother wanted her to argue about the pearls, at which point attending the ball would be potentially withheld as a punishment.

Of course, then Susannah would not be able to attend, either. Constance knew Julia had to chaperone; she just didn't like it. Therefore, she wanted to remind Julia that any good thing could be taken away.

"All right," Julia said, getting up. "I don't need the pearls. My gown and slippers will suffice." She was unable to stop the next tart reply. "Though I could roll about in the dirt a few times. That way, I wouldn't run the risk of appearing too presentable."

"Dear child." Constance *tsk*ed. "At *your* age, it will be a miracle if you're even noticed. Don't sulk, Julia. I am only looking after your well-being, as your dear father would have wished."

Julia knew that this was the precise opposite of what he would have wanted. She liked to imagine that her dear papa looked down from heaven, smiling at her before making a rude gesture in Constance's direction.

Papa would probably remind Julia that she had the Beaumont spirit. The Beaumont line stretched all the way back to the Conqueror, and King William himself was rumored to have called Julia's ancestor "the most exhausting man alive." Beaumonts never gave up.

"Very well, my lady. I shall endeavor to be appropriately dull and spiritless this evening."

"Good." Constance nodded in approval. "Fetch me the *Lady*, and you may go. Oh, and fluff my pillows," she added when Julia picked up the magazine.

Julia almost offered to fan Constance with ostrich feathers but worried her stepmother would take it seriously.

Julia left the chamber and descended the stairs with even greater determination than before. Tonight she would dance with a wobbly heel, laugh, and catch some gentleman's eye. She would be charming and witty. She would not turn away anyone, even a shaved walrus, so long as he was prepared to marry her.

As far as Constance was concerned, Julia's ending had already been written. However, a great revision was about to be made.

CHAPTER TWO

So far as duels went, this one had been almost pleasant.

Gregory Carter, Duke of Ashworth, returned the smoking pistol to his second with a smile.

"I feel we've settled our differences amicably," he said.

"Ashworth." Percy Randall, his second, best friend, and semi-constant drinking companion, glared as he put the pistol away. "You shot at each other."

"We both missed! Deliberately." Gregory looked back at Winston Falkes, his opponent. The dewy young man handed over his own gun and continued to glower in Gregory's general direction. "At least, *I* missed deliberately."

"You're lucky Falkes is a terrible shot." Percy groaned as he climbed into his saddle. Gregory did the same. They had to hurry; dueling was a gentleman's activity, but it was still bloody illegal. The respective parties cantered off as the dawn rose over Hampstead Heath.

"The whole thing was madness, anyway." Gregory's horse trotted alongside Percy's at a leisurely pace. "I never touched the man's wife."

"Then why did you agree to the duel?"

"I felt rather sorry for the poor sod." Gregory had returned to town for the Season a mere month ago. Already, the married ladies of the *ton* had set their collective cap at him, a rather racy cap with salacious notes tucked into the brim. Mrs. Falkes had been particularly aggressive, trying to seduce him behind a potted fern at the Duchess of Fenwick's gala. "His wife loathes him. Who knows, this dueling episode might make him more attractive to her."

"You're a true philanthropist," Percy drawled.

"What I am," Gregory said, "is tired. I'm two-and-thirty, and every married woman from Oxford Street to Hyde Park keeps trying to slip into my bed."

"Poor bastard." Percy chuckled. "My heart bleeds for you."

"Point is I'm well past the age for affairs. It's time to settle down."

"Marriage?" Percy asked.

Gregory shuddered. "I hate it when you joke in that obscene way."

"Come on, Ashworth. You're quite serious about never taking a duchess?"

"The second kindest thing I could do to any woman is not to marry her," he replied. "The first is unmentionable in the presence of innocent horses."

He was serious, though. His entire life, Gregory had been surrounded by matrimonial shipwrecks. Everywhere he looked in London, he saw women stranded on deserted islands with fashionable addresses, desperate to be rescued from their boorish husbands. Gregory knew that at least some of those unions had been love matches, and look how those had turned out. Then, of course, he only had to remember his own parents to put him off the idea of marriage entirely. "No, the best thing to do now is mellow into eventual middle age and attend brothels in peace."

He wished the *ton*'s matrons would take the hint. Though really, Gregory only had himself to blame for this sordid state of affairs. Over much of the past ten years, he'd solidified his reputation as London's most devastating rake. There was said to be a whole society, the Carter Club, which met for tea twice annually to recall their fondest memories and most pleasurable positions.

But as his notoriety had grown, so had the number of embittered husbands wanting their honor satisfied. Today's duel marked the second in four weeks.

"You're going to get yourself killed," Percy said, as if reading Gregory's mind. His friend was uncomfortably good at that. "Or end up on trial for murder."

"I'm sure the Carter Club has a betting pool on when precisely that'll happen," Gregory mused. "I wonder if I could lay my own wager. Though I'd be dead, which would make collecting the winnings difficult…"

"Must everything be a joke with you?" Percy appeared irritable.

"I only joke about serious things, Perce. You know that."

Percy sighed. "All I'll say is that marriage to a respectable lady is the surest way to save yourself from being dead in a field or at the end of a noose."

"I could also leave town and never return. Travel to foreign parts where no one knows my sterling reputation." Gregory considered for a moment. "The Canadian wilderness, perhaps. Though I'm told the bears are territorial."

"I don't know why I bother with you," Percy grumbled.

"Yes. It does suggest something rather questionable about your character." Gregory winked at his friend.

They said their goodbyes, agreeing to meet at their club later in the week, and Gregory finally turned for home. He arrived at his address in Grosvenor Square and entered Carter House to find his butler, Peele, waiting for him with a silver tray of calling cards.

"Already? It's barely midmorning." Gregory picked up one after the other. Mrs. Edmund Travers, Lady Cosgrove, the dowager Duchess of Gateshend. Half of these had been sprayed with scent. One woman had even planted a rouged kiss on the back of her card. At least none had left behind a lacy garter. Again.

"There was also a Mrs. Worthington, Your Grace." Peele gave a hefty sigh. "And a, er, Mr. Worthington arrived not ten minutes after her."

When married couples called on him in sequence, it was never a good sign.

"Perhaps His Grace might reconsider attending the ball this evening?" Peele furrowed his graying brow. He'd always been protective of Gregory, ever since the duke was a small boy in an empty house.

"Don't worry, Peele. The Weatherfords are old friends. I'll make a brief appearance before climbing over the garden wall and running away."

"An elegant solution, Your Grace." Peele bowed as Gregory went up the stairs, loosening his collar as he did. He hadn't been to bed last night. Not going to bed before dawn was something of a habit with him, though preparing for a duel was not the most enjoyable way to spend an evening. Perhaps he should be a bit more careful.

Ironic, wasn't it? Neither of his recent duels of honor had been merited. Gregory was living every man's dream: more women than he could handle were chasing him, desperate for a single night in his arms, yet he didn't want any of them. Since his return to England, he hadn't engaged in a single dalliance. Perhaps he really had grown tired, or older, or both. The wives of London, however, were anything but tired *or* discouraged. Mrs. Falkes had been so desperate for his attentions she'd nearly pulled them both into the punch bowl. Gregory couldn't blame the ladies, not really. After all, the tales of his prowess *were* warranted. Though he'd only tied a mistress up that one time, and now *everyone* yearned for the same treatment. He shook his head. That would teach him to experiment.

On the second floor landing, he paused beneath the family portrait. Gregory always thought or spoke the word *family* with a small amount of irony.

The three people in the painting looked as if they couldn't wait to be away from one another.

His father stood behind his mother, who was seated upon a chair with a small dog in her lap. Off to the side, like an afterthought, there was a small boy with dark hair and gray eyes. Gregory vividly remembered standing for that portrait. It was one of the handful of times he had been in the same room with both his parents. As soon as the portrait artist dismissed them, his father had called for a carriage and his mother had gone back upstairs, reminding Gregory's governess that she had no wish to be disturbed for any reason to do with the boy.

The boy.

Well, the boy was quite the man now, and he was determined never to make the same mistake his parents had. Gregory didn't avoid marriage purely for his own sake; he could never saddle any woman with the burden of a lifelong commitment to him. He could never be that cruel. If the thrill of affairs and romantic conquests had diminished, perhaps the time had come to retire to his estate at Lynton Park or resume his global travels. The life of a dukely recluse could suit him well.

But before all that, there was this ball. Gregory shambled toward his chamber, rubbing his eyes. First he'd get an hour or two of sleep, then he'd break his fast and prepare for tonight. He must look presentable, after all. Even exhausted rakes had appearances to maintain.

CHAPTER THREE

"You'd think these men had never seen a lady older than five-and-twenty before," Julia said. For the past three hours she'd been stuck on the sidelines, only able to watch the spectacle of the Weatherford ball. A shame, because she hadn't danced in ten years and particularly loved it. Her feet tapped in time with a waltz, her right heel wobbling away.

"All these men have the debutantes memorized," Lady Weatherford said. "Along with the size of their dowries."

"My first plan doesn't seem to be working." Julia sighed. "Time for my second strategy: knock some fellow on the head and place him in a bag."

"A most useful accessory for the London Season."

"The Husband Bag would net me a solid fortune indeed."

The women laughed. At least Julia had finally been able to spend time with her oldest friend. Laura Daldry, now the Viscountess Weatherford, had become one of London society's most esteemed hostesses. Throughout the evening, an assortment of gentlemen had come over to thank the viscountess for such a splendid event. Laura had urged the bachelors to meet Julia, her "particular friend." The men were quite happy to make her acquaintance. More than one gentleman smiled as his gaze trailed up and down her form. An older fellow had even licked his lips while staring at her bosom. But admiration never translated to an invitation to dance, or further conversation. The men always moved on to circle some doe-eyed girl of eighteen or twenty.

"At least Susannah's doing well." Julia smiled to see her stepsister waltzing about the ballroom in the arms of the Earl of Wilstshire's eldest son. Beautiful, rich, and sweet as sugar, Susannah might find her match this very night. "Laura, are there really no older widowers hunting for a bride?"

"There was one. Sadly, Baron Pomfrey married a young heiress whom he met in Bath only last month."

"Baron Pomfrey? Is he not all of seventy-eight?"

"A *spry* seventy-eight, so he says. And the girl is barely eighteen."

All men were the same. They wanted innocence and youth, a wife who would accept everything they told her with a loving smile.

"If only I'd been in town these past ten years," Julia said. "I might have found someone even as wonderful as the viscount."

"Well. I may be partial, but I don't believe Lord Weatherford can be matched." Laura beamed, her cheeks still brightening after almost ten years of marriage. She laid a hand upon her stomach, where Julia knew the bump revealing the Weatherfords' third child would soon begin to show. Julia smiled at her friend's happiness, even as her heart sank. As a girl, she'd dreamed of marriage and family.

Ten years ago she'd almost had both.

Wishing for the past would change nothing. Julia had to be assertive, but carefully so. It was important to let men believe that everything was their idea, even though it very rarely was.

"Perhaps I might swoon," Julia whispered. Lady Weatherford laughed.

"We must be on the lookout for a single gentleman of good fortune who appears adept at catching fainting women."

"I doubt that describes most men here," Julia drawled, surveying the ballroom of handsome but decidedly pampered-looking prospects. "I daresay most have never caught anything more challenging than a cold." She lowered her voice further. "Or even the clap."

"Julia!" Lady Weatherford almost choked on a laugh. "Darling, you really must keep a civil tongue in your head until after your wedding day."

"True. A man must never suspect a woman of having a personality until it is far too late."

There was a sudden commotion on the ballroom floor. Heads swiveled as people watched someone make their way through the crowd.

"Oh dear." Lady Weatherford sighed. "I'm not surprised he's late."

"Who is he?"

"The Duke of Ashworth." Laura sounded shocked by her ignorance, but the name meant nothing to Julia. "Oh, I forgot. You've been hidden away in the country for the past ten years. You don't know him."

"Has he murdered someone?"

Half of the ballroom appeared incensed at the man's approach. The male half.

"The married women of London were quite delighted when the duke returned from his travels abroad," Lady Weatherford said slyly.

As the man appeared, Julia understood their excitement.

This duke was the most handsome creature she could have imagined. He moved through the crowd with the innate grace of a predator, causing the lesser men to simply melt out of his path. He was tall and broad-shouldered, with hair of a dark, gleaming sable that curled in a most becoming way. Julia imagined running her fingers through that hair; her hands tingled with the mere thought.

She caught only his profile, but the face would have been beautiful if not for the masculine lines of his jaw and nose. His lips were full, though, and his high, sharp cheekbones set off a glittering pair of eyes. Julia wondered what color they could possibly be.

Goodness, her mouth had gone dry. She swallowed as the duke glided past, the eyes of the room turning with him.

"I imagine he's unmarried," she said.

"I'd introduce you, but I'm afraid it would be a waste of time." Laura sighed. "Ashworth really is a decent man beneath it all, but he has a most active social life. He's told Weatherford that marriage is not for him, nor he for it."

Of course. Besides, a man that breathtaking would have all of London in a tizzy. If he were to ever marry, he would choose a wealthy debutante like Susannah. Ah well. At least Julia had been able to glimpse such a gorgeous beast.

Susannah arrived, escorted back by the earl's son. The young man bowed and left the women. Julia's stepsister was positively glowing.

"Look!" She displayed her nearly full dance card. "Lord Caldwell was most insistent on two waltzes. Can you imagine?"

"You deserve it." Julia smiled tenderly. She wanted Susannah's happiness more than anything, though when her stepsister married that would leave Julia all alone with Constance. Julia pursed her lips. There had to be some way…

"Pardon." A woman abruptly shoved Susannah aside.

"Excuse me!" Julia said, but the woman didn't look back. She merely rushed through the crowd, cutting a path toward the other end of the ballroom. "What on earth was that?"

"Mrs. Worthington." Lady Weatherford clucked her tongue in disapproval. "I feared this might happen. She would love to be the duke's particular—"

"Friend," Julia said. They mustn't scandalize Susannah too terribly.

"Poor Ashworth. If he isn't careful, he'll have a third duel before the month's out."

"A third? In a month?" Julia gaped.

"The duke has been a 'friend' to nearly every married woman in this room at one time or another," Laura remarked. "Their husbands are only too ready to call him out."

"He doesn't seem particularly interested in Mrs. Worthington's friendship." Julia noticed the duke duck out of the ballroom. Mrs. Worthington vanished after him in hot pursuit. Well. That was the risk a handsome rake took in their society.

Feeling parched, Julia went in search of a glass of lemonade, leaving Susannah under Lady Weatherford's expert eye. On the other side of the room, Julia sipped as she watched all of London society on display. She sighed as the clocks struck the hour; she hadn't made headway with a single man, no matter how old or awkward he might be.

Perhaps Constance truly had won. Perhaps it was Julia's fate to tend to the woman, fluffing her pillows and pouring her tea.

She set her jaw. No. She refused to let that happen.

"Excuse me."

Julia startled as a florid-faced man stormed past her, out the ballroom and into a corridor.

"Worthington," someone said with a chuckle. "Missing his wife?"

Worthington. Oh dear. Julia set her glass down and watched Mr. Worthington stalk away in hot pursuit of the duke. Julia imagined that this Duke of Ashworth was about to be called to that third duel. One he actually might not deserve.

• • •

How had the woman found him so quickly? This Mrs. Worthington must have been a randy blood-hound in another life. He'd never even met her before, but she'd certainly known him, introducing herself the instant he entered the ballroom. He'd only just managed to get away.

Gregory hurried down the corridor before slipping into a darkened parlor. He shut the door and breathed out in relief. In all the tumult, he hadn't even been able to greet his hostess. Damnably rude. But he'd never dreamed some woman would literally be lying in wait. His notoriety must have somehow increased in his absence. How was that possible?

Gregory walked to the window and looked out upon the Weatherfords' back garden. He noted a little rope swing that hung from the branch of an oak tree. Yes, the viscount doted upon his children. Not only that, but he was clearly still in love with his wife after almost a decade of marriage. Whenever Gregory came to dinner, he'd see the many soft looks and casual touches that passed between them.

The Weatherfords proved that love existed. Gregory gave a grim smirk. If only it weren't so bloody rare. He adjusted his cravat and straightened his lapels. Enough time must have passed. Surely he could return to the party.

Just then, the door flung wide open.

"Your Grace," a woman said breathily.

Oh shit.

Mrs. Worthington shut the door and pressed her back to it. She had wild, curling dark hair, and a carefully penciled mole at the corner of her lip. The woman thrust her chest forward. "I knew it was fate that we should meet."

"Fate? You chased me in here."

"We have only so long before my husband should find us." The woman loosed a ribbon on her bodice, and the front of her dress dropped away to reveal a red satin shift. Well, she'd certainly come prepared. "Ravish me."

"I don't know what they told you about me," Gregory said, "but at least some of it was a lie. Now kindly put your bosoms away and allow me to pass."

"You mustn't tease me." She moved toward him, arms open, breasts jiggling. Gregory dodged around her. "Your Grace!"

The door flew open to reveal a furious-looking man, stopping Gregory cold. The fellow's jaw quivered with rage as he beheld the underdressed woman. "Gladys!" he cried.

"Philip!" she shrieked.

"*Fuck*," Gregory said.

"You have sullied the honor of my wife, sir!" Mr. Worthington tugged out his handkerchief and threw it in Gregory's face. "I must demand satisfaction!"

"How can you have satisfaction? *I* haven't had it yet!" Gregory attempted to talk the man down. If he had to fight one more duel, he was going to fall asleep with his finger on the trigger. He'd never been this exhausted in his life. "This is all a misunderstanding. The lady followed me in here."

"Are you calling my wife loose?"

Worthington's face grew beet red.

"Well, she's not exactly screwed in tight, is she?" Gregory had an inkling that had been the wrong thing to say. Mrs. Worthington made a furious, squished noise.

"It wasn't my fault, Philip! He dragged me in here. He wished to ravish me!" She flung herself onto a chaise and sobbed dramatically.

"You blackguard! I can contain myself no longer." Mr. Worthington snatched up his handkerchief and threw it again. This time, it landed on the toe of Gregory's shoe; the duke didn't have the energy to pick it up. "You shall answer for this insult to my wife. Pistols at dawn!"

"Could we make it a mid-afternoon duel? I've been up for two days straight," Gregory said.

All three turned as the door opened yet again.

"Your Grace?" A woman spoke in a low, musical voice. "There you are, my dear duke. I wondered where you had got to."

Gregory came face-to-face with a goddess.

She was tall, dressed in a gown of periwinkle satin that highlighted the extraordinary blue of her eyes. Her golden hair curled in becoming ringlets; Gregory imagined that hair tumbling about her naked shoulders. He could only dream of the generous curves hidden by this gown, if the ample swell of her bosom were anything to go by. The woman smiled, which drew attention to a full lower lip. Gregory became hypnotized by that lip. He wished to bite it. He wanted to hear that sultry voice whisper in his ear, *Gregory. Oh, Gregory.*

Blood thundered through every part of his

body. Who was this vixen? He'd never seen her before, but she had to be married. No one this gorgeous could be still on the shelf.

"Lady Weatherford wondered where you might be, Your Grace." The beauty gestured. "Come. You promised me the next dance."

"Ah yes, my dear Lady Somersome." Gregory gargled the name as he left the Worthingtons to their astonishment. "I couldn't find you."

"Is that why you came all the way over here? Looking for me?" The woman beamed, a dimple forming in her left cheek. No dimple had ever made Gregory hard before, but this one was doing the trick.

"I would look for you anywhere, my lady. You have all my attention this evening." Gregory checked the Worthingtons and saw that the ingenious woman had played this scene faultlessly. Mrs. Worthington appeared crestfallen, while Mr. Worthington blustered.

"It appears I, er, made an error, Your Grace. My apologies."

"Think nothing of it. Good evening, sir. Madam." Gregory closed the door on the Worthington marriage and moved into the hall. The delectable lady kept a few steps ahead of him. Gregory felt a stirring throughout his whole body. It was the thrill of the hunt. "Might I know the name of my rescuer?"

"Rescuer is far too grand a title." The lady sounded breezy, but also a bit nervous. "We must hurry. I can't be seen dallying in private with... well, with *you*."

"Yes, you must have a care for your reputation." Gregory swept in front of the woman. She looked at him with such an earnest expression in those blue eyes that he felt momentarily dumbstruck. But only momentarily. "At least, you must take care your husband shouldn't find us."

"Well. On that score, at least, we needn't worry." She bobbed a curtsy. "Miss Julia Beaumont, Your Grace."

Miss? Gregory nearly snorted at what had to be a joke. The woman was in her mid- to late twenties. What kind of depraved society would allow such a creature to mellow into spinsterhood? It was evil that no one had kissed those lips or stroked those supple curves. She had a body designed for touch. For ecstasy.

But Gregory was a rake, not a cad. He had never compromised an unmarried woman. No, this vixen couldn't be his. He ought to escort her back to the ballroom, thank her for the assistance, and leave. Anything further ran a risk for both of them.

But this Julia Beaumont had appeared in the midst of dreary London society like an oasis in a desert. And Gregory was dying of thirst.

CHAPTER FOUR

Oh, this was dangerous. Idling in a deserted corridor with a notorious rake would sink Julia's reputation. No decent man would marry her, and she did not believe that this Duke of Ashworth would do the respectable thing and wed her out of obligation. Three duels in one month suggested that he didn't care a fig for respectability.

She must leave this man, but found it impossible to move. His gaze was too captivating.

His eyes were the dark gray of a storming sky, but also warm. Almost playful. The duke studied her as if she were some marvelous toy. No man had ever looked at Julia like he wanted to swallow her in one sinful bite. Julia's body grew heavy at the mere thought of his hand upon her skin. Her breath hitched when she imagined the duke slipping his fingers beneath her bodice, tracing his fingertips around and around her—

I must leave. Now.

"Your Grace. You're blocking the way to the ballroom." She must make him believe she had no interest.

"An astute observation, Miss Beaumont." A wicked smile played upon his lips.

"Perhaps my veiled request was too subtle. Please move, Your Grace."

The duke stepped aside and gestured for her to proceed. Julia walked quickly. Soon, they would part. She would be off to Susannah, he to some new, nameless conquest. Julia's indignation flared. Really, he knew she was unmarried. She had much to lose in this game, and yet he still played with her? This duke was no gentleman.

"I don't believe I properly thanked you for your assistance," he said.

"Words aren't necessary, Your Grace. Actions would be better proof of your gratitude."

"You're a woman of action, then?" The duke stepped before her again, halting Julia in her tracks.

"I believe in getting things done."

"So do I." The seductive purr in his voice let her know exactly what he meant. Julia felt her face flush. This man was being impertinent. He was shocking her with suggestion. He was more than a rake; he was a fiend. Yet she didn't want to move, idiot that she was. No other man had ever captured her attention in this way, so quickly and so completely.

Except this duke probably made every woman feel like the center of his world. That charm had allowed him to make many conquests. Julia refused to become one of them.

"And what, pray tell, occupies your time in the day to day? You must be a busy man indeed if you arrive to Lady Weatherford's ball three hours late. What matter of grave import could have detained you? A cravat that would not fluff? A grievous cologne shortage?"

"You are out to wound, madam." He sounded delighted by it. Perhaps appearing listless would send this man away from her, but Julia did not want to feign disinterest. She hadn't felt this alive in months. Years. *Ever.*

"You're detaining me, sir. That puts my reputation at considerable risk. A gentleman would care, but such a thing hasn't crossed your mind. Given what Lady Weatherford has told me of you, that hardly surprises."

"Oh? She's spoken of me?" The duke lifted his brows. "What a shame. She's failed to mention anything of *you.*"

"Why should she?" Julia's pulse pounded. She became so aware of the small distance between their bodies. It felt as though heat were building in that space, a spark about to ignite. "There's nothing to tell."

"I doubt that you and the word 'nothing' are in any way acquainted." The Duke of Ashworth prowled about her with sinuous grace that left Julia breathless. She could leave if she wished, but her feet seemed rooted to the floor. It wasn't that she felt helpless in this man's presence. Rather, she did not want to miss out on the challenge of trouncing him. "Indeed," he said. "There's a very 'something' about you."

Julia looked the duke in his wicked, storming eyes.

"And you, sir, are a man who must have everything, it seems. The married women of London no longer interest you, so you toy with the spinsters as well."

"Yes. That raises a significant question." He seemed genuinely curious. "How is it a woman of your considerable gifts hasn't secured a husband?"

The truth only irritated her. Besides, why should she tell this man her private struggles?

"I've yet to find the man who matches me," she replied.

"Now *that* I can believe." The duke took one step nearer. Though she was tall, he was well over six feet. Julia rarely had to lift her eyes to meet a man's gaze. She felt, for the first time in years, that a worthy opponent had presented himself. Her blood was fire in her veins. "You must allow me to show my gratitude. With actions, not words. Come." The duke held out his hand. "A dance, perhaps? A waltz, to thank you for my rescue."

"As I've said, Your Grace. No thanks are necessary." Julia smiled. She must not let him know he'd rattled her. Shaken her to her core. He could not know how much she enjoyed it. "Merely refrain from fighting duels on Lady Weatherford's property. At least until all of the guests have gone."

Julia stepped around the duke. She couldn't decide which urge was stronger: the desire to get away, or the wish to be detained.

To her suppressed delight, he stopped her yet again.

"Duels in the plural? You must think me a very naughty—and busy—man." The words *naughty* and *busy* upon his lips conjured heated, dreamlike images of the velvet dark of a bedroom, the silken rustle of sheets. Julia was innocent, but not naive. She knew the specifics of what went on between a husband and wife, though she lacked all experience.

This duke was a true demon. He took no care for her reputation, or her innocence. How infuriating. How exciting.

"I don't think. I know," Julia said. "I don't wish to play your games. I'm here to find a husband, not dally with a seducer." For the first time, the gleeful light left his eyes. The duke's whole expression darkened. Had she succeeded in wounding his pride?

"You believe one of those puffed-up dandies in the ballroom has a hope of matching you?"

Her skin prickled with gooseflesh. He sounded almost jealous of the idea.

"I'm afraid I haven't much choice if I want to marry. I'm no longer some fresh-faced debutante. A spinster, particularly a clever one, must take whatever she finds." Julia had never bared her true thoughts this quickly to anyone before, not even Laura or Susannah. She was being much too forward. If she wanted to find a husband, then time was running out. "Good evening, Your Grace."

Julia hurried away, but the man was not done.

"If you want to attract male attention, taking to the floor with me is the wisest decision you could make."

Julia imagined his arm slipping about her waist as he led her in a waltz. The idea left her breathless.

"One dance with me, and every man in that ballroom will find you fascinating. They'll lay themselves at your feet," he said.

"I don't need all of them," she replied. "One will do quite nicely."

"He must be the right one, though."

The duke's entire body radiated temptation as he held out his hand yet again. Julia believed that his touch would scorch her, burn its way straight through her glove. She drank in the simmering heat of his eyes.

"Yes. He must be," Julia whispered. "And he is not here."

Triumphant, she walked away from the bloody Duke of Ashworth.

Snap. The wobbly heel of her shoe broke when Julia put too much weight upon it. The treacherous heel shot across the hallway, upsetting Julia's balance. She gasped as she began to fall.

Arms encircled her. The duke held her with the greatest ease.

Well. At least we know he can catch a falling woman.

She remained in his arms. Even after the duke righted Julia he kept her close. Surely he had to feel the way her heart throbbed in her chest. Should she free herself? It was the wisest thing to do, but then the duke lifted her chin to meet his eyes. The force of that gaze was like the ocean coming at her during the height of a storm. Others might have been swept away, but Julia knew how to stand her ground.

She did not budge, which delighted him.

"I don't think I've ever met such an obstinate lady before," the duke said.

"I assure you, sir. You've barely got the measure of me."

"Oh, I believe that. Nothing's more attractive than a beautiful, headstrong woman with a smart mouth."

No man had ever looked at Julia as if she were temptation itself. Every inch of her quivered at the thought that he might...

"That smart mouth," he growled, "has me hypnotized."

Julia forgot what she was going to say as he bent his head to hers. At the first touch of his lips, she was lost. The duke kissed as though he were hungry for her, like Julia was a dish that had been long denied him. His lips were soft, and his stubbled jaw scraped her cheeks. Julia should have pushed him away, but instead she wound her arms about his neck and deepened the kiss. Heat pooled between her legs, leaving her sore with wanting as she felt his tongue stroke just once against hers. She moaned, and he growled in reply. She could feel his burning, very masculine pride at reducing her to something so wanton.

When he pressed her closer, she could also feel the very masculine evidence of his arousal.

Julia had little experience in the way of kisses, but she could tell that this duke was devastatingly good. He pressed one scorching kiss after another upon her lips. She dug her fingernails into his shoulders, wishing to feel more. To feel all. The next time he broke a kiss, she took his bottom lip between her teeth. She had never felt more animal—or more wonderful.

"Damn," the duke whispered, his voice hoarse with lust. "I knew it the moment I laid eyes upon you. You're a vixen."

"I…" All of her words had flown away. Julia's smart mouth wanted to be kissed, and kissed again. Her eyes fluttered shut as the duke kissed her jaw and all along her neck. Julia tilted her head back, lost in the blissful sensation of being in his arms, of his body pressed to hers, of his lips… everywhere. She adored the spicy, masculine scent of him. She…

She was about to ruin herself. The instant anyone laid eyes upon her, all hope was lost. Ashworth would walk away unscathed. People might judge him harshly, but none would deny him access to society. Whereas Julia's hopes of finding a husband would be destroyed. Forever.

"No," she gasped.

Ashworth stopped. Julia shoved out of his embrace and smoothed her skirts, looking this way and that. The corridor was empty, but that was no guarantee that they had not been seen.

"What have I done?" Julia had been given one chance to escape her fate as Constance's drudge. She'd wasted it on a few moments of pleasure. The greatest pleasure, yes, but…she had to leave. After this exhibition, she must disappear before anyone could put her face to her name.

"Miss Beaumont?"

"This didn't happen." She touched her burning cheeks. Julia looked around, but didn't see her broken heel. "Don't follow me!"

Entering the ballroom, Julia slowed but did not

loiter. She didn't try to catch any gentleman's eye. It was too late. Heart sinking, she made her way to Laura and Susannah.

"What's wrong?" Her stepsister frowned. "Darling, where were you?"

"I'm so sorry," Julia said to the women. "But we need to leave."

• • •

Gregory had never been so consumed by a kiss. Miss Beaumont had set every nerve in his body sparking with delight. She'd been so soft, so yielding, and yet so strong. Her luscious mouth had been exquisite. She was ecstasy itself.

Intelligent as well. Perhaps her wit and intellect made the chase even sweeter. He'd never enjoyed speaking with any woman so much before. Hell, perhaps he'd never enjoyed speaking to anybody that much, period.

Fuck, his loins ached. He'd been reduced to a beast so quickly. In a kind of heady madness, he realized he needed to find her. Her touch had been fiery and also soothing, a burn and a balm.

Gregory scanned the ballroom for Miss Beaumont and caught sight of Lady Weatherford. Julia had said they were friends. Gregory made his way over, bowing his head in greeting.

"Your Grace. How wonderful to see you tonight." The viscountess smiled, but Gregory could barely return the greeting. He searched the crowd for periwinkle satin and curling golden hair.

"A young lady," he said. "That is, I was just

speaking with a Miss Julia Beaumont. Do you know where she might have got to?"

"Miss Beaumont and her stepsister, Miss Fletcher, left moments ago." Gregory could feel the lady watching him closely. "I believe they've ordered their carriage."

He made excuses, and then Gregory was on the hunt. As he left the ballroom, he pushed past a few gentlemen who "accidentally" blocked his path. They wanted to intimidate the duke, but he was not in the mood for stupid games. He was in the mood for nothing but her.

Gregory exited the Weatherford house just in time to see Miss Beaumont hurrying along the front path with another young lady in tow. Julia looked back over her shoulder, saw him, and sped up. She grabbed her stepsister's hand as a carriage arrived. The women hurried inside, closed the door, and clattered off.

She was gone. *Damn*.

Gregory walked to the street, watching her carriage as it vanished into the night. Miss Beaumont had done the correct thing. Gregory knew that he was a damn scoundrel to have taken advantage of an unmarried woman in such a way. How much lower could a man like him sink?

Even if love existed, a bastard like him didn't deserve it.

Gregory turned back, and nearly tripped over something lying on the pathway. He picked it up and inspected it in the lamplight.

It was a beaded lady's shoe, missing a heel.

CHAPTER FIVE

Julia sat in the morning room, pen in hand, staring at the last three lines she'd crossed out on the otherwise pristine page. For the past two hours she'd been attempting to work on her (proposed) pamphlet. The Society of Ladies for the Expansion of Female Literacy was a club that most fashionable women did not elect to join, but it was one of the charitable endeavors that mattered most to Julia. As an unmarried woman, she did not have much of a position in the Society—or in any society—but Julia did what she could for the cause, including writing up pamphlets to be printed at club expense and distributed to the public. It was useless, though. Her topic was supposed to be The Importance of Scholarly Education in the Development of Moral Character, but every sentence she wrote, no matter how urgent or packed with meaning, conjured images of the Duke of Ashworth. *To improve her spirit, a woman must first improve her mind*, morphed into: *To improve the Duke of Ashworth, a woman must first improve her Duke of Ashworth.* She put down the pen and slumped in a most unladylike manner.

"You mustn't worry," Susannah said. The girl was seated at the pianoforte, her fingers dashing across the keys as she played a piece by Mozart. Brilliant, as always. Susannah needed music in the way Julia required books, as if she would die without it.

Though the Duke of Ashworth was rapidly putting Julia off reading or thinking entirely. Last night she'd attempted to peruse Wollstonecraft's *A Vindication of the Rights of Woman* in order to settle her nerves. It had turned into *A Vindication of the Rights of the Duke of Ashworth*, and she doubted very much that the duke needed any help protecting his bloody rights.

"If Constance ever learns what happened, she'll confine me to the attic for the rest of my life." Julia left the writing desk and flopped onto the sofa. "I'll become something out of a Gothic tale, singing mad songs and knitting sweaters for mice."

"I'm sure no one saw you." Susannah finished her concerto with a flourish. "We'd have heard something by now."

"It's only the morning after." Julia sighed. "Do you believe the papers would carry such news? I can see the headline. Spinster Compromised at Weatherford Ball: War Against Napoleon Deemed Trite In Comparison."

Julia glanced around the room, resigning herself to its four walls. They were not unpleasant walls. Indeed, they were painted a buttery yellow, and sported glass-paned doors that opened upon the rose garden. But she would never move outside of this cloistered world. This and Pennington Hall, her family seat in Kent, were the only two places she would ever again be allowed to go. At least Julia could remain in her ancestral home.

The Beaumont heir, Sir Hugh, was a distant cousin who resided in America and took little interest in an impoverished estate. Still, this would be her entire world. A comfortable one, to be certain, but limited. She'd have her pamphlets that no one would read, and once in a while, she'd be permitted to dote upon Susannah's children like a good aunt. That certainly wasn't a shameful life, but it was too constricting for a woman of her temperament. Such a quiet existence was as good as a prison sentence to Julia.

How could she have been so foolish? Julia had always prided herself on good sense, but one infuriating, brutally handsome man had reduced her to a creature that cared only for its own pleasure. Sensational pleasure, yes. The greatest, most intense pleasure she had ever experienced, or ever would.

"Why are you so flushed?" Susannah asked.

"It's warm in here." Julia grabbed a book, opened it, and stared at a page for several moments before realizing it was upside down. Her stepsister came and sat beside her.

"Perhaps he'll call on you." Susannah sounded so earnest. "Maybe he's on his way right now to propose."

"Not if Lady Weatherford's description was accurate. I'm certain His Grace found another lady to woo after I left. Perhaps two at once."

"Julia!"

She couldn't help smiling. "You're so easy to shock, darling."

For a chaste gentlewoman, Julia read a great

deal of "sensational" literature. Of course, women like her never ended well in those kinds of stories. According to Gothic novels, most fallen women ended their lives in Castilian nunneries or died of spontaneous illnesses. Even so, the lurid tales suggested there should be fire between a man and woman. Last night had been an inferno.

"Really," Susannah said. "He might surprise you."

"Surprises are rarely pleasant."

The girls stopped speaking as Constance entered the room. Julia's stepmother was back on her feet today, though still somewhat sickly. Her eyes were puffed, and she fluttered that lace handkerchief to and fro, ready to catch a sneeze.

"My deaw Zoozannah." Constance discreetly blew her nose. "Ah, dat's beddah. Dow. Ahem, *now*, whom do you think will be calling on us today?"

"I'd hoped Lord Caldwell might visit, and Mr. Dorchester. They seemed to enjoy dancing with me last night."

"Susannah was the belle of the ball," Julia said.

"Indeed." Constance fixed Julia with a withering glare and blew her nose. "She might have made more conquests if you hadn't forced her to retire early. A broken shoe, puh. Of all the insipid reasons to leave!"

"I'd already danced my fill," Susannah said.

"And I wouldn't have helped Susannah's chances by falling into the punch bowl." Julia stared wearily at Constance. She imagined looking at this woman for the rest of her life. Bringing tea, mending clothes, carrying small, yappy dogs from room to room. Why hire a lady's maid when one had an unmarriageable stepdaughter?

"I'm certain most gentlemen wouldn't have noticed. Truly, your delusion knows no bounds, Julia."

"My delusion?" Julia rarely lost her temper, but today might be special.

"You are on the shelf. Men pay no attention to spinsters!"

Julia was tempted to brag of her exploits with the Duke of Ashworth, but knew that Constance would immediately stuff her into a sack and return her to Kent by post.

"I'm sorry I didn't lock myself in a closet until the ball was over. In future, I'll remember my place."

"Nonsense. I'm quite well again." Constance gave another angry honk into her handkerchief. "I'll chaperone Susannah for the rest of the Season. You will remain here, do needlework, and listen politely to the stories of her exploits."

"Mamma," Susannah cried, but Julia pressed her stepsister's hand. If Susannah became angry, Constance might accuse Julia of turning the girl against her.

"Understood, my lady. From now on, polite listening is my greatest pleasure. My only pleasure. I may never speak again, in fact."

"You make everything so dramatic." Constance sniffled.

The lady brightened as Hodge, their butler, entered. Hodge's presence meant there were callers. For Susannah, obviously.

"Yes, Hodge?" Constance beamed.

"The Duke of Ashworth, my lady."

Julia lost momentary feeling in her hands and feet. Susannah squeaked.

"Well! Susannah, you certainly made an impression. A duke, of all things!" Constance appeared giddy.

"Calling for Miss Beaumont," Hodge said.

All color drained from Constance's face. She looked as if a gust of wind or even a moderate sneeze might knock her over.

Susannah beamed as she hurried to her pianoforte. Meanwhile, Julia was too stunned to speak, which had never happened before. Perhaps the duke *had* come to make her an offer.

Freedom might be on its way to this very room, wrapped in a handsome package.

When Ashworth entered, Julia made certain to rise slowly. He mustn't know how eager she was. The duke greeted Constance with poise and charm.

"Lady Beaumont, I presume?" He bowed his head. "A pleasure."

Constance gaped. Julia understood her stepmother's reaction. Yesterday evening, he'd been enthralling. In the broad light of day, this man was the epitome of masculine beauty. Constance managed a curtsy and a mumbled excuse before fluttering out the door. The duke appeared bewildered, as well he might. Leaving two unmarried women alone with him was hardly respectable behavior.

"She's been ill," Julia said. "Unfortunately, it's

not serious." She gestured to a chair. "Will you have a seat, Your Grace?"

"Thank you, Miss Beaumont." He bowed to Susannah at the instrument. "Miss Fletcher, I presume?"

"I'm not here." Susannah played a merry tune. "Don't speak to me."

"Er. Quite."

As they sat, Julia cursed in silence. She'd promised herself she'd be calm if they ever met again, but that was impossible. The Renaissance masters might have thrown down their brushes in dismay upon seeing this man. What artistic genius could capture the essence of such perfection?

Meanwhile, Julia recalled being in his arms, his mouth covering hers. She forced her heart not to quicken at the memory.

Ashworth sat with an easy grace, at once relaxed and yet somehow commanding. He wore a suit of dove gray, his dark hair swept back. The sharp planes of his face and the sensual curve of his mouth were oh so touchable. Susannah softened her playing, giving Julia a chance to speak.

"Did you enjoy the ball, Your Grace?"

"Perhaps too much."

The duke's brows knit in concentration, and Julia's heart beat faster. Did Susannah have it right? *Was* he working up the courage to propose? "I came to tell you," Ashworth began.

"Yes?" Julia leaned forward as the duke reached into his deep coat pocket...and pulled out a shoe.

"I found this last night. Since it's missing a

heel, I thought it might be yours."

Julia took the shoe, cursing her own excitement. The duke had not come to ask for her hand. His regard had been only for her feet, the monster.

"Thank you. These slippers belonged to my mother. I'm happy to have them reunited."

"Yes. It's unfortunate when one loses its mate." He cleared his throat. "Slippers, that is."

"I've often thought life would be easier as a shoe. You come into the world with your match already made."

"You've often thought this?" He arched a brow. "How unusual."

Most men would have sounded off put, but he appeared amused.

"Spinsters have plenty of time to entertain eccentric thoughts."

"That seems a paltry benefit compared with what you're missing," the duke said. His words delivered in that deep, rich voice sounded suggestive. Susannah missed a note in her surprise.

"I beg pardon?" Julia asked.

"Well. That is…" His Grace realized the slip he'd made as he glanced at Susannah.

"Susannah knows about last night," Julia said.

"Yes. I *do* think you're an abominable cad, but I now understand how my dear stepsister lost her head." Susannah played something that conjured the idea of thunderstorms and horrible shipwrecks. Fittingly romantic.

"Ah yes. Stepsister. Lady Weatherford mentioned that."

"You spoke to the viscountess?" Julia snapped. "Have you been telling all of London? Perhaps you'd like to make a formal announcement of rakishness in the *Times*."

"I'd never considered such a thing," he mused. "Perhaps all rakes should advertise. How modern."

"Be serious, please."

"I may have lost my head, madam, but I would never spread ruinous gossip about a lady." The Duke of Ashworth sounded serious. "I merely asked the viscountess where you'd gone. You left in a hurry."

"You can't be surprised." Julia lifted her chin in defiance. "After your shocking disregard for my virtue."

"Forgive me, but you were only too happy to disregard it yourself."

The cheek of it all shocked Julia. Gentlemen in these circumstances were supposed to either beg forgiveness or look disdainfully upon a fallen woman. They weren't supposed to trade barbs with her. This duke was unlike any other man she'd ever met before.

"That doesn't matter. It was your duty to protect me from, er, myself."

"Come now, Miss Beaumont. You seem like the type of woman who knows her own mind."

He sounded rather attracted to the idea. Attraction was not the problem between them. Or rather, it was the greatest problem.

"Either way, last night ruined any chances I had of securing a match."

"It shouldn't. No one knows, and the Season's

only begun. Though you may be a spinster, you're the comeliest one I've ever come across."

He and Julia held each other's gazes, both refusing to be the first to look away. This man was a fascinating oddity. He was smug and self-congratulatory, but his admiration for her was real. Fierce, even.

"My stepmother says that the Season's over for me."

"Does she know what happened between us?"

"No. She likes to think of me as furniture. Something reliable that never leaves the house." And that didn't mind being sat on.

The duke frowned.

"So that's why you're still unmarried," he said.

"This is my first time in London since I was seventeen years old. Maybe when I'm fifty I'll be allowed back." Julia hated to be self-pitying, but she felt like a bird trapped under glass.

"Damn cruel," Ashworth muttered. "And a damned waste, if I may say."

"You may not." Julia drew herself up.

"But I must." The duke stood and went to look out onto the garden. His movements were swift, and Julia could sense the anger simmering beneath that handsome facade. "A woman like you, reduced to being a nursemaid? Someone with your wit should be out in society, commanding attention. Someone with your...evident charms," he growled, "should be married. You're the kind of woman that men yearn to satisfy. Though I doubt the lucky bastard who could match you exists."

Susannah gasped. Gentlemen did not curse in front of ladies. Julia had always hated that custom. Most men treated women as if they were children. This duke was no gentleman, but in his own odd way he'd shown her respect. He didn't find her merely desirable. He found her capable.

But knowing that he'd walk out and leave her to this dismal little life only infuriated Julia.

"Well. Thanks to you, my one chance of escape was ruined. A true gentleman would have come here to offer a hasty marriage, but you've offered me a shoe. A broken shoe, at that."

"Meaning?" Now the duke appeared cross, which did nothing to erase his irresistible charm. How unfair.

"Meaning I don't want your pity."

"I don't deal in pity." Ashworth leaned against the wall. The powerful line of his body relaxed, making him still more attractive. Damn the man, he was impossible.

Julia realized that Susannah had stopped playing anything resembling music. Rather, she plinked one note on the pianoforte again and again as she watched their scene with widened eyes.

"Susannah! Play something else."

Susannah obliged by playing *two* notes over and over.

"Honestly, you don't strike me as that intelligent, Your Grace," Julia said. The duke narrowed his eyes.

"With all due respect, madam, my experience suggests otherwise. I have a lot of experience."

"If I hadn't rescued you last night, you'd have fought another duel over a woman's honor. You might have been killed! Yet directly after escaping, you attempted to seduce me."

"Attempted?" The duke smirked.

"Only a fool would chase women the way you do. You're lucky I have no father or brothers to call you out."

Ashworth seemed to realize she had a point, which caused him to appear even more aloof and charming. Men were ridiculous.

"It was an unfortunate lapse in judgment," he said. A lapse in judgment. What every woman hoped to be called. "You see, Miss Beaumont, I hadn't anticipated that a beautiful woman *and* a delectable sparring partner could exist in the same exquisite packaging."

By the devil, he was insolent. And charming. Insolently charming.

"Lady Weatherford tells me you've seduced nearly every married woman in the *ton*. That means every husband wants to shoot you. An intelligent rake wouldn't antagonize so many powerful men in possession of so many well-oiled pistols."

"What would you know of a gentleman's oiled pistol, Miss Beaumont?" The duke spoke low to spare Susannah's ears.

"I've read a great deal," she drawled.

"You think so little of me, yet I returned your slipper. Surely that's the mark of a gentleman."

"No, it's the mark of a prince from a fairy story."

"Ah, but in those tales the prince offers his

hand along with a maiden's, er, shoe."

"Yes, and you'd never be so honorable."

Julia toyed with her mother's shoe as she pondered their fascinating predicament. In a way, they had opposite problems. She strained toward marriage, while he risked getting shot to avoid it.

An idea made Julia drop the slipper. Ashworth cursed as he picked it up.

"You seem hellbent on losing this blasted thing."

"I've had a thought," Julia said.

"Only one?"

She studied the duke as he lounged in his chair. A handsome rake. A witty scoundrel. The type of man women dreamed of, but who was too much a cad to ever make a devoted wife happy.

No, marriage to a sweet, romantic girl wouldn't suit him at all.

Fortunately, Julia was neither of those things.

"You and I," she said, "make quite a pair of rogues."

"A charming rogue on my part."

"Neither of us has met society's expectations. We have that in common."

"What are you saying, Miss Beaumont?"

"A normal gentleman would've proposed marriage, but you're no ordinary gentleman and I'm certainly no ordinary lady." Julia waved her retrieved slipper. A warped fairy tale, indeed. "Therefore, *I* will propose to *you*. My dear Ashworth, we should marry as soon as possible."

CHAPTER SIX

The woman surprised Gregory at every turn. He'd come expecting tears, for her to call him a monster and a seducer. He'd envisioned Miss Julia Beaumont flinging herself facedown upon a sofa and wailing over her lost virtue. All spinsters were the same deep down. Shielded from the world, they nurtured foolish romantic hopes and wept when the brute reality of man revealed itself.

Instead of weeping, Miss Beaumont had taunted him, insulted him, and now was proposing to him with a broken shoe.

She was the most insolent minx he'd ever met, and every second in her presence served to increase Gregory's appetite. He knew she could be soft and passionate; this reminded him of how damned stubborn she was. Again, he thought of devouring that sumptuous, smart mouth. He dreamed of pulling up her skirts and tracing a creamy expanse of leg before reaching that heavenly space at the juncture of her thighs. Parting her. Plundering her.

They were pleasures he must deny himself. Even he wasn't enough of a bastard to deflower a poor, naive innocent.

And now, she was telling him they'd be married. Not asking. Not pleading. Issuing orders as if she were the most desirable general in military history.

Even though his body ached for her touch, Gregory felt horrified. Not for himself, but for Julia. A woman like this, fearless in the face of a duke, ought to be married to a true fairy tale hero. Some prince with a pure soul and a kingdom made of gold.

While Gregory's estate entailed enough land, money, and servants to be luxurious as a kingdom, he was the exact opposite of a charming prince. Despite his hunger, he had to make Julia Beaumont let go of this absurd idea. She deserved the perfect man, and Gregory was as far from that as Canterbury was from the earth's core. Maybe farther.

"That's a kind offer, but I have to decline," he said.

"Oh no." Julia smiled, well pleased with herself. "You're not declining."

"My lips moved, and the words 'I decline' came out."

"Marrying me is the best chance you have to be happy."

His eyes went out of focus as Gregory envisioned the woman lying naked upon a bed, her abundance of hair spread along the pillow. He pictured skimming his hands up her curves, cupping her breasts, then sliding inside of her one silken inch at a time.

Oh, that would make him a very happy man. Those forty to fifty minutes would be paradise itself. It was the next forty to fifty years he worried about.

"I think debauchery and gardening are the

best ways to make a man happy," he said.

"There's no reason married men can't debauch and garden in peace."

"This isn't just about my happiness," Gregory snapped. Honestly, the appalling selflessness of some people. "You don't know what you'd get, marrying me."

"An estate?" Julia ticked off the list on her fingers. "A title? A house in town? Several carriages? A great deal of money? Lines of credit at all the best shops?"

"I stand corrected, you mercenary wench."

"We each have something the other needs." Julia kept brandishing that shoe at him like a gaudy weapon. "You help me escape a lifetime of fetching Constance's smelling salts. As your wife, I can protect you from the ladies of the *ton*. They won't feel as free to chase you if I'm by your side."

This was…rather ingenious, actually. A buffer between Gregory and the Mrs. Worthingtons of the world was just what he required. Besides, Julia needed rescuing from this life. Even if she could enjoy the Season, Gregory knew London was filled with vain, preening idiots who wanted a wife to be wealthy, twenty, and dumb as a block. Julia was a woman, not a girl. Quite a woman. She shouldn't live and die a spinster. Julia deserved to be a duchess. As his wife, she'd take her rightful place in society.

And her rightful place in his bed.

But Gregory remembered the "family" portrait. His parents had exchanged perhaps fifty words in all twenty years of their marriage. When their boat sank off the coast of Ireland, they must have been relieved. Drowning meant they wouldn't have to struggle for conversation over dinner.

Gregory was their son through and through. Nothing in him was either worth loving or capable of love.

"I'm not the sort of man to be tied down," he said.

"You prefer to do the tying?" Julia asked, an innocent question that conjured images of her naked, blindfolded, and with her wrists bound in silken cord above her head. Oh, that one night in Naples would be *so* tempting to repeat with her.

"I'm very good at it. I mean," he said, trying to avoid growing aroused. "I can't give you what you want."

"You're a single man with a pulse. You're everything I could dream of."

"I'm not the doting husband type. I'm the type that mocks doting husbands, ruins wives, and talks at the theatre. I wouldn't make you happy."

He expected Julia to turn her face away in despair when she realized what a reprehensible beast he was.

He didn't expect her to throw a shoe at him. Gregory caught it with ease as Julia stood, looking the picture of beautiful exasperation.

"I don't expect romance! I want freedom, and you want protection. Anything else can be negotiated."

"Negotiated?" Now it was Gregory's turn to point the shoe in righteous fury. "You're speaking as if I were some commodity to be sold on the open market."

"Now you know what it is to be a woman."

She had him there.

"Well," he said, "I don't like it."

"Of course you don't!" Julia threw up her hands. "Do you think we ladies adore feeling like cattle at auction?"

"You misunderstand." Gregory rose, forcing the woman to turn up her eyes. A becoming blush warmed her cheeks. "If this is a negotiation, we should *both* negotiate."

"Very well." Julia attempted to look unruffled, but her oh-so-kissable lips parted as her breath quickened. Those lips and those eyes and those breasts and those…everything…could be his. Gregory didn't believe in ownership of a woman, but he believed in possession. He wanted to possess this woman's thoughts and desires, to be what she craved, even if he disappointed her in the end.

Because the thought of any other man touching her drove him to the brink of madness.

"I'm willing to offer you my name, my wealth, and utter freedom to do as you please. In return, you'll keep the most aggressive society ladies from nipping at my heels. And other, more vulnerable parts."

"I'm happy to say yes to that." God, he wanted her to say yes. Yes, and yes, and *oh yes*. Which brought them to the second problem.

"You understand we'll be married in name only."

"Your name's all I need." But Julia's

expression wasn't as brash as her words implied. She wanted romance, even if she didn't know it yet. God, he wanted to give her every bit of ecstasy but knew he'd never satisfy the cravings of her heart. Gregory hadn't realized it was possible to despise himself more than he already did. What a revelation.

"It'll be better if you have your life and I have mine," he said.

"Yes. Your life will undoubtedly be quite active."

True. She probably imagined that Gregory would elect an existence filled with uninterrupted carousing and scantily clad ballerinas. Though he'd grown weary of all that, it was good if she believed it. Julia needed to consider him the most worthless libertine alive; that way, she would never feel tenderness for him. Gregory could swallow much disappointment, but he'd never be able to stomach letting down a woman such as Julia. They'd be married, and then he'd be gone traveling the globe in solitary contentment.

After he got over the temptation of his own wife.

"This is a marriage of pure convenience."

"That's what makes it perfect," Julia said.

"I'm not romantic. Don't expect picnics and poetry and, I don't know, swans or something."

"Swans are rather nasty birds." Julia snatched the shoe back and toyed with it, which drew Gregory's eye. God, she had the most gorgeous hands. If only she had something better to fondle than a lady's slipper. He could help in that department.

You won't burden her. She needs an escape; that's all you are. You need a wife to stand between you and London's most lascivious matrons. That's all she is.

Of course, Julia Beaumont was much more than that. It's just that Gregory couldn't hope to match her.

"So. Is it official?" Susannah squeaked. The young lady slammed her hands upon the pianoforte keys in her excitement, creating a sound like a cat being squashed. "Are you engaged?"

"It would seem we've agreed to satisfactory terms," Gregory said.

"My dear Ashworth, your way with words makes me swoon." But Julia's entire expression lit up, as if a great candle had begun to burn inside of her. She was a ravishing woman, an intelligent lady, a statuesque goddess. She was to be his bride.

Hopefully she wouldn't come to regret it.

• • •

Julia's thoughts were like fireworks at a fairground, whizzing about in all sorts of fantastical colors and configurations. She was going to be married! More than married, she was to be a lady. More than a lady, a duchess.

A duchess married to the most disreputable rake in England, of course. Perhaps on the entire Continent. But that didn't matter, because she would be free from Constance's groans and complaints. She'd have her own house. Her own household. Her own husband.

Even if the marriage was in name only. Well, Julia only needed the Duke of Ashworth's name. Not any other part of him.

Even the parts that were so tempting. Not only his full lips, but the satisfied curve of them. She had never seen a naked gentleman before but could only imagine the physical perfection lying in wait beneath those immaculately tailored clothes. He was the most maddening, boastful, ungentlemanly duke in the world. Julia knew she'd soon grow exhausted of him, happy to have her own separate life.

But for today, well, the sight of him caused her breath to stop.

"Julia!" Susannah rushed over and embraced her. Julia hugged her stepsister tight, still stunned by her good fortune. Perhaps she'd wake up in a few moments to find this had all been a dream. God, she didn't think she could handle such a thing.

But the dream didn't end. It was real. So was the rakish Duke of Ashworth and Julia's new, exciting future.

The door opened and Constance reentered the room. She'd taken extra care with her appearance, applying the faintest touch of rouge to conceal her sickly pallor.

"Forgive me for earlier, Your Grace," she said. "I took a sudden turn but have recovered nicely." Julia's stepmother noticed the slipper now laid upon the floor. "Oh! Is that Julia's?"

"Yes, Miss Beaumont lost it on the

Weatherfords' front path last night," the duke said. "I took the liberty of returning it."

"So *that* explains your visit. Ha!" Constance fluttered her handkerchief. "Oh, that girl can be such a mischief. Well, I do hope you'll take some refreshment, Your Grace? Perhaps you might listen to my dear Susannah on the pianoforte. She's most accomplished."

"Yes, you should stay, my dear Ashworth," Julia purred. She sidled up to him and felt his own amusement radiating outward. They made an excellent pair of coconspirators. "My stepmother will want to help us plan the wedding."

"The... I'm sorry, what did you say?" Constance's handkerchief ceased fluttering.

"Oh, I also popped 'round to propose marriage to Miss Beaumont," he said with casual ease.

Constance wavered, a tree about to fall.

"Isn't it wonderful, Mamma?" Susannah beamed. "Julia's to be a duchess!"

Constance opened her mouth as if to scream.

Instead, she gave a great sneeze.

CHAPTER SEVEN

"Please hold still, Miss Beaumont." Mrs. Maxwell knelt upon the floor, hemming the white satin of Julia's soon-to-be wedding gown. "You will be the most ravishing bride of the Season. His Grace does have fine taste, does he not?"

"He's a very surprising man," Julia said. More than surprising. Ashworth—Gregory—had delivered shock after shock this past week. The morning after their engagement, he'd sent a carriage to collect the ladies. Julia was to have a whole new wardrobe courtesy of Mrs. Maxwell, the most fashionable modiste in London.

Julia felt dizzy as she regarded herself in the three dressing mirrors. She could imagine they were the three versions of herself. A past spinster, a future duchess, and, presently, the toast of London society.

She had to admit, her future husband had negotiated all of this perfectly. The instant they became engaged, Julia had wanted to get a special license to marry. The sooner she was safe from Constance's manipulations, the better. But Gregory had other, craftier ideas. He was 80 percent crafty ideas, 15 percent smug virility, and 5 percent effortless smolder.

"If we marry in haste, the society harridans won't believe I've fallen in love," he'd told Julia over dinner the next night. The engaged couple had spoken with Susannah while Constance remained frozen in horror at the end of the table. She'd looked like a living waxwork for almost a week now.

"Isn't there plenty of time to woo me in front of the *ton* after I'm your wife?" she'd asked.

"Our romance must fool everyone in London, from chambermaid to queen. I'm afraid I'll have to lavish you with gifts and attention, Miss Beaumont. *Julia*."

The way her name sounded upon his lips sent a rush of heat throughout her body. Between her legs, especially.

"I'll do my best to endure such trials. Gregory."

He had laughed with delight at her use of his name. The sound of that laughter was like soft fur rubbed along her spine.

Gregory had more than kept his word. Expensive flower arrangements arrived daily, each more lavish than the last. Julia hadn't known this many roses existed in all the hothouses in England. Boxes of marzipan, strings of pearls, even a milk-white Arabian mare turned up one after the other. Then came the engagement ring, a round, brilliant cut sapphire the size of a thumbnail and the exact shade of Julia's eyes. Susannah helped Julia sort the gifts, giddy as a child. Meanwhile, Constance remained mute, disappearing behind the boxes as they piled up.

Every morning, Julia would open the cards Gregory sent with the bouquets, and she would struggle not to burst out laughing. He wrote her private little "endearments."

To my lovely ball and chain, from your devoted future prisoner.

She dashed off notes to be sent back to him. *Ball and chain? I prefer to be called the Iron Maiden, sir.*

She'd get a reply back within the hour. *Only until we're married. Then you'll be the Iron Madame.*

Julia almost hated that it was so easy for him to make her laugh.

As the days passed, she had to acknowledge Gregory's cleverness. Their grand romance was in every society paper and gossip column. All of London called theirs a true Cinderella story. After all, every last detail was in place: the couple met at a ball, the lady lost her slipper, and the gentleman returned it with an offer of marriage.

Within days, Julia's wedding had been deemed the social event of the season. As the gifts poured in through the front door, so did endless rounds of fashionable callers. At least three duchesses had visited this week, and an eccentric gentleman poet had offered to compose a sonnet in Julia's honor.

Gregory was paying for Julia's wedding gown, trousseau, and a whole new wardrobe befitting a duchess. No expense would be spared.

No white satin would be left in London, either, by the time Mrs. Maxwell had finished. Julia had suggested she wear her best Sunday gown on the walk to the altar, the standard attire for a bride. But Gregory wouldn't hear of it; she must be the height of fashion, outfitted like a queen. The modiste had sewn pearls all along Julia's neckline, and there would be over a dozen white roses placed in her hair and tucked into the folds of her clothing. She'd look and smell heavenly on her way to be married.

But the dress and the new pelisse and the morning and afternoon gowns weren't the only attire the duke had arranged. There was also the matter of the six satin night rails. The sheer stockings held up with ruffled, riotously lacy garters. The drawers of brilliant crimson silk.

When Julia asked her fiancé why he'd ordered so many risqué choices, he'd smirked. "I have to show London I've fallen in love," he'd replied. "But I also have a reputation as a rake to maintain."

"You're going to look gorgeous." Susannah appeared in the mirror beside Julia's reflection. Her own bridesmaid's dress of peach silk had nearly been completed.

"I'm sorry, darling." Julia hugged Susannah as Mrs. Maxwell allowed her off the stool. "This whole wedding has eclipsed your first Season."

"Are you joking? It's increased my notoriety. I'm part of the fairy tale, after all." Susannah laughed as she flapped open a lace fan and fluttered it under her chin. "The wicked stepsister."

"Anyone who calls you wicked shall have my glass slipper shoved right up his—"

"Language, please." Lady Weatherford swept into the shop and seated herself upon the velvet settee.

"Would you care for tea, my lady?" Mrs. Maxwell beamed. Tea, port, champagne, she'd served them all to Julia and Susannah the last few days, alongside sugared almonds and candied plums.

"No, thank you." Laura blew out her cheeks as she patted her stomach. "Ugh. Bearing children is wonderful, but I shall be *so* glad when the first few months are over. She's already her father's daughter, dashing and somersaulting all over the place."

"So certain it's a girl?" Julia laughed. "Wouldn't Weatherford prefer a boy?"

"Please! We have two already. The viscount's had the nursery painted pink, and he's even told me the name: Daphne Josephine."

"What if it's a boy?" Susannah asked.

"Then Daphne will be the most original boy in all England."

Julia sat beside her friend as Mrs. Maxwell summoned Susannah, eager to see to the brides-maid's hem.

Meanwhile, Laura turned Julia's hand this way and that to admire the cut of her sapphire.

"I don't think I've ever seen a bigger stone," she marveled. "Ashworth must like you very much."

"I suppose it's better not to marry someone you detest," Julia said. Really, she was unbeliev-ably lucky. Every single detail of this wedding would be top-shelf. Constance would never have paid for such extravagances, not for Julia.

"You do like him, don't you?"

"Because of the duke, I'll never have to mas-sage Constance's shoulders ever again, read her the gossip pages, or remake her tea three times because something's always off." Julia suppressed a shudder. "I'm ready to throw him a parade every morning when he comes down to breakfast."

"Speaking of the morning..." Laura checked on Susannah, who was deep in discussion with Mrs. Maxwell. "Do you need any, well, advice?"

"On what? Awakening?"

"No. I know you've read a great deal, Julia, but some parts of married life can only be, er, experienced."

Laura's meaningful expression made it clear she was discussing the wedding night. The point of no return. Consummation.

Whenever Julia imagined Gregory standing above her, his shirt opened to display his sculpted chest and its perfect canvas of tawny flesh, she almost became faint. Her throat swelled, and her tongue felt thick and clumsy.

But she remembered the magic words: marriage of convenience. Nothing more. She'd never asked what that arrangement meant to Gregory, but she couldn't think why he'd want to, er, consummate the union. Even if the marriage weren't technically official until they did, who would know? It was all pretend, anyway.

This beautiful, expensive wedding gown, this sapphire ring, and all of those gifts and gestures were only pretend. Julia had accepted that, at her age, she would have to settle for a marriage of convenience, but she never dreamed she'd have to behave like a woman in the midst of a fairy tale. Sometimes she could almost fool herself into believing that this was real, that this man truly loved her. This sinfully handsome man with the face of an angel and the mind of a devil. A brilliant, wicked, amusing man.

Then she'd remember that this was all an act, and that she was gaining her freedom and comfort, nothing more. She pretended that thought didn't hurt at all. Julia had sharpened her wits to guard her heart, but she sometimes wished she could be that open, warm girl again. The one who didn't know the pain of disappointment.

The one who believed in love, or at least, who believed that she would find it.

"I don't think we need to worry about any of that." Julia studied the glinting ring on her finger. She wasn't a shy or melancholy person, but she couldn't pretend cheeriness she didn't feel.

"Why not?"

"You know why," Julia whispered. She was afraid Mrs. Maxwell would overhear. "This is an agreement, not a love match."

Laura and Susannah were the only women in London who knew the truth about the upcoming Ashworth wedding.

"Yes, but you *will* be married. Ashworth must want an heir at some point! Besides, you didn't see him the night you ran away from the ball." Laura's smile was pure mischief. In some ways, she was still the same optimistic girl she'd been when they were children. "He searched the entire room for you and scarce listened to a word I said."

Those words shouldn't have thrilled Julia. She knew Ashworth...Gregory...found her attractive, but he found *every* woman attractive. He was a ravenous wolf, and she was far too wise and world-weary to be a sheep.

"He doesn't want to complicate things, and neither do I," Julia said.

"Are you sure?" Laura frowned.

No. Not at all. But whenever Julia imagined speaking with Gregory about this, of placing herself in such a vulnerable position, she remembered only too well being seventeen years old. The last time she'd trusted any man. The last time she'd ever been a fool.

That was why marrying Gregory—no, the Duke of Ashworth—was so perfect. He would never fall in love with her. And while she believed he'd enjoy their wedding night, and that she would as well...

"I don't want to make this complicated," she whispered. "We both know what we're getting. We shouldn't try to arrange anything else."

Laura took her hand.

"That sounds rather like Lady Beaumont speaking," she muttered.

As if on cue, Constance waltzed in from the front of the shop, where she'd been examining a row of bonnets. Julia's stepmother wore an ice-blue afternoon dress, one that matched her glacial expression. Constance had a smile for Susannah, at least.

"My darling, you look quite beautiful. I'm certain you'll outshine the bride."

Laura cast a commiserating look at Julia before she went to admire the detail in Susannah's dress. That left Julia and Constance alone. Whenever Julia looked at her stepmother, she tried to spot what had made her father decide to marry the woman. Julia's mother had died when she was two, and for over a decade afterward her father had been her world. They'd been such good friends, and when he'd told Julia he was remarrying she'd been delighted. She didn't want to think of her father being alone, especially after she found herself a husband.

There must have been a time when Constance was kind to Julia, but it was hard to recall now. She and Julia's father hadn't even been married a full year when he died of a sudden illness, and from then on Julia had felt like a nuisance. If she'd been a boy, she could have inherited. Instead, the estate had gone to a distant cousin and Constance and the girls had been reduced to existing as tolerated guests in their own home.

"I think my gown's coming along rather nicely," Julia said. She wanted a pleasant afternoon.

"Mmm. His Grace has fine taste." Constance sniffed. "Though at *your* age, dear, wearing white is perhaps a touch inappropriate."

"Well, when I'm a duchess I'll help to set trends in society." Julia's blood pressure began to rise. "Women can wear any color they like, no matter how old they become. And I won't stop there. I might encourage any number of wild things, from large feathered headdresses to female suffrage."

"You have such an appalling sense of humor." Constance shuddered, her mouth puckering like she'd chomped into a lemon. Appalling. Too tall. Unfortunate. Irritating. All words that had dropped from Constance's mouth into Julia's ear over the years.

"I joke when I'm nervous," Julia said, her patience strained.

"Only weak women complain of their nerves."

That was more than enough. Julia stood, towering above her stepmother.

"If you could show me even the smallest kindness, we'd both be so much happier," Julia said. Her throat tightened as she fought a swell of emotion. She wished she could have even a few good memories of a mother's love, but Constance had made that impossible. Still, Julia had to believe that things could be fixed. For Susannah's sake, she didn't want there to be all this anger. "We could use this wedding as a chance to start over. There doesn't need to be competition any longer."

"Competition?" Constance appeared incredulous. She placed a hand upon her chest, a gesture of shock. "You think I feel in any way threatened by *you*? My Susannah is more beautiful and more charming than you'll ever be, and if you hadn't entrapped the duke, she'd have remained far wealthier, as well."

"How exactly do you mean entrapped?" Julia hissed. Constance walked away, summoning Julia. They didn't want Susannah to overhear, after all.

"I'm no fool." Constance's sneer could have chilled blood as they stood near a spool of lace, pretending to inspect it. "You think a man like the duke is marrying you for love? No, he wouldn't

have done such a thing if you hadn't gone and ruined yourself."

"That's not true," Julia snapped, even as her
face heated. Because it *was* true. She'd kissed
Gregory in that corridor, and if she hadn't happened to lose her shoe he likely never would have
sought her out. She'd still be ruined, and a spinster.

"You think you caught his eye?" Constance bit
back laughter. "You little fool. Even if you didn't
ruin yourself, you know that he's only using you.
I've heard of his reputation. The man's using you
to protect himself from scandal. A plain-faced
bride is just the ticket to make him look respectable."

Julia's stomach clenched. Constance had hit so
near the mark without even trying. The rest of
society would do the same. Even when Julia was
Duchess of Ashworth, her guests would greet her
with smiles and then whisper behind her back.
They'd pity Gregory, or else congratulate him on
using a pathetic spinster to keep from the dueling
field.

But his kisses at the ball had been passionate.
They had scorched Julia. Even if this marriage
was convenient, he did like her. She grew more
confident as she faced down Constance.

"You simply can't bear it, dear stepmother.
You've spent years trying to break me, all so I'd
be an obedient doll who'd follow your every com-
mand." Julia loomed; how lovely that she was tall
enough to loom. "But I won. I'm marrying far
above my station, and yours, and there is nothing

you'll ever be able to do or say to me again that can hurt me. I will be very happy with my husband, and Susannah will be always welcome at our home. But you will have to wait for a formal invitation, like the rest of the *ton*," Julia snapped.

"You may have this wedding." Constance's voice was sugared ice. "You may become a duchess, and you may even fool society into believing you're in love. But you know as well as I do that this wedding is a fraud." Her stepmother's lip curled. Constance had been passively cruel before. This was aggressive, as if now that Julia was leaving, Constance had to get in as many final jabs as possible. "That's the only way any man could ever marry you. You have a sharp tongue and an ugly countenance, my dear. You're the opposite of what a gentleman wants in a wife."

"How dare you?" Julia pulled herself up, but Constance knew just where to aim to deliver the greatest amount of damage.

"I'll always recall the seventeen-year-old girl who stayed outside of Pennington Hall all night, waiting with packed bags for a man to spirit her away. An elopement, puh. I also recall that girl trudging back inside come the morning, soaked to the skin and crying because her beloved never came. He thought better of it, and he abandoned you." Constance smirked. "Even when you were in your prime, Julia, you weren't enough to satisfy a man. Remember that."

Julia had never been tempted to strike another human being before. At least, not a woman. But her gloved hand clenched into a fist as she imagined walloping Constance right in her shrewish mouth.

She's right, you know.

Even if Constance had allowed Julia to spend her best years out in society, Julia likely would not have made many conquests. Men enjoyed looking at her, but when she opened her mouth they often lost interest. It wasn't that she was an idiot. Hell, if she'd been stupider she might have secured a proposal. Having opinions, especially educated ones, was a bad decision when one was female in this hideous society.

"When I'm the Duchess of Ashworth, I won't strike at you for Susannah's sake." Julia fought to keep her voice from quavering. "But I don't want to speak to you ever again, you spiteful old woman."

Constance gasped. Finally, Julia had managed to wound her vanity. As Constance stalked off to admire Susannah, Julia took a moment to compose herself. She gazed out the shop window to the bustling London street and noticed her reflection in the glass.

She saw a woman in a bridal gown, but even dressed in white Julia knew she was fooling herself. She wasn't a real bride. She recalled in vivid detail the day when she was supposed to elope. She could still feel the sting of the early morning rain against her cheek. When she'd realized that he hadn't come for her—that he would never come for her—she'd pretended that her tears were raindrops.

She'd been a fool before, but she would never be a fool again.

CHAPTER EIGHT

Gregory swallowed another brandy, feeling it burn down his gullet in a line of fire. The excellent liquor did nothing to burn away his thoughts of Julia, though. Nothing he tried could erase the memory of her generous curves, of her willful mouth and those kissable lips.

Here he was at the Wolf's Den, London's most luxurious club, surrounded by scantily clad beauties, and he couldn't get his future wife out of his head. He'd cast nary a glance at the women clad in velvet and diamonds, offering to share a glass of champagne and perhaps something more. Bloody Helen of Troy could've draped herself across his lap, and he would have forgotten she was there in a matter of seconds.

"This is a real problem."

"Isn't it good to fancy your fiancée?" Percy drawled as he sipped a beer. They were ensconced in a private booth with silk curtains to either side. The silhouettes of high society flashed by like a shadow play. "From everything you've told me, Miss Beaumont is a fine match for you."

"That's just the problem." Gregory pulled on a velvet cord, summoning a waiter to order another several brandies. "She's perfect. She's brilliant, and gorgeous, and God help me she's funny. She makes me *laugh*, Perce."

"You poor man." Percy snorted and drank.

"No, poor Julia. She deserves more than some dissolute libertine." Gregory scowled into his replenished glass. He found a shimmering, brandy-colored duke glowering back at him. One of Gregory's few virtues was honesty. He knew how ill equipped he was for married life. A worthy man would have been a lovable child. Gregory's birth should have been enough to give his parents something to cling to in their marriage, but they had been able to ignore each other—and him—with the greatest ease. If even his own parents couldn't love him, how would he be worth anything to a woman?

He'd taken to enjoying himself, giving every lady he bedded a night of sensational pleasure. If Gregory couldn't achieve love, he could at least have satisfaction.

But now he'd entrapped a fierce warrior goddess of a woman. Julia would soon realize that all the money and estates he possessed couldn't give her what she truly wanted. Affection. Companionship. Love.

Then she would despise him, and Gregory hated to think of seeing disdain in her eyes.

"Maybe you should ease up on the brandy," Percy said. "Besides, aren't your fiancée and her family coming to dine at Carter House tonight?"

"I'm on a liquid diet," Gregory drawled, swallowing another glass.

Someone parted the curtains and intruded on their dissolution. Gregory squinted into the dewy face of Mr. Worthington.

"Your Grace!" Worthington grinned. His

cheeks were flushed, the tip of his nose bright red. He'd already had a few. Or more. "We wished to congratulate you on your forthcoming nuptials!"

"We?" Gregory blinked in stupefied horror as an assortment of London's richest husbands crowded in on him, lifting glasses and cheering raucously. His eardrums rattled.

"My wife's been in tears since word started getting round!" one fellow crowed.

"Mine's sulked for days." Another appeared blissful at the notion.

"You've made our lives so much easier, Ashworth." Worthington seized Gregory's hand in a viselike grip. "We've been drinking toasts to you and Miss Beaumont all week!"

Gregory wrenched his hand away, though the news did give him a lift. All the London matrons believed this love match to be real. That meant he was safe. No more duels; no more wives chasing him through parks or crawling after him under carriages. (He'd only been pursued beneath a coach once, but once was more than enough.) Julia had saved him. She'd given him a new life.

And he was ruining hers in return. The thought set him to brooding into his glass once more.

"Chaps, why don't you say your goodbyes?" Percy asked. He seemed to intuit what Gregory was thinking. Smart fellow. "This is a private party."

"Of course." Worthington clapped Gregory's shoulder, which almost caused the duke to slosh his drink. "What a choice of a wife, too! A dowdy spinster for your duchess, why, it's a stroke of genius!" Worthington wobbled back and forth, unsteady on his feet.

"What did you say?" Gregory's vision sharpened as he rose to his feet. "About Miss Beaumont?" Dowdy? How could anyone look at a woman like that and see dowdiness?

"It was sporting of you not to take any of the prime girls from the marriage mart." Worthington gave a lazy smile. "Some of the men might have felt resentful. But taking an older, dried-up spin—"

Gregory clobbered Worthington across the jaw, dropping the fellow in an instant. The crowd of men backed up as Worthington blustered and tried crawling to his feet. Gregory's knuckles stung, but he hardly felt the pain.

"Anyone who has something rude to say about my intended is welcome to get the same treatment," he snapped. The fellows all inched farther away, regarding Gregory with fearful looks, or curled, angry lips. He didn't care. Were all men so idiotic that they could pass up a desirable woman because she wasn't what society mindlessly told them they should want?

"How dare you!" Worthington tugged that stupid lace hankie from his pocket.

"I know, I know," Gregory said. "Pistols at dawn."

Before Worthington could issue the challenge, something heavy slammed atop the table, rattling the glassware.

A silver wolf's head snarled up at Gregory. A chip of ruby glinted in its eye socket.

"You know how it goes, gentleman," a low voice rumbled. "No issuing duels in my establishment."

The rest of the celebrating husbands vanished, terrified as always to be confronted by the Wolf himself. Gregory only smiled at the surly fellow.

"Hello, Rafe. Care to join us for a drink?"

Rafe Winters gripped the silver-headed knob of his cane and gave a friendly sneer. The so-called Wolf of Mayfair, Rafe was the wealthiest and most notorious businessman to ever come out of the Camden slums. His club specialized in the finest of everything, from crystal chandeliers to vintage wines to the most genteel clientele.

Everyone knew the Wolf, but only Gregory and a select few didn't fear him.

"I don't drink on the job, Ashworth. You toffs know that." Rafe gave another crooked, fearsome smile as he stalked away. The tall, black-haired man cut a swath through his club, that cane *thunking* with every step. Rafe's knee had been smashed during a fight in his early days. He'd gotten himself a cane, and then used it to beat in the head of the prick who'd injured him.

Worthington quivered on the floor like a pale, landed fish until Rafe had vanished.

"Still care to call that duel?" Gregory smiled as the man crawled away.

"An evening with you is always an adventure." Percy drained the last of his beer, then summoned a waiter for the bill. "But we should go home, Ashworth. Your young lady will be arriving soon enough."

"At least she'll be impressed by Carter House." Gregory tried to fumble his clothes back into something resembling order. "Perhaps the sheer bloody size of the place will distract her from what she's saddled herself with."

"Will marrying her be so very terrible?"

Percy didn't understand because he still had a soul.

As they rattled back to Grosvenor Square in his carriage, Gregory watched the London evening fly past his window. His thoughts flew to Julia, and how badly he wanted to see her. It had been two days since they'd last met. She must have had another fitting for her trousseau at Mrs. Maxwell's. The thought of the delicate silk and lace items Gregory had arranged for his new bride tightened his loins with pure longing.

After all, even if this were a marriage of convenience, it would have to be consummated at least once. Otherwise, Julia would never feel certain that she was safe from annulment.

Gregory imagined entering the bridal chamber to find her lounging across the bed, her voluptuous curves caressed by the finest silks. He pictured removing the garment, finding the heavenly display of her naked body ready for his. Ready to be filled by him.

His fist clenched. God, even if he couldn't give that woman everything she deserved, he could at least make her happy she'd married him for one wild night. In that way, at least, he'd see her satisfied.

• • •

"I don't know what I was expecting." Julia became breathless as their carriage pulled up to Carter House and the footman opened the door. "Perhaps not quite so many windows."

Indeed, the enormous, three-story house rose up into the night with spiral turrets at east and west, and every single window blazed with brilliant candlelight. This was only Ashworth's London home. His estate itself would be even grander.

Susannah bounced from the carriage with excitement. Constance still hadn't looked at the house, as if it couldn't possibly interest her. Julia ignored her stepmother as she climbed down.

The front door opened just as they arrived, and a distinguished-looking butler with gray hair bowed the ladies in. Julia went slack-jawed as she entered the front hall.

The floors were laid with the creamiest Italian marble, which had been buffed to a shine. The wood-paneled walls were decorated with sumptuous velvet hangings, many of which bore the Ashworth crest in gold. Gleaming suits of medieval armor stood on either side of the doorway, swords and shields at the ready.

The works of art that adorned the walls were so plentiful that they made Julia dizzy. She saw an oil painting of a reclining courtesan that had to be hundreds of years old. The woman lay on a bed of silks and smiled knowingly at the viewer. She was naked apart from the wild flow of her golden-red hair.

That certainly seemed like the type of woman Ashworth craved. A voluptuous goddess. Julia blushed to think of how she might compare to such a beauty.

But that thought made her pull back her shoulders. A living, breathing woman was more complicated than some flawless image created by men, for other men. Julia wouldn't be cowed by other people's expectations. Women spent far too much time apologizing for their insecurities anyway.

"Ladies." The duke came to greet them as the women entered. He gave a small, formal bow. "Welcome."

Every time Julia saw him, it felt like lightning rippling under her skin. The candlelight glowed upon Gregory's cheekbones, both highlighting his face and casting it into shadow in the perfect ways. The duke was as much a work of art as the masterpieces hanging in his hallway.

"So this is Carter House." Julia glanced around the splendid room once again.

"You approve, my dear?"

It felt as if he was truly interested in her reaction. Well, he had excellent taste, after all. He must want to hear it praised.

"Do you think it's large enough?" she asked. Julia's voice echoed in the vast space. Gregory smiled, his eyes flashing. He did like when she teased him.

"Absolutely." He kissed her gloved hand, his

eyes never leaving hers. Julia's whole body heated from that small amount of contact. "Despite what other men tell you, size *does* matter."

Julia's heart knocked against her rib cage. God, why did the man have to be so bloody good at being so deliciously bad?

The group went through to dinner, joined by Percy Randall, Gregory's friend and best man. The soup and fish and duck courses moved one after the other like perfect clockwork, and throughout the meal Percy charmed everybody while Gregory drank a great deal.

Every time he glanced at Julia across the table, he took another swallow of some very good wine.

Perhaps he's started to regret it. Julia couldn't shut out that sensible voice inside of her. After all, Gregory was shackling himself to a woman he did not know out of a simple need for protection. Once the desperate wives of the *ton* left him alone, the duke would look at Julia and see what everyone else saw: a lonely spinster who'd managed to ensnare him in a moment of weakness. His gratitude would vanish, and he might even come to scorn her for taking away his perpetual bachelorhood.

Julia became sick just thinking of it. No, more than sick; bloody furious. She wasn't about to spend her life feeling like a burden. After Constance, she could never live like that again. She'd seen enough of life to know that wealth and status without self-respect meant nothing at all.

Not that she was going to call off the engagement. She wasn't out of her mind. But before they went any further, she and the duke needed a few things cleared up.

After dinner, the women waited in the drawing room for the men to finish their brandy, another absurd custom that only delayed the important conversation. Julia was almost bursting out of her skin by the time Gregory and Percy came through. Constance and Percy soon gathered at the pianoforte to listen to Susannah's beautiful playing. While music lilted about the room, Gregory approached Julia.

"What do you think of your future home?" he muttered.

"Perhaps too many windows."

Gregory chuckled at that, which gave Julia the courage for what came next. "Is there a more private location? I'd like a quick chat."

His face became neutral and stony. Julia's gut tightened; it looked like he'd been thinking the very same.

"Follow me."

The duke led her into a smaller, book-lined chamber. He left the door open only a crack, so that the music slipped inside.

"Oh!" Julia gasped as she surveyed the room. "It's…astounding!"

She'd never seen so many books in one place before. The ten-foot tall shelves scraped the top of the ceiling, and every bit of space was crammed with leather-bound volumes. Julia hurried to a shelf and picked up a copy of *Robinson Crusoe*. She riffled through the velvety pages, admiring the book.

"You like to read?" Gregory asked.

"I love it. It's one of my favorite hobbies." She glanced slyly at him over her shoulder. "Don't tell me *you* are a reader, Your Grace."

"Now, why should that be so surprising?" The duke sounded genial, but she might have detected a note of something else beneath the good humor. Something almost wounded. No, she must be making all that up; men like Gregory never had their feelings bruised. Then again, her perception of Gregory mainly consisted of three things: he was handsome, he was a duke, and he was a rake. The thought of a great seducer sitting down before a winter fire, a book propped open in his lap, a cup of tea at hand, seemed like a grand joke. But Gregory wasn't a simple rogue in a story book. He was a man. A man with contradictions, thoughts, and appetites.

At the notion of appetites, Julia slipped the book back in place, steeling her nerves before she turned to face him. "Ashworth, we need to discuss something important."

"Yes. I agree," he said. The man also looked like he was preparing for something. Something unpleasant.

God, was he trying to tell her he'd thought better of it? That he wanted to call the wedding off?

Julia had planned to rush ahead, but he beat her to it.

"It's about our wedding night," Gregory said.

CHAPTER NINE

It was as he'd feared. Mention of the wedding night stole all color from Julia's cheeks. She looked as if the idea of giving herself to him like some virgin sacrifice was repulsive.

She had grown somehow more beautiful in the days since they'd last met. Maybe it was the dress she wore, one of the concoctions Gregory had paid Mrs. Maxwell to create. Julia glittered like a diamond in a gown of cream silk with crushed blue velvet accents. And there was something about the way she came alive when surrounded by books that excited him further. It was one thing to desire a beautiful woman, but a beautiful woman with a keen mind only fed the ache in his loins and the fire in his blood. Because ladies were discouraged from anything too mentally taxing, Gregory adored a woman who devoured knowledge for its own sake. It was the most glorious kind of selfishness, to become who you wanted to be without a thought for the narrow constricts of society. He was delighted by Julia's boldness.

But she appeared so terrified at the idea of giving herself to him that it forced Gregory to look away from the gorgeous vision. His reputation repulsed her, and she was sacrificing so much of what she truly desired in order to marry him. She was his for show, but not for touch. Julia Beaumont was a fantasy. It's all she could ever be.

"Forgive me for bringing it up," he said. "I merely wanted to let you know that we don't have to consummate our union." He swallowed; his throat felt quite dry. He couldn't let her see how bloody disappointed he was. "In fact, it would be best if we didn't."

"Of course." She turned her back on him, studying the spines of his books with rapt fascination. Doubtless she was trying to hide her giddy relief.

"You don't need to worry about an annulment. I never planned to marry or have children, so I won't try to weasel out of our arrangement even after the *ton*'s wives and dowagers have moved on."

"That's very considerate of you." Her tone was tart. Somehow, he found her desirable even when she was snapping at him.

"You sound as if you're about to throw a book at me."

"I am not."

"Just don't make it the complete works of William Shakespeare. That could kill me if you aimed wrong."

"I never aim wrong." Julia snatched one of the volumes from off the shelf and, just as he'd anticipated, chucked it at him with a short, sharp cry. Gregory caught the book as it sped toward his face.

"Christopher Marlowe. Excellent choice," he said, reading the cover.

"You really can be a monumental ass, Your Grace," Julia snapped.

"I don't know why you're spitting venom at me now." Gregory went and shoved the volume back into its spot, coming face-to-face with the delectably furious Miss Beaumont. "I've just tried to respect your decision."

"Oh, naturally. This has nothing to do with *your* desires, not at all!" Julia's cheeks flushed. Gregory couldn't help wondering if other parts of her naked body colored with passion. He clenched his jaw, trying to will his desires away. "If you can't bear the thought of a proper wedding night between us, Ashworth, then say so. I'm not a child. I'm perfectly capable of behaving like a rational adult!"

"Says the rational adult who threw a book at me."

But the world seemed to disappear all around Gregory as he beheld the infuriated vixen. She was angry because she thought he didn't want to consummate their union. If he didn't know better, he might have thought that meant that Julia wanted to consummate. That she was *eager* to consummate.

His breeches tightened at the very thought that she wanted him on top of her, thrusting in and out of her sweet, soft wetness. Desire almost fractured Gregory's vision. He had to force himself to stay standing, and quiet.

"You made my 'decision' for me, just as I would expect from some overprivileged aristocrat."

"Then tell me, madam. What do you decide for yourself?"

The color fled her cheeks once again. Julia looked away from him, feigning disinterest. Gregory's heart quickened, and he heard his pulse in his ears. Had he gotten it all wrong? Was she as eager for a wedding night as he was? Was such a thing even possible? He wanted her to capitulate into his arms with a cry; he was terrified she'd do just that.

"Answer me, Julia. It's up to you. I leave the decision totally in your hands." He couldn't help the mocking edge that sharpened his voice. "Do you want a proper wedding night?"

Say yes, God. Please say yes.

No. You have to say no, damn you.

Gregory wanted her to say yes; for her own sake, he begged her to say no.

"I..." Julia chose another book from his shelves, this time a collection of poetry by Shelley. As she turned the pages, the lady absently bit at her full lower lip. God, she was sensational. "I don't see why we need to discuss any of this. It's insulting."

"Oh? A man insults a woman by giving her a say in her own destiny?" Gregory moved toward the door, willing her anger. He wanted a reaction worthy of her. Something volcanic and passionate. Something that matched the heated blood flowing in his own veins. "I didn't realize you were so old-fashioned, Miss Beaumont."

"You really are an incorrigible ass!"

"On that, at least, we can agree." Gregory turned and came face-to-face with the girl. Anger brightened her eyes, just as it whetted his wits...

and engorged certain body parts. He noticed her gaze trail along his form, stopping at his rapidly developing excitement. She bit her lip, blushed, and looked away. "Tell me what you want, Julia."

"What I want?"

"Has no man ever asked you that before? What do you want?" He drew nearer to her. She wrapped her arms around herself, as if out of protection. Likely no one ever *had* sought such an answer from her before. "Tell me what you want from me. I'll do what I can to meet your expectations," he whispered.

At least in the bedroom, he believed he could satisfy her. Even if it was only the one time. Even if it was just a few blissful hours before the rest of their lives began, apart.

"You're being impertinent," she whispered. But she couldn't hide the way her body quivered for one moment, a leaf about to fall from a tree. She wasn't afraid of him. Gregory realized that she feared herself. But why? Did she fear her desire? Her reluctance? Her passion? He wanted to know her, all of her. Beyond the superficial details like her age, her beauty, her spinsterhood, she was something rare. It was obvious. He just wanted to bloody see her.

"Do you hate my impertinence?" Inch by inch, they drew closer together. Her lips were warm, inviting, begging to be claimed and kissed once again. They had not kissed since that night at the Weatherford ball, but now much was permitted. Even if society would be scandalized by their being alone, entwined in passion, surrounded by books, they *were* engaged. In two simple weeks, everything would be allowed.

"I hate the way you toy with me." But she didn't try to move away from him. If anything, she inched closer. Gregory wanted to bury himself inside of her, his head in her hair, nestled in the slope of where her neck and shoulder met. He wanted to lift this fragile silk dress and have his way with her on the library's velvet settee. His balls tightened at the mere idea of her soft inner thigh, of the sleek wet of her sex. He wanted to make himself one with this impossible, vibrant woman.

I want a wedding night. Just once. Even if it's all I ever get from you, I'll die happy knowing how you feel just the once.

But he needed to hear those words from her lips. He needed those words like he craved oxygen.

"Apologies, my lady." Gregory did not move. He didn't take her in his arms, or press his lips to hers. He needed to let her tell him the truth; whether she actually wanted him or not. "What would you have me do?"

"Just be honest with me. I know you don't love me." She was blunt, so straightforward. She didn't sniffle, or look at him with doe eyes, pleading him to contradict her. The woman looked at him like he was an equal, not a fairytale prince she was desperate to create in order to satisfy her fondest dreams.

"Men like me aren't capable of love, it's true," he said. "But it has nothing to do with you, Julia.

I'm the one who's deficient."

"And that means you're trying to protect me, then?" She took one step closer, so that their breaths mingled. Gregory felt her nearness, her body warming his in the narrow space between them. "You don't want to hurt me, is that it?"

The thought of hurting her ate him alive, and it was made worse by the certain knowledge he would do just that. No matter what he did, stay or leave, he would hurt her in the end because that's what he did. That's all he truly was, a worthless man whom fate had given a fortune and title.

"Enough of these games," he growled. She was driving him to distraction with her body, the heady scent of rosewater perfume that clung to her hair. "Tell me what you want, madam. Tell me, or God help me I'll make the choice for both of us."

"What do you choose?" she whispered. He felt her hands sliding up his chest, her fingers winding together as she clasped the back of his neck. Her luscious mouth twitched as she fought a smile. The vixen was teasing him.

Gregory couldn't think. He couldn't think of Percy and the two ladies in the other room, of the scandal of being alone with this woman. His brain could think of nothing clever to say, not when she was this near and her body this warm and her mouth this frustrating.

"I choose to silence you," he whispered. "I've had enough of your talk."

"I'm afraid I rather love talking," Julia purred. "You'll have to find something I enjoy more."

She wanted him. Gregory's breath caught in his throat, triumph shouting all through his soul.

"I have a few ideas," he said.

Then he claimed her lips with his.

• • •

The first kiss had been ravishing. The second made her want to be ravished.

Gregory clasped her to him, fisted her array of golden, curling hair as he pressed her close. Once again, Julia was drowning in his embrace. He tasted heavenly, of secrets and wine, and his lips seemed to burn her with their passion. Julia had wanted to make him kiss her. She'd wanted to see him lose control and feel smug in how superior her own control was.

But she was lost in his arms again. This time, he did more than kiss her. As his tongue stroked against hers, as he moaned into her mouth, his hands roamed across her body. Julia quivered when he traced a hand along the curve of her back before cupping her bottom. She gasped, but he didn't release her mouth. He kept kissing her greedily as he squeezed the plump swell of her backside, then reached down to claim her thigh. He lifted it, causing her to wrap her leg around his hip as he slowly, effortlessly laid her backward.

Julia found herself lying upon the settee, gasping for breath and sanity as the duke aligned his body with hers. She groaned as his fingers skated along her neckline until his hand landed upon her breast. He squeezed her through the silk, causing her to grow slick between her legs. She pulsed, desperate to feel him pressing down inside of her.

"Does this tell you what I want, you minx?" He kissed her neck, his whiskers scraping her delicate skin. Julia's hips bucked at the unexpected surge of pleasure. His breath was hot against her ear. She whimpered when he took her delicate lobe between his teeth, when he sucked it into his mouth. Gregory slid up her skirt, one daring inch at a time, before running his hand along her calf.

He brushed his palm across her knee…and then went higher. Julia shut her eyes in blissful rapture at the sensation of his fingers on the soft canvas of her inner thigh.

Lord, he was coming to the tops of her stockings. A few inches beyond those, and he would touch her where no one else had ever been allowed to go.

She wanted him to explore her. She wanted his hands to be the first to touch her in every conceivable, secret place. Julia knew that this wasn't love, that it could never be love between them, but she wanted all of this if only for a single night. She wanted consummation.

Even if it meant he never touched her again afterward, that they lived separately so that he could have his dalliances and she could have her freedom.

"You asked me what I want?" she whispered.

"Tell me," he growled. It was difficult to growl as he kissed her lips, but he managed it skillfully. His attentions left her breathless.

"I want a proper wedding night." Her voice

almost hitched, but Julia managed to keep from sounding afraid. Gregory's pupils dilated so that his eyes were dark, hungry pools of need. "And then that will be that."

"You mean once, and never again." His nostrils flared as he breathed deeply. The duke's hand squeezed her breast, and Julia saw bright pinpoints of light all around the room, her own private constellation of stars.

"I need to be sure of my place." She lifted her chin, regaining control. "I need to be the true duchess, not just some imitator. But I don't want to complicate matters, so we'll be together one time only. Then we'll go our separate ways. Do you agree?"

"Do I have a choice in the matter?" Gregory's voice came out as little more than a snarl. It made her flush, to hear how near he was to losing control of his senses. Because of her.

"You mean you don't want to?"

"Does it feel like I don't?"

True. Julia's heart pounded as she could feel him pinned between her thighs. She didn't need to be told what part of him had grown so rigid, and what he wanted to do to her. The very idea made her want to laugh with delight.

"This isn't going to be a proper marriage. We both agreed to that. Being like, well, *this* for more than one night will set up expectations. It will create problems. I want to avoid that."

A muscle feathered in his jaw as Gregory narrowed his eyes. He assessed her as a predator might before it went in for the kill. But he didn't seem to realize that he hadn't felled a deer. Julia was a female panther ready to claw his own eyes out should he deserve it.

The duke smirked.

"You're a wise chit, I'll grant you that."

"Call me a chit again and I'll grant you a fast, messy death."

He struggled against laughter, a sight that always warmed Julia's heart…and quickened her blood.

"Then we'll have a wedding night," he said. "A proper one. A mutually satisfying one." His voice was like aged whiskey. Julia held her breath as he leaned over her, lips tracing hers as he spoke. "And the next morning, I'll depart England. Alone."

"Taking a honeymoon all for yourself, Your Grace?"

"Nothing could be more peaceful."

Julia's nipples hardened as he claimed a kiss from her one last time. Her toes curled as he moaned into her mouth. So she'd have this for one night. She'd consummate her union with this exasperating man.

And then their happily ever afters would commence, entirely apart.

"Speaking of peaceful," Julia said. "If we don't want Constance screeching and flying about, we'd better quit this room at once."

"Indeed. You should straighten yourself up first, though." He lifted his body from hers, and smoothed a hand through his wild, luxuriant hair. Julia sat up, adjusting her gown and stockings. She smiled with swollen lips.

"And you'd better calm yourself." She couldn't help how her eyes tracked to the prominent bulge at the front of his trousers. Julia felt her face go scarlet as she slid a foot into a lost slipper. "After all, we don't want to cause a scandal."

CHAPTER TEN

Julia found herself standing in the center of her wedding breakfast, her head still in a whirl from the events of the past two weeks. On her walk up the aisle this morning, hanging on Lord Weatherford's arm as he gave her away, she'd seen the faces of high society staring at her from the pews. It was unusual to have such a crowd turn out for the ceremony itself, but then again there was nothing typical about this marriage. Julia had seen rows of so many smiling men…and so many tearful-looking women.

She could scarce recall the vows. Julia only knew that she'd said them, and Gregory had said them as well, and now a gold band fit quite snug on her left hand. Every once in a while she'd gaze down at it as if in shock. There was such a rush of excitement in her veins, but also fear.

Her life as Constance's drudge had been small, but it had been safe in its own way. She had known what each day would bring. But now she was a wife, a duchess, and she had taken her place as one of the leaders of high society. Last week's pathetic spinster had become today's *ton* darling.

"All because a man put a ring on my finger and swore an oath," she muttered to Laura. They were standing in Beaumont House's main gallery, where white roses adorned the tables and the cook kept bringing out rounds of salmon on toast.

"They don't care a fig about a woman's mind or abilities. All they care about is whether or not some man finds her worthy. Honestly!"

"It's shameful." Her friend nibbled a corner of toast in agreement. "But at least now that you're the Duchess of Ashworth you could try turning the peerage on its antiquated head."

The Duchess of Ashworth. The words almost made Julia giggle, like a rude joke someone had let fly.

"The turning has already begun." Julia beamed. "I'd a letter from the Society of Ladies for the Expansion of Female Literacy. I thought they wanted to know where my next pamphlet was, but they were most adamant about meeting to discuss plans for a charity ball. In fact, they're eager for my opinion on all sorts of initiatives."

"Oh?" Laura shook her head. "Unbelievable. You were almost a glorified secretary two months ago."

"Yes, writing essays on the more minor points no one cared about. Now they want to talk of giving me the position of chairwoman! They said no one has done more to champion the cause over the years than I have." Julia wanted to laugh; people were so ridiculous. "Well. If becoming a duchess has given me power over the lot of them, I intend to use it."

"You'll become quite a tyrant," Laura said. "Worse than Bonaparte himself."

"Indeed. By the time I'm finished, every charwoman in England will be able to read and write with proficiency. And I may not stop there. Wait until I've got them digesting essays on female suffrage."

"Is Ashworth aware he's married such a dangerous woman?" Laura grinned.

"We both of us know exactly what we're getting in this arrangement." Julia surveyed the room. Virtually no one else knew the truth or would ever know. Here she was with over two hundred members of the *ton* fawning over her and weeping at the beauty of her "fairytale romance," and all the while Julia felt like she was playing an enormous prank on the lot of them. A prank that would last the rest of her life.

They thought she and Gregory were a love match? Julia couldn't imagine ever loving a man like that. Desiring him, yes. God, yes. But a witty and charming rake was still a rake. Anyway, Gregory himself had stated plainly he had no capacity to love. Julia would be a fool not to believe his own words.

At least, as a rake, Gregory would know what to do tonight when they...consummated.

"I need to ask you something," she whispered to Laura. The viscountess put down her plate and snuck off with Julia to stand in the hall just outside the gallery. "So. Ah." Goodness, Julia wished she wasn't blushing quite so hard at the moment. She blamed it on the three sips of champagne she'd had. Two hours ago. "Ashworth and I have agreed that we will, in fact, be having a wedding night."

"Oh." Laura's eyebrows lifted.

"Just the one, of course."

"I don't think you get more than one wedding night. At least, not with the same husband."

"I'd rather set myself on fire than ask Constance about something like this, and I think she'd feel the same. I know all about the, eh, anatomy of the situation."

"Julia, you're scarlet. You're almost mauve!"

"Oh, blast it all. Is there anything I should know that might come as a surprise?" Julia wasn't like Susannah in these matters. Dear Susannah was so open with her feelings, and so comfortable expressing them to those she loved the most. Julia had learned long ago that anything she revealed could be used to hurt her later on. Constance had proved that. She didn't want to show what she truly felt: that she was terrified and elated all at once. That she was curious about what she'd feel.

Well, maybe not curious, because she knew precisely how she'd feel. The mere thought of Gregory's body atop hers could leave her panting and breathless. The entire day, part of her had hoped the sun would never set, while the other had begged night to arrive.

"You don't need to worry." Laura took Julia's hand in both of hers. "If I'm sure of anything, it's that the duke knows exactly what he's doing. In that way, rakes make the most wonderful husbands."

"I don't know why I'm afraid. I hate even admitting that I am!"

"Are you afraid of the pain?" Laura frowned. "As long as he doesn't rush, it lasts only a moment."

"Not the physical pain." She sighed. Julia meant the other, emotional pain. Not that she'd be abandoned, by any means. She knew that Gregory was set to sail on the morning tide, bound for Spain, and from there, perhaps deeper into the Mediterranean. He said he'd "business" to attend, but "business" could only be coded language for pleasure. Well, that was fine with Julia. They would both go about their lives as if nothing had happened. "I think I'm afraid that I'll be so terrible at it, he'll feel sorry for me."

"Julia!" Laura clapped a hand over her mouth but couldn't help her laughter.

"I won't be pitied by anyone! Especially my own husband." But even Julia had begun to chuckle.

"Any man who expects you to be both a virgin and a true proficient at the same time is a dreadful prat. I believe he'll be both good and kind to you."

"How can you think that?" Julia was surprised.

"Well, the Carter Club wouldn't exist if he weren't adept." Laura shivered. "Ugh. Half of them have gone into mourning since news of your engagement broke."

"No, I mean how can you believe he'll be kind to me? He's notorious for seducing women and dueling men. How could anyone go from that to being kind?"

"Well, I'm one of the few married London women who knows Ashworth well, but not intimately." Laura smirked, her eyes twinkling with merriment. "And I know that he's not as wretched as people say he is. Also, I know what I've witnessed with my own two eyes. And I've seen how he looks at you."

"It's a marriage of convenience," Julia muttered.

"And wouldn't it be convenient if you fell in love with your own husband?"

For the second time in her entire life, Julia found herself tongue-tied. She wanted to keep arguing with Laura about this but wasn't even certain what she was fighting. Or who. Maybe what she truly feared was what Laura had said. That she *would* fall in love with her husband.

And that he would never be able to love her in return.

"Julia! Lady Corwin is asking after you." Susannah dashed into the hallway, looking as delighted as if this were her own wedding day. Her stepsister was the only person on earth who could fully melt Julia's heart. "Isn't this most exciting? Though I'll be sad waking up tomorrow and finding you gone."

"Well, that's why I'll need you to come and visit often. Call every day. Why, just come and live with me the rest of the Season. I can do a much better job of chaperoning you now than Constance."

"Oh, that'd be lovely." Susannah cocked her head at a quizzical angle. "But won't you be quitting town for your honeymoon?"

"Gregory will be going away. I won't." Julia made sure to smile, so that Susannah didn't worry. "We both agreed it'll be for the best. Honestly, most wives would love the thought of a honey-moon spent on their own."

"I adore my husband, and you're quite right on that score." Laura headed back to the gallery. "Come along. You can't afford to neglect your guests, especially now that you're one of the great ladies of the *ton*."

Julia reentered her wedding reception, chatting and smiling with so many people that she began to lose track of who everyone was. Her thoughts kept spinning to Gregory. Every time she caught sight of him looking decadent in his wedding clothes, she noticed him smiling, laughing, or telling some story with animation. She also noticed that most of the women were leaving him well alone, which could only add to his good mood.

Once, just once, he caught her eye across the crowded room. God, she wanted a chance to speak with him in private, but as the bride and groom they had no opportunities. As Julia moved among her guests, accepting compliments and congratulations, she wondered what the duke could possibly be thinking.

· · ·

I hate clothes.

Specifically, Gregory hated Julia's clothes. Not that there was anything wrong with them—indeed, he'd spent a considerable sum to make sure they were top-notch. But he wanted her to take them off, and if this bloody wedding breakfast didn't end soon, he might have to just get on top of a table, summon the guests' attention, and politely urge them to get the hell out. Yes. That was just what a respectable gentleman did on his wedding day.

At the altar this morning, he'd been stunned to realize what was happening. He stared at Julia in her white satin, with the gold band glinting on her finger, and realized that he had married this enchantress. Somehow, Gregory had found himself in the exact position he swore he'd never take. He'd become a husband.

Even if it was mainly for show, even if he'd only know his wife for one short evening, he'd taken a duchess. Julia couldn't have suited him better. She was everything he needed: beautiful, brilliant, courageous, and so very practical. She didn't ask for anything he could not give.

Gregory had a sudden flash of inspiration: perhaps he could tell her some further truths about himself. For starters, he could explain what his true business was in heading for the Continent. Julia probably thought he was off for an erotic escapade, but he could disabuse her of those notions. Honesty, why, it could be just the thing to change her opinion of him. To have her see him with clearer eyes...

"I don't understand." His mother put down her quill, leaving the letter she'd been writing unattended as she gazed at Gregory in befuddlement. "What's this doing here?"

"This," said his nurse calmly, "has finished his tea and would like to spend an hour with you in the parlor."

The memory made him flinch. Gregory had been all of five years old at the time, but he hadn't dared to approach his mamma for a hug. He didn't think he could recall ever receiving one, in fact.

"Take him to the park if he's got nothing to do. Honestly." His mother returned to her letter. She didn't even notice when Gregory left the room.

He looked out the window, giving himself a moment to calm down. Though his parents had been absolute beasts, even beasts loved their children. Gregory himself had been deficient, that was the only explanation.

"Your Grace, may I have a word?" Lady Beaumont simpered up to him. She wore a lavender frock that on any other woman would have appeared springlike. On her, it looked chilly.

"Certainly."

He led his new mother-in-law, or stepmother-in-law, or whatever-in-law to the side of the room. Her lips pursed. She looked as though a disgruntled man had appeared stark naked before her. It was a very specific type of look.

"Yes?" Gregory tried to be polite. A little.

"There's the matter of Julia's dowry. As you may know, my late husband was an excellent man, but not particularly good with money. Julia's dowry is small, a mere three thousand pounds." She scoffed, as if embarrassed by an amount of money that could have supported most families for their entire lives. "However, there is also the matter of the enormous expenses she's created since her father died. Especially since it took her so long to be married."

"Yes." Gregory forced his pleasant smile to remain in place. "If only she'd been taken to London sometime in the last ten years, she might have made a match sooner."

"Er. Quite. Though I'm certain you're only too relieved she didn't marry anyone else."

Gregory tried to keep a handle on his temper.

"I'm asking if you'd be prepared to receive a smaller sum in place of the three thousand, so I may reclaim some of the costs," the woman said.

"Forgive me if I'm wrong, but you were married twice, weren't you? Wasn't your first husband, Susannah's father, quite wealthy when he died?"

Constance turned an unflattering shade of green that clashed with the lavender frock.

"That's Susannah's money. Surely you don't think I'd favor Julia over my own daughter?"

"I think if you'd favored Julia at all, her life would be different." The poor girl likely wouldn't have stayed on the shelf this long. She wouldn't have needed to settle for marriage to the country's most notorious rake. She could have had a happier life, one with children and a true marriage, a future that a man as warped as Gregory could never provide. And now Lady Beaumont wanted to stick one last knife into Julia? "I don't want her dowry. Consult Julia about it and give her whatever is 'left over.' Is that all?"

"Well. You don't need to take such a tone." Whenever someone was in the wrong, they always complained about tone. How fascinating.

"If you wanted one last opportunity to

humiliate Miss Beaumont—beg pardon, the Duchess of Ashworth—then I'm afraid you haven't succeeded." Gregory kept his voice level and silken, all elegance. If anyone saw him, they'd claim he looked perfectly cordial. "The only one you've humiliated, my lady, is yourself."

"You really do deserve each other," she said, pursing her lips.

"You've been wrong about everything else in the short time we've known one another. No surprise that you're wrong about that, too. Julia deserves far better than both of us."

Gregory gave a polite bow and walked away, leaving Lady Beaumont to sputter all by herself.

"I saw that."

Gregory paused as Julia glided up to him. He had never seen such a spark in those blue eyes before. In fact, she appeared almost giddy.

"You saw only my most charming performance, as usual." He lifted a brow.

"I know Constance's smallest ticks. Whatever you just said knocked her flat out."

"Such violent language, madam. And now that you're a duchess, why it's positively…" He leaned just a bit nearer, so that he could whisper close to her ear. "Enthralling."

He heard the hitch in her breathing, which thrilled him too much. It also made him want to take her into his arms and finally do what he'd yearned to do since the moment he laid eyes upon her.

But first, they had the rest of this damned reception to get through.

• • •

Once the guests had left and Julia had changed into a pale blue going-away frock, she descended the stairs of Beaumont House for the last time. She blew a kiss to her father's portrait while she walked down to meet Gregory and Susannah. Constance had vanished, saying something about a headache.

Julia was grateful to that headache.

"Oh, I'll miss you." Susannah flung her arms around Julia. It was the only time that day Julia had been forced to fight against tears.

"You'd better call. Tomorrow, if possible."

Even though they didn't share a drop of blood, Susannah was her sister in all the ways that mattered. The girl dashed tears away as Gregory regarded the women.

"Come then, Your Grace." He extended his hand. "Your carriage awaits."

Julia allowed herself to be helped into the gold-accented coach with the Ashworth crest gleaming on the lacquered door. She waved out the window to her stepsister as Gregory seated himself opposite her. The door closed, and the horses' hooves clopped on the street as they pulled away from Beaumont House.

And then it was just the duke and Julia.

"You made a ravishing bride," he said.

"Thank you." Julia believed she could taste her heart in her throat. She tried to think of something light and teasing to say, but her nerves wouldn't permit it. She couldn't stop staring at her husband. What a strange word, husband. Gregory watched her carefully, as if she might dash out of the carriage at any moment. "You needn't worry. I'm not going anywhere."

"I should hope not." He looked at her with hunger. "I'm enjoying this sight far too much. You in my carriage. Us alone. No chaperones. No sisters."

And soon, no clothes between them. Julia pressed her thighs close together, trying to quash the bloom of desire deep within her body.

Ugh, she hated waiting. She'd already waited so damn long for this moment. Even if it wasn't everything she'd expected, today had been everything she craved.

Tonight should be as well.

When they arrived at Carter House, the servants were lined up and ready to greet their new mistress. Normally the newlyweds would have vacated London to begin their honeymoon, but this was anything but a conventional wedding. Gregory wouldn't have time to show her Lynton Park, his ancestral estate, before he left England, but Julia could make her way to Somerset whenever she liked.

Alone.

We agreed to this. She remained calm as she met Peele, the butler.

"Welcome, Your Grace. We're ever so delighted to see you," he said.

The butler and the servants all did appear pleased. In fact, Julia believed that if he could have, Peele would have organized a festival in her honor.

"They're glad I shan't be dueling anymore," Gregory murmured as he led his new bride into the house.

"Because they care for you?" She was surprised to see him appear almost bashful.

"You know how servants are. They like having a secure position."

But from the way a chamber maid wiped a happy tear from her cheek, Julia thought Gregory might be downplaying the truth. Any man who inspired love and loyalty from his staff was usually a good man, however wild.

Julia flushed to think that she'd married a man who was not only wicked, but good.

No. She brushed that thought aside as she was shown upstairs to her chamber. Gregory was charming, and perhaps intelligent, and maybe an original, but that was all she'd allow. Julia was not going to make the mistake of forgetting what this arrangement was. She'd wanted freedom and security, and she'd found both. If she wished for anything more, she'd only make herself miserable.

Julia tried not to stare in awe when she was ushered into the duchess's chamber. The walls were papered in pale-blue silk, and the large, canopied bed seemed soft and lush as a cloud. Tall windows let in the London sun as two maids bustled about, getting her all settled in and unpacked. There was a washroom in an adjoining chamber, one with a deep, claw-footed tub that looked like it would make for a heavenly soak.

Julia couldn't recall the last time she'd enjoyed such luxuries. Even though she hadn't been a servant, at Pennington Hall she'd been used to attending on Constance at all hours of the day. The moment she'd begun to settle in with a book or a bath, she'd be called on to do something else. But here, she'd have so much time and peace.

And all because of Gregory.

Julia thanked the maids as they left, and paced across the room, casting glances now and again at the bed. The sight of it turned her whole insides to butterflies.

The sun was beginning to set when she decided to simply enter Gregory's chamber. The wait was turning her mad. But as she touched the handle, the door opened.

"Oh. Hello."

Gregory stood before her. Julia's gaze went out of focus as she saw him without his coat. She had never seen a man so undressed before. The shirt clung to his broad chest, and she could see that his arms were corded with dense muscle. Julia felt faint as her husband shut the door and put his back to it.

His cravat was undone, and she could see the pulse jump in his throat. He smelled of sin and pine and musk. Julia hated that she felt so uncertain, but didn't know how to proceed.

"Are you hungry?" he asked.

"No." She licked her lips. "I'm full from the reception."

"Yes. Good."

He, however, seemed ravenous as he beheld

her. Julia backed up as Gregory approached. They both stopped on opposite sides of the bed.

"In that case," he growled. Gregory strode around to meet her. "Shall we?"

He kissed her before she could reply. But it was a *yes*.

CHAPTER ELEVEN

Julia hadn't known it was possible to be frightened and elated at the same time as she kissed Gregory without any concern. No one would enter this room, or tell them to stop, or shriek that she had ruined herself. This man with his titles, estates, and wicked suggestions was entirely hers.

For one night.

Julia flushed as she felt his hands on her body. Her eyes fluttered shut as he laid her down upon the bed. A soft moan escaped her when the duke lifted her frock, revealing her legs all the way to the tops of her stockings.

"Sheer bloody perfection," he rasped. Gregory began to untie her stockings, and Julia propped herself on her elbows and watched in a lustful haze as he unrolled them. Her husband's lips caressed the soft skin of her inner thigh. Julia shuddered as she felt his stubbled cheek, the heated rush of his breath as he parted her legs. As he—

"Wait." Her whole body tensed.

"Hmm?" The duke stopped at once, though he appeared almost unsteady as he pulled back from her. Gregory's dark hair was mussed and curled over one eye in a devilish manner.

"Are you all right?" she asked. Julia pushed down her skirts.

"Yes." He blinked. "Though you may have to

give me a moment. A gentleman has only enough blood to operate his mind or his manhood at any given time."

"Yes." She bit her lip as Gregory stood, the evidence of his…manhood…on prominent, straining display against the front of his breeches.

"Did I hurt you?" He looked concerned.

"No."

"Are you afraid?"

She hadn't expected him to sound quite so concerned. Based on Gregory's reputation, Julia had expected a sinfully passionate wedding night, but not a gentle one. She'd thought she wanted passion. Hell, she *did* want passion. But she also wanted—

"Dinner."

"Excuse me?"

"I find I'm hungry after all." That was a lie. The thought of food made her ill, but now that the moment was here Julia had begun to panic. It was stupid, really, but she felt seventeen all over again. She could still picture herself standing out under the open sky, gazing at the horizon for hours. Waiting for her fairytale prince to come riding to fetch her. Waiting for her life to begin.

He'd left her standing there, the rain pouring down upon her head. One man had already found it so easy to leave her behind. Now she was supposed to give all of herself to this man, her husband, but she knew he'd leave tomorrow morning and not return. The thought of it made Julia feel too raw and bruised.

She just needed a few more glasses of wine,

and then she'd be ready.

"Of course." Gregory rang for the servants and had them bring supper up to the room. Julia made certain to stand by the wall; she didn't trust herself to be anywhere near a bed right now. "I won't pounce, you know. I only go in for the kill when I've been expressly invited."

"Shame that the animal kingdom doesn't work the same way."

"Yes. Imagine lions sending engraved invitations to a herd of gazelle, asking them to formally agree to be eaten. If only nature modeled itself off the English upper classes."

"Then the natural world would be insufferable," Julia said. They both grinned at that, but she still felt the strain between them. It had nothing to do with attraction. The way her new husband prowled back and forth before the fire put her in mind of those lions he'd mentioned. Wasn't that the way of men and women? The man devoured, and the woman yielded.

What a bloody stupid system.

Her heart pounded as the servants entered to set up a table and chairs before the hearth. Julia glanced out the window as they brought up silver trays of food and crystal decanters of wine. She noticed that dark clouds had blocked out the rising moon and swallowed the stars. The whole world right now was illuminated by fire and candlelight.

When the servants bowed and exited, Gregory motioned for her to take a seat.

"I'm afraid it's a light meal," he said. "Cream

of turtle soup, braised lamb shank, and a fifty-year-old Bordeaux."

"It's a wonder you haven't starved by now." Julia allowed him to hold her chair. She seated herself, and placed a napkin in her lap while her husband sat across from her. He poured wine, but didn't take anything to eat. "You're not hungry?"

"I'm ravenous." His roving glance told Julia the sort of delicacy he wanted to savor. A line of heat went straight down, making her body full and heavy. She had never felt so desired before. No man had ever looked as if he wanted to flip over the table and have her on the carpet if she gave even the slightest hint she wanted it. Julia shivered, feeling the power charge in the air like a lightning strike between them.

Maybe it was the power that scared her. Or the fear of losing control of it.

"Maybe we should talk," she said. Julia took a spoonful of soup as something to do. God, but it *was* delicious.

"Well, let's see. Being English, we can discuss the weather and cricket. Being upper class, we can discuss money and how very much we secretly hate everyone that we know. That gives us four exciting topics from which to choose."

"I suppose I could start by saying thank you."

Julia's heart palpitated a bit. Laying herself bare before another had never been easy, but she was going to do that tonight. For some reason, the idea of lying naked in this man's arms didn't scare her as much as the thought that she wouldn't be able to hide anything from him. He'd see her every feeling, and in that way he'd have power over her. If there was anything that scared her more than the thought of being powerless, Julia didn't know it.

"For the food? My staff took care of it." But the duke's attempt at humor badly disguised his embarrassment.

"If it hadn't been for you, my life would have been very different."

She was surprised when Gregory's face appeared to darken at the words. He watched the fire with an almost sullen expression.

"I hope it won't be worse than what you left behind."

"You've met Constance. You know not much could be worse." Julia toyed with her soup. "I suppose I'm not very good at this."

"That makes two of us," he growled. The duke drank his wine while Julia felt a small, hot ember of anger ignite in her belly.

"You don't have to look so disappointed."

"Disappointed?" Gregory scoffed. "You'll have to expand your vocabulary, my dear. *This*," he said, gesturing to the inhuman perfection of his face, "is irritation. Not disappointment."

"I don't know what rankles more." She tossed her spoon aside and crossed her arms. "Your condescension or your irritation."

"I'm told condescension is my most attractive quality." But Gregory stood up and went to the window, speaking to his reflection rather than her. "Forgive me. I'm sure this is anything but the wedding night you dreamed of as a girl."

Yes, and no. If anything, Julia could never have envisioned a husband as handsome, as wealthy, or as frustrating as this one. Nor could she have imagined being as fascinated by him. Gregory was surly, straightforward, charming, and infuriating all at once. Most men couldn't be anything other than bland. Blandness was not this man's problem.

"Tell me about yourself," Julia said. She held up a hand. "And no pithy remarks. No quips. No evasions. I'd like to know you a little more intimately before we become, well, intimate."

"What a novel idea."

But he approached her, pulled his chair over to the other side of the table so that they were quite close. The hair on her nape prickled; Julia had never been so aware of anyone's presence before. Wherever he moved, her eyes instinctively drew to him. The duke toasted her. She clinked glasses.

"What would Her Grace care to know?"

There was so much about him that remained a mystery.

"How old were you when you inherited the Ashworth estate?"

"Seventeen. Both my parents died in a boating accident."

"I'm sorry." She put a hand over her heart. "That must have been dreadful. To be alone so young, that is."

"Honestly, I feel like I became less alone after they were gone."

He said it in that infamous way of his, with a smirk and a shrug. But Julia couldn't believe that anyone truly felt that way.

"Are you serious?" she asked.

"One thing you should have learned by this point, my dear. I am never serious."

Julia swallowed the rest of her wine and poured another glass. The duke watched her with puzzled admiration.

"I see this is truly a marriage between equals," he murmured as she downed a second helping.

"Do you know what this feels like?" Julia wiped her lips with a napkin. "It's as if we were two Spartan soldiers armed with only our shields. No spears or swords, nothing that can be used as an attack. We keep circling each other, putting our whole energy into defense when in truth we're perfectly safe because the other would never dream of making a move."

Gregory nodded slowly. "I suppose I take your point. Though I must say, it's unusual for a lady to nurture an interest in the military habits of ancient Greece."

"The Spartans encouraged their own women in the study of combat," Julia replied.

"Well, now I see why they would fascinate you."

"Bother all that. Do you comprehend what I'm saying?"

"You want us to stop protecting ourselves and be open. Yes. Either that, or you'd like me to lower my defenses so you can stick a blade in."

"Either suits me," Julia drawled, pleased when Gregory laughed. It was rare to find a man who enjoyed a droll woman. For the sake of protecting her heart, Julia wished Gregory *was* nothing more than a shallow, womanizing rake, yet something about him continued to clash with that image. Because a man who was that awful and insipid wouldn't appear delighted by her wit, nor would he look at her with such piercing concern.

Concern for Julia and her welfare.

She startled when a low growl trembled the windowpanes. Thunder boomed outside, and the steady patter of spring rain began on the roof.

"My." Julia was at a loss for anything to say other than, "It's raining."

• • •

Gregory could feel his pulse in his throat and at the very tips of his fingers. The candlelight caressed Julia's face, turning her radiant. His gaze slid to her legs, concealed once again by that thin sheath of blue silk. The sensation of her against his hands and lips, the way she had quivered on the precipice of ecstasy, had almost undone him. Even watching her take a spoonful of soup was like quiet torture. The sight of her tongue, the way cream glistened upon her lips, they were enough to drive a man insane.

Just watching her throat move as she drank was enough to get him half hard. He gripped his knee, trying to keep control of himself. Maybe in his own way he was as frightened as she was. Gregory wanted to lose himself inside of her, but what if she saw how undone he was by her mere presence? Wouldn't he love to lower his defenses and show her all of himself? Take down that

Spartan shield, bare his breast for her dagger? If she wanted to carve out his heart, he'd be only too delighted to give it. But the idea of such intimacy made him want to be sick. Gregory could not take another major rejection. He'd ordered the entirety of his bloody life around shielding himself from such an upsetting possibility.

But his thoughts and fears faded into the background as he gazed upon her bosom. It rose and fell with her breathing, and he wanted to feel the swell of her breasts as they filled his hands.

"Gregory?" She sounded like she'd said his name a few times already.

"Yes. Raining. I'll see if they can make it stop," he muttered.

Julia laughed. The sound was as tinkling and gentle as the rain itself, and sent a rushed shiver of delight up his spine.

"Let's talk about you," he said. His new bride watched him over the rim of her glass. He felt her assessing him, a predator suddenly reduced to being prey. He liked that. "You must have gotten along with your father."

Her expression cleared. God, her face was so lovely when she smiled.

"I did. He was the dearest person in the world to me. At least I had Susannah when he passed away."

"How old were you?" Bloody hell, what morbid conversation for a wedding night. But Gregory didn't think he could seduce this woman the way he had so many other ladies over the years. He couldn't simply pour sweet nothings into her ear.

He found he cared, wretched as that made him.

"Fourteen. And soon after, Constance locked me away in Pennington Hall."

"I'm awfully glad that you managed to slip her lead that night at the Weatherford ball."

Was it his imagination, or did she blush at his words?

"Oh. Yes. Because now you're safe from the rest of the *ton*."

"Also because it's led me to this moment." Gregory took her hand. Her lips parted in evident excitement, but he could still feel the tension in her body. He kissed her palm, never taking his gaze from hers. "I can't recall the last time I found myself this enraptured by any woman."

And he meant it, too. So when Julia pulled away from him and got up to stand before the fire, it felt like plummeting from a great height. All the way from heaven, in fact.

"It's kind of you to flatter me, but you don't need to lay it on quite so thick."

Ah, there it was yet again. Normally he adored the tartness of her tongue, but now he felt downright surly.

"I'm not the lying type. If I were, my life would be a great deal easier."

"Yes, and you wouldn't have had to marry a perfect stranger."

Gregory rose, feeling at a loss for words before this suddenly implacable goddess. He reminded himself that this had to be nerves. She'd waited for so long to be married, to be with a man, and this was no ordinary wedding night.

He prowled toward her, standing before the fire's blaze. A log snapped in the grate. Julia's eyes widened as he wrapped an arm around her waist. She placed her hands upon his chest, but didn't shove him away. Her breath hitched as Gregory leaned down to whisper in her ear.

"If I had to wed a stranger, I couldn't have dreamed of one more perfect than you."

She moaned as he kissed her throat. She tasted sensational as his lips crept up her neck, as he nibbled upon the delicate lobe of her ear.

"Ah. Gregory," she whispered.

"Julia."

Enough. He had to do this, or he might explode. His new wife clung to him as he lifted her into his arms. He kissed her greedily as he carried her to the bed, as he laid her down and then lowered himself upon her. Their kissing grew heated, and she nipped and sighed as he lifted her skirts again and ran his hands along her silken legs. By now, he was painfully hard.

Her hands fumbled at his buttons, and he helped her. He undid his shirt fast, ripped it from his body. Gregory did feel a moment of smug satisfaction to hear his new lady moan at the sight of his physique. Though he wanted nothing more than to rip the clothes from her body and have her, he allowed her to trace her palms along the contours of his torso. He leaned over her as Julia explored him, her fingertips trailing across the light dusting of hair upon his chest. Her pupils were dilated, and she seemed to be in a trance.

"Is Her Grace pleased?" He smiled.

"Oh yes."

He fell back upon her, claiming her mouth as he hitched her skirts higher, as her legs wrapped around his waist on instinct. Lightning flooded the room in blinding white as he slid one strap of her gown from her shoulder. Gregory bared his teeth in animal anticipation as he freed her breast from the constraint of silk. Her naked breast was in his hand, the nipple pink as a rose. He leaned down and traced the tip of his tongue around and around it, feeling it harden beneath his attentions while Julia writhed and groaned in anticipation.

Thunder broke over the house, so loud that his bride screamed out of fear rather than desire. Gregory looked up at the ceiling, shocked to hear the rain begin to pound. Damn, the bloody house might shake apart in this storm.

But right now, he didn't care. The lady beneath him was too delectable. The damn room could have been on fire, and he wouldn't have been able to focus on anything except her. He returned his attention to her breast, and to peeling the last scraps of clothing from her body. Already, he salivated to think of the sweetness that lay between her legs, waiting for his expert exploration.

Gregory passed his hand up the slope of her thigh, to the tender curls that protected her sex. He moaned in ecstasy as he cupped her, as he began to part her with his finger.

"Wait!" Julia cried. "Stop."

He stopped, though he feared he'd combust.

"Are you all right?" he rasped.

This time, the thunder pealed so loud over the house that Gregory himself almost rolled off the damn bed. Torrents of rain began to ripple against the windows.

And Julia appeared caught somewhere between ecstasy and fear. Though he doubted she was afraid of the storm.

After all, he could dress this up with honeyed words all that he wanted, but it was still a bargain between them. An exchange of favors. This was more of a contractual obligation than a romance, and no amount of passion could pass it off as anything else.

As more lightning streaked across the sky, Gregory sat up.

"I don't think I'll be traveling tomorrow," he said.

"Probably not." Julia frowned as the wind howled outside. "Thank God we didn't have an outdoor reception."

He laughed despite himself. "I doubt I'll quit London until next week. So. There'll be time."

Julia understood his meaning and appeared so relieved that he got off the bed and collected his shirt without another word. Gregory dressed himself again, wincing at the pain of his rather engorged manhood. It wouldn't take much work to release himself as soon as he was back in his room.

What a wedding night. A storm outside, utterly quiet within.

"Perhaps tomorrow," Julia said.

"Yes. Tomorrow."

Gregory found himself back in his room, with himself in his hand. It took barely two strokes and a thought of *her* before he finished. As the storm raged outside, he realized that beneath the frustration, he felt simple relief.

Selfish as it was, this way he didn't have to say goodbye to her so soon.

CHAPTER TWELVE

Julia tossed and turned in her dreams throughout the night, as though she were on board some storm-struck boat with Gregory. They argued through the wind and rain, about what she could not recall. She did vividly remember that his torso had been bare the entire time. When they hit a rock and began to sink beneath the waves, she awoke with a gasp.

The storm outside continued to pound as she got out of bed and parted the curtains. The world was misty, the glass fogging from the weather. Julia leaned her forehead against the window, delighted by how cool it felt on her fevered brow. But she couldn't help sneaking glances at the bed. The sheets were rumpled from her body, but not from his. They needed to change that. Julia needed to consummate this union in order to feel secure, but last night…

She'd wanted him so badly that she felt liable to erupt out of her own skin, but when she'd felt his hand upon her sex, her mind had gone blank. It was like two Julias were sharing her body at the same time. The first one wanted to lock the bedroom door and devour every perfect naked inch of the man she'd married, while the other couldn't shake the fear that had dogged her for over a decade now.

Perhaps she ought to tell Gregory about her

fears and where they came from, but that only felt pathetic. Julia was well aware that she didn't make for a fantasy bride. She was too old, too stubborn, too frustratingly human. Maybe she couldn't have Gregory's love—which she didn't even want—but the idea of him pitying her was too galling to contemplate.

Maybe I ought to kick down the door and launch myself on top of him and have done with it.

Julia steeled herself as she turned for the door connecting her room to the duke's. She would enter and take what was hers, as the Duchess of Ashworth. Then she'd be safe forevermore.

The sound of voices in the corridor outside froze her in her steps. It was a pair of servants murmuring some conversation. Julia glanced around and saw no clock, but imagined it couldn't be much later than six in the morning. After years of living as Constance's nursemaid, she was incapable of sleeping in.

She didn't catch much as the servants passed her door, but she discerned two words: the mews.

Oh dear. Julia chewed her lip as she glanced outside yet again, this time looking across the courtyard. The carriage house and stables were grand at Carter House, but not especially well-equipped for violent weather. In the distance, Julia could see stablehands trudging in and out of the building, toddling with buckets full of rainwater. There had clearly been a minor flooding of the stalls. The poor horses.

Julia's thoughts fled to Boudicca, the white mare she'd received from Gregory as a wedding gift. Named for a Celtic warrior queen who'd valiantly battled the Romans, Boudicca the horse seemed hardy and able to withstand any kind of foul weather. However, when thunder pealed yet again over the house, Julia swore she could catch the sound of frightened neighing all the way across the courtyard.

Horses were spirited, and creatures like Boudicca were often half wild. Julia understood that quite well and made up her mind.

She didn't ring for a maid. There was no need, as she had become well used to dressing herself back home. Constance had gone on and on about the unnecessary expense of employing an extra maid to help Julia with her toilette, and so she'd learned how to sort herself out. Within moments, she was dressed in a simple gray morning outfit, and pulled on her boots. Julia put her hair in a quick, messy braid and wrapped a shawl about her shoulders as she left the room and hurried down the stairs.

She knew that Gregory's servants would have everything well in hand, but Julia liked to make certain of things for herself.

• • •

Gregory groaned as the bedroom door opened. In his current sleep-addled state, he thought it might be Julia stealing into his room, ready to fling herself into his bed. The thought of her forced him into immediate alertness, and he sat up in hopes that he'd find her wearing a sultry smile and absolutely nothing else.

Unfortunately, it was Peele. Fortunately, the butler was entirely dressed.

"What is it?" Gregory croaked. He frowned; normally his valet, Tomkins, would awaken him just before noon.

"Beg pardon, Your Grace. It's about the Duchess of Ashworth." The butler appeared concerned.

Damn. Within instants, Gregory was out of bed and stepping into his clothes with grunts and growls. He refused to wait for the damn valet to help him. The storm appeared to have passed sometime during the night; as Peele opened the curtains, yellow sunlight soaked into the carpet.

"Is she all right?" Gregory muttered. His heart almost stopped as he considered she might have run away. Not that there was anything to run from—Gregory would never keep her against her will. But perhaps last night he'd shocked her with his forwardness. He should have kept his damn shield up and his…spear…down.

"Oh yes, Your Grace. Her Grace is perfectly well. Er. That is…"

"Peele, before my heart stops, come out and bloody say whatever it is."

"Yes, Your Grace. The duchess is in the mews."

Gregory blinked, leaving his shirt half unbuttoned. What the devil was Julia doing down there?

"Is she hurt? Are any of the stablehands hurt?" His mind spun. "How are the horses?"

"Entirely fine, sir. Her Grace is…well, perhaps the duke might come and see?"

Gregory found himself hurrying across the

courtyard with his thoughts in a whirl. He scarcely even noticed a puddle as he stomped through it. The sky overhead had brightened to intense sapphire after a full night's storm. As Gregory headed for the mews, he found two of his stablehands standing around talking...and laughing. Smiling. Enjoying themselves.

Gregory's servants tended to be a happy bunch since he insisted upon giving them high wages and treating them well, but as he'd been prepared to find something amiss, the jovial spirits on display unnerved him.

"Where is the duchess?" he asked.

"Gregory? Is that you?"

Her voice came out from the stable door, and Gregory entered to find his wife holding a pitchfork.

And cleaning out a horse's stall.

All this while her hair was down in a flyaway braid and damp mud clung to the hem of her dress. Gregory had seen high society women in every conceivable position, but he had never, in his wildest dreams, imagined he'd see one of them in the mews. Working.

"What the devil are you doing?" he snapped.

Julia wiped the back of her hand across her forehead as she straightened up. The chit looked at him as if *he* were the mad one.

"Isn't it obvious?" she drawled.

"Am I paying my own servants to stand around and gawk at their mistress while she does *their* work?"

"Well, if you'd rather one of our stablehands

go inside and embroider a cushion, I'm happy to trade off. This sort of thing appeals to me much more, anyway." With that, Julia continued mucking out the damn stall of her white Arabian. The mare was contentedly munching on a breakfast of hay and oats, and her tail swished as her mistress patted her rump.

"You seem to think this a much more everyday sight than it actually is."

"Honestly, Your Grace. You never struck me as so conventional." The cheeky wench rolled her eyes at him. The sight of her insolence in this real, earthy setting did something wicked to Gregory. He felt rather like an animal himself, desperate to fling his wife down upon a bale of hay and claim her in the manliest fashion possible. "Surely you've mucked out a stall before."

"I've never boiled my own water for tea before."

"Lord, then you really do need to live a little bit." Julia scoffed as she finished her chore, handing over the pitchfork to one of the stableboys as he entered.

"Er. Thank you, Yer Grace." The youth blushed scarlet as Gregory gave him a withering stare.

"Don't you dare be harsh with them." Julia pulled off a pair of gloves as she shook her head. Her golden curls bounced with the movement, loosening further from her braid. "I forced them to let me help."

"Help?" Gregory stared at the woman in disbelief as she made to fetch a bucket of water. "Unless you'd like to give me a fit, do not pick that up."

"That does sound awfully tempting." Julia faced him with her arms crossed, a willful expression on her face. That one, fiery look from her was enough to turn his blood molten. Somehow even the sight of her doing physical labor could get him hard.

Christ, he needed to take her inside, away from all the servants and horses. They shouldn't see everything he wanted to do to her. The list was too extensive and much too vulgar.

"Why are you even out here?" Gregory passed a hand through his hair, trying to get himself under control.

"When I woke up, it was still storming and I could see that they were overwhelmed here in the stables. I'm used to helping with horses; my father insisted I learn to care for my own mare personally when I was growing up. He felt a true lady should know how to look after her animals. Anyway, I decided to muck out Boudicca's stall while I was here. I helped feed everyone while the stableboys worked to keep the place from flooding. Really, it was no trouble whatsoever." Julia frowned in bewilderment. "Why are you so flushed?"

Because you are the most frustrating wench I've ever known, and I want to take you now did not strike Gregory as the most appropriate thing to say.

"You named the horse Boudicca?" he asked instead. "After the warrior queen?"

"My. You've read a book before." She seemed

genuinely impressed.

"I was at Oxford."

"That doesn't make much difference. Many wealthy men of the *ton* are educated at Oxford and Cambridge, but they seemed to spend less time studying and more time indulging themselves at their clubs."

"You take a very dim view of the educated male upper classes." Gregory approached his wife, having to force himself not to throw her over his shoulder and cart her bodily back into the house.

"Only because I've spent time with them." She turned up her chin in that delightful, arrogant manner of hers. "If I'd ever been allowed a spot at university, I would have been in heaven. I'd have studied history, philosophy, the giants of literature. Instead, I've had to spend my life simpering over needlework, pretending to be enthralled by the latest gossip from some country squire's wife."

"You also take a dim view of your own sex. At least you're consistent."

"Oh, hardly." Julia appeared indignant at his comment. "I have far more pity for my own sex than yours. We're supposed to maintain a ridiculous balancing act, knowing enough to make good conversation with you while knowing so little we require you to explain everything to us." She fluttered her lashes in a comical way that delighted him to his core. "This is what your lot requires, after all. To feel like masters of all you survey."

"For a newly minted leader of the *ton,* you seem to hold us all in some contempt." He smiled.

"I didn't want to marry simply to plan balls

and flaunt my status, you know." Gregory couldn't help but enjoy Julia's irritation. "Being a duchess means my voice shall be heard louder than ever now. I can initiate real change on behalf of my sex, no matter their station."

Gregory was truly surprised. He'd known Julia wanted to escape her stepmother but had thought she wanted him for the most obvious reasons: freedom and wealth. He saw now how ungenerous that opinion had been.

"It might please you to know that I like an educated woman," Gregory murmured. He advanced upon her, wanting to scoop her into his arms. "And, in fact, I did take my studies seriously. A true gentleman knows his way around a library and his private club equally well."

Julia tugged her shawl tighter around her body, even though the air hadn't chilled much in the last few minutes. Gregory always took a great deal of pleasure from watching her cheeks redden as he approached. He took her chin in his hand as he stood before her, turning her gaze to meet his.

"This isn't quite the way I envisioned my honeymoon beginning," he said.

"Indeed. You should have been by yourself on a ship bound for Barcelona at seven thirty this morning."

"Oh no. Eleven. Even if the house were on fire, I could never think of rousing myself before nine."

Julia scoffed. "Hard to believe I married such a layabout."

The word "lay" only seemed to tease him.

"I'm a duke. And as you're a duke's wife, you would do well to remember that you're now a woman of complete leisure."

Julia shuddered. "Lord, what's the fun in that?"

Gregory had married a perverse lady, indeed.

"You don't understand the keen pleasure of spending an entire day in bed, do you?" he whispered. He put an arm around his bride, who yielded with sublime ease. Gregory wondered if she could feel the outline of his ever-hardening manhood pressed against her. He kissed the corner of her mouth, and the breathy sigh she gave only fanned the flames. "I can teach you all the finer points of indulging yourself."

"Oh, can you?" She sounded challenging, but she shivered in his embrace. How wonderful.

"It's one of the things I'm best at. Along with horsemanship, fencing, the finer points of art curation, and…this."

His mouth closed over hers, and Gregory swore he could feel her entire body vibrate with pleasure. Enough waiting. The time had come to conclude their bargain.

Conclude it three times, perhaps. Just to be certain.

Gregory lifted Julia into his arms and made for the door.

CHAPTER THIRTEEN

This time, Julia knew there would be no stopping. He was going to take her upstairs and have his way with her, and she was going to love every minute of it. A full morning's physical work had gotten her out of her head, where Julia tended to live. Now, her body aching with want for Gregory's touch, her thoughts had blissfully quieted.

She couldn't bloody wait.

As Gregory carried her into the house and made for the staircase, though, Peele arrived.

"Devil take you, Peele, can't you see I'm busy?" Gregory snapped. The butler didn't seem surprised to find the duke carrying his bride around.

"Beg pardon, Your Graces, but there are three callers who wish to speak with the duchess."

"They're for me? Is my stepsister among them?" Julia asked. If so, she'd have to send regrets and tell Susannah and probably Laura and maybe even Constance to come back another time. In a few hours, say, at the earliest. Or maybe tomorrow morning.

"No, Your Grace. They are all dressed in mourning, I might add." The butler offered a silver tray of calling cards while Gregory set her on her feet. The description of women in mourning tended to dampen the fire of arousal. Julia wondered if she could kick grieving widows out of her house, but it seemed wrong.

"Mrs. Woodhouse. Mrs. Pankhurst. Lady Clifton. Do you know these women?" Julia glanced at her husband. One glance was enough. Based on the tightening of his jaw, Gregory must know these women intimately indeed.

"We're acquainted."

Julia felt a strange surge of frustrated jealousy. These women were more "acquainted" with her husband than Julia herself.

"Shall I tell them you are, er, otherwise engaged, Your Grace?"

Gregory extended his hand for hers, ready to lift her back into his arms and carry on with the deflowering in merry peace. Julia narrowed her eyes.

"No, Peele. See them in and make them comfortable. Let me make myself more presentable and I'll be down in fifteen minutes."

"Very good, Your Grace."

"I believe there are other matters which require your urgent attention." Gregory seethed with impatience, though he struggled to maintain composure before his butler. It was beautiful to watch.

"I won't be able to concentrate on such matters if I'm wondering what these particular women want to see me about." That was the truth. Also, it gave Julia diabolical pleasure to thwart the duke's passions. If three of her husband's past mistresses had come to gawk at her, then Ashworth could fume until Julia was prepared to alleviate his agony. "Why don't you go upstairs, my dear, and wait for me?"

Peele's face turned a tomato-ish red with barely suppressed laughter. Clearly, this was a rather amusing reversal of positions. The duke probably was used to having his women tied up in knots, in every conceivable way. Gregory glared at his amused servant.

"*Et tu*, butler?" he muttered. Then, with a beleaguered sigh, said, "*Fine*. Tell your maid to hurry it up, and not dress you in anything too complicated. I'm impatient enough as it is."

His eyes blazed with desire, the sight of which almost made Julia send the women away. But she was too damn proud and too damn stubborn to submit to even the most enticing man she'd ever met.

"That reminds me. I'll need to hire a permanent lady's maid," Julia said as she hurried up the stairs.

"You don't have a *what?*" Gregory snapped.

• • •

Exactly fifteen minutes later, Julia swept into the morning room where her guests had been made comfortable with tea and biscuits. The women all stood as she entered and curtsied to her. It was so unusual to see anybody curtsy to her, but then as a duchess Julia outranked virtually everyone she met.

"Your Grace." One of the callers, a smiling, attractive blond woman in her early thirties, stepped forward. "Oh, congratulations!"

"Yes!" The other two cheered. One even applauded. The sight of three women dressed in full black—one even wore a veil of mourning—was strange enough, but to see them all so high spirited only added to the insanity.

"Thank you?" Julia said.

"I'm so thrilled to meet the woman who accomplished the impossible." The blond lady clasped Julia's hand in both of her gloved ones. "Elizabeth Woodhouse, Your Grace." Julia tried to place the name, but couldn't. It was so strange, because she was certain she'd seen this Elizabeth Woodhouse before. Something about the woman was so familiar. "Forgive the intrusion, especially as you were only just wed, but we couldn't keep ourselves away. You're all our club has been able to discuss for nearly a month now!"

"Ah. Yes. Your club." Julia looked from grinning face to grinning face and tried to understand. "What precisely *is* your society?"

"The Carter Club, of course!" A taller, dark-haired woman sighed. She looked positively blissful as she glanced at the ceiling, lost in a haze of memory. "His Grace gave me the three most pleasurable weeks of my life down in Bath."

Julia did not consider herself much of a prude, if at all. She supported all forms of women's liberation, socially as well as educationally. But even for her, this was bizarre. An entire society founded upon the recollection of extramarital activities with her husband was one thing; having three of the members come to tea was quite another.

"I hope you ladies won't be offended, but calling here seems a little perverse."

"I *told* you she'd find it odd," the third woman hissed. She crunched a biscuit apologetically.

"Oh, we're not here to intimidate you, Your Grace. We only wanted to congratulate you! And, I confess, to glimpse the remarkable woman who managed to tame that savage beast of a man."

Elizabeth Woodhouse snapped open a fan and fluttered it, having apparent palpitations with the memory. Julia didn't know whether to be proud or horrified. Strangely enough, she was leaning toward proud. These women were…unusual, to say the least, but they seemed sincere and quite friendly.

"This is like a most marvelous day at the zoo," the biscuit-chomping woman said before chomping another biscuit.

Well. What a fascinating compliment.

"Is it true?" Elizabeth asked. "How you and the duke met? Did you really lose a slipper in your flight from the ball?"

"Every word is true," Julia said. The women all tittered (except the biscuit eater, who crunched).

"I do love a good Cinderella story," the brunette said. "Though I must say, the duke is far more of a catch than any boring old prince."

"I quite agree," Julia said faintly.

"Is he not the most *marvelous* lover?" Elizabeth heaved a sigh.

"I have no one to compare him to," Julia said, which was true. Carefully evasive, but true. "And I don't wish to be rude, but this is teetering on the overly personal."

Far from being offended, Elizabeth rolled her eyes in rapture and clasped her hands to her breast.

"I see how the two of you make such a splendid match. Ashworth does enjoy a challenge."

"Indeed. He *loves* to take on a strong-minded woman." The brunette, who'd introduced herself as Lady Clifton, lifted an eyebrow. "That is, provided she succumbs in the end."

"And she's *always* happy to!" Elizabeth fanned herself again. The women shrieked and giggled with delight. "Ah. I must admit, the Carter Club's been a bit disheartened since Ashworth was scooped up."

"Hence the, er, mourning?" Julia asked.

"Yes! Our hearts are not broken, you understand. But we are grieving for other parts of our anatomy."

Julia didn't know whether to laugh or scream.

"Well. Thank you for calling, ladies," she said. It verged on outright rudeness, but if ever a circumstance allowed for a little discourtesy this surely was it.

"Oh yes! We won't disturb you any longer. Is Ashworth upstairs? Awaiting you?" Elizabeth might have drooled. She dabbed a quick handkerchief to conceal it. "Oh, you lucky thing. Do give him our best!"

"And our congratulations!" Lady Clifton said.

"Would your cook be willing to part with this recipe?" Mrs. Pankhurst had finished off the plate of biscuits.

"Whenever you emerge from your cocoon of newly wedded bliss, we would like to make you an official, lifetime member of the Carter Club!" Elizabeth beamed as the women headed for the door. "The perpetual guest of honor, in fact."

"Er. Thank you."

"Oh, and have you tried the Neapolitan Knot yet?" Lady Clifton whispered.

"No. Not yet."

"Well. If I were you, I'd request it. It's ordering off the menu, as it were, but you'll be *so* satisfied." The women winked, and giggled, and chattered as Julia led them down the hall and Peele ushered them out the door. When the ladies had gone, the butler frowned.

"Are you well, Your Grace?"

"What's a Neapolitan Knot?" Julia muttered.

"Pardon?"

"Nothing, Peele. Thank you."

Julia walked up the stairs, the skirts of her pink silk day dress bunched in her hand. At the top of the stairs waited her husband, a man so prodigious in the bedchamber that three of his most devoted fans had come simply to cheer Julia on in her conjugal endeavors. The thought of Gregory waiting for her, and the thought of his clothes coming off, his hands upon her skin, her breasts, and between her legs turned her almost giddy with anticipation. Many men liked to imagine themselves great lovers, but Julia doubted that most men of the *ton* had women who recalled their time together with ecstatic fondness.

Gregory wasn't just an adept lover. He was

clearly sensational if he left these women not only physically but also emotionally satisfied.

It almost frightened Julia, because it kept reminding her of how damned inadequate she was in this department. And it became clear yet again how easily Gregory moved from one woman to the next. To pleasure them, yes. To thrill them, oh yes. But there was nothing Julia could offer this man that would excite him more than the legions of women he'd already had.

Women wanted a husband who knew what he was doing, but maybe they wanted one who didn't know, well, *everything*. There was nothing that Julia would be able to teach this man, certainly, and nothing they could experience for the first time together. She would be one more on a long list of conquests.

You didn't want romance. You told the man yourself that all you wanted was freedom! Was that a lie?

No. It hadn't been. Julia had to march in there, consummate the marriage, and then Gregory could be on his way. They would both be so happy, all their dreams fulfilled.

When Julia opened the door to Gregory's chamber, she entered and found the room empty. The bed before her lay pristine and vacant.

"Gregory?"

Julia jumped as the door shut behind her. Gregory leaned against it, a wicked smile playing upon his lips.

"You startled me," she said.

"That's a fair place to begin." He prowled

toward her. "But I'm aiming for shock. Then rapture. Then perhaps ecstasy. We'll see where the day takes us."

Lord, somehow this man could tear past all her usual defenses and reduce Julia to some insatiable creature. Every time he kissed her, it seemed more heated than the last. At this rate, she'd melt before he'd finished taking her. She must not let that happen.

"Ah." She whimpered as she tilted her head back and his lips traced the line of her throat. Her husband bit lightly upon her neck, and sucked so that she knew it would leave a mark. A badge of their passion for all to see.

A way to show the world that she was his.

"What did the ladies have to say?" he growled in her ear.

"They wanted to congratulate me." Julia leaned back in his embrace as Gregory's mouth continued to do the most marvelous things. "I'm married to the most sensational lover in England, apparently."

"Not just England. Those French bastards think they've got the market cornered on pleasure." To Julia's shock, Gregory lifted her up. Her legs instinctively clasped about his waist, and she felt her blush deepen as one of his hands cradled her bottom. "But the English always triumph."

She thought he'd lay her on the bed, but Gregory pushed her up against the wall. Julia moaned as one of her feet found the floor, and as his hand disappeared beneath her skirts. Again, she felt his touch on her thigh. All the way up to her sex.

Again, she groaned with pleasure as she felt him cup her.

"We never got to the best part last time," he whispered against her lips.

"What—? *Oh*."

He opened her. He slid one finger inside of her body. Julia clenched around him in surprise, which made him growl with delight.

"That's very promising." He gazed deep into her eyes, masterful. The playful, witty side of him had vanished. This was the beast emerging. "I'll be inside you soon enough. But I need to make you ready."

"H-How?" She hated how weak her voice sounded. But she'd never known such pleasure and couldn't imagine how it might be topped.

Until approximately three seconds later.

Julia had read that women experienced an "ecstatic union" in all her trashy Gothic pamphlets, but she'd had no idea how that worked.

Now she did.

While his finger thrust in and out of her in slow, rhythmic strokes, Gregory pressed a thumb to the very apex of her thighs. She could feel it, the pressure on a little nub of flesh.

That pressure created a feeling of the most massive excitement. She felt as if she were racing down a hill, the wind in her hair, and near the bottom as she went faster and faster her slippers began to lift from the earth. She was starting to fly.

"Oh God. Oh," Julia gasped.

"Is that good?" His voice was low in her ear, husky with need.

"Gregory. God."

"I'll take that as a yes."

He continued to trace his thumb around the little bundle of nerves, and then, as she started to lift off the ground and into the heavens, he pressed hard in exactly the right spot.

Julia screamed as she shuddered, as her body clenched. Gregory laughed in triumph when she tightened on his fingers, as she rippled around him. Julia screamed again, her whole being electric until finally she was reduced to bonelessness. She slumped in his grasp, her head upon his shoulder, trying to catch her breath.

What had he done to her?

Please, let him do it again.

"What a promising start," he whispered in her ear, his voice hot as sin. "Let's proceed." He carried Julia to the bed and sat her upon its edge. "Remove your boots."

She wasn't the type of woman who took orders from anyone, but Julia did exactly as requested. When he made her stand and turned her around, she didn't breathe a word of protest. The pleasure was still pulsing through her.

"Women's clothing is much too complicated." Gregory undid her frock with ease and let the garment pool about her feet. He made quick work of the stays as well, and soon Julia stood there in only her shift. "Now."

His hands slid to her hips, then inch by inch he began to ruck the fabric up around her thighs.

Julia shivered when she felt him undo the untidy braid of her hair. Her curls spilled around her shoulders.

"Better by the second," he hissed.

Julia turned around and kissed him. The duke kissed her back, his hands touching everywhere on her body. She allowed him to shove her backward so that she bounced upon the bed. Gregory took her by the hips and dragged her so that her legs dangled over the edge. On instinct, she again wrapped her legs around his waist. Though he was still clothed, she could feel the rod of his manhood throbbing against her. They were almost united.

"Should I take you like this first?" The duke's lazy smile and the wicked glint in his eyes both vanished. Surprise, even concern, replaced them. "Julia? Are you all right?"

"F-Fine."

Only she wasn't. Against her will, her body had begun to shake as though she were freezing. Her teeth chattered, though she clamped her jaw shut to fight it.

"I don't think that's true." Now his brow furrowed. "Did those women do something?"

"No." She swallowed, managing to keep her chattering teeth under control. But she couldn't stop the shivers. Again, she was on the very precipice of everything she wanted—and she wanted it so badly, both the consummation and the security it would bring. But she was back in her head, exactly where she did not want to live right now. Her thoughts wouldn't cease churning, and she kept recalling "Neapolitan knot" and the memory of walking back in to Pennington Hall, sodden from the rain and sobbing with a broken heart.

People wanted her so long as she could be useful to them. As soon as she wasn't needed, they discarded her, or else treated her badly. Julia had never been like Susannah, adored for the mere pleasure she brought to everyone's lives. She'd always known that she had to be functional and practical, because anything else was setting herself up to be a fool.

She knew all of this. So why was she so frightened?

Because I care what he thinks of me? Do I want him to like me? Respect me?

Not love her. Never that. She wasn't an imbecile. But what if she enjoyed it too much and felt the sting of rejection once he left her? What if she came to miss him?

"If we go on like this, I'm going to die of a heart attack." Gregory released her legs and leaned against the bedpost, breathing out in a long, slow stream. Julia waited for him to begin reproaching her, chastising her for not doing her duty as a wife. That was how husbands were supposed to act when disappointed in this way. Julia prepared herself to fight back, to tell him that she needed more time.

Instead, the duke looked at her with evident concern.

"If you don't like something, you can tell me," he said.

"I do like it. Very much." That was the truth.

"I'm pleased to hear it. Then what's wrong?"

Again, she should just talk to him about what she felt, and again she came up short. She couldn't even tell him of her failed elopement. Julia had never thought herself much of a coward, but she was too cowardly even for that. Instead, she came up with a logical excuse. Something calculating, something he'd expect of her.

"Those women reminded me of how close we're being watched by society. If we consummate and you leave tomorrow or the next day, they'll be able to tell something is amiss. I wanted the security of a position and the freedom to live my own life, but I don't want to be an object of scorn for the entire *ton* in order to get it. I don't want to be known as the jilted wife, the spinster who trapped a rake and had him leave her soon after."

"I see." Gregory winced again as he shifted his body. His arousal didn't seem to be going down. "What do you propose?"

Julia bit her lip and thought.

"They expect us to go on a wedding trip of some kind. Take me back to Lynton Park. It'll look like we're off on our honeymoon. We stay a few days over there, finally consummate our union, and then you can travel to the coast and set sail. Meanwhile, I'll remain at the Park and sit out at least a month of the Season. When I return, your absence won't look so egregious."

Gregory raked a hand through his hair.

"Sometimes I wish I hadn't married a woman with such a damned competent brain."

She tilted her head and narrowed her eyes.

"We need at least one of those in this marriage."

"Such a barbed tongue, too." Gregory bade her stand. Julia could feel the power of his heartbeat as he pulled her against his body. God, she wished she could give in. Just submit and let the demons of her past die. "Very well. I'll have our bags packed and order the carriage. We'll leave as soon as possible."

Her cheeks colored. So, she was to have a honeymoon after all. A strange and abrupt one, but one all the same.

"In the meantime." He released her and looked down at his still evident arousal. "I'll have to manage this."

"Perhaps I should do something to help." She cleared her throat. Her voice sounded weak, which she despised. "It's my duty, after all."

"I don't want duty from you." Gregory lifted her face to his. She had never seen him so utterly serious. "I want passion. I want you burning with desire in my arms when I take you. Anything else would feel unearned."

"Oh."

"But." He kissed her, his lips tracing hers as he spoke. "I'll have that passion before too long. And then, my lady, there'll be no force on earth powerful enough to stop me from having my way with you."

With that, Julia left him and returned to her own chamber. She rang for the servants and instructed them to pack her trunks. While they worked, she went out into the hall and shut her eyes, trying to still her thoughts.

He wanted her passion? The bloody fool didn't know he already had it.

CHAPTER FOURTEEN

The miles between London and Somerset had been fleet, mostly due to Julia's interest in her new husband. The talk had been as playful and easy between them as ever before, and she feared she would miss the conversation when he left her for his journey across southern Europe. Still, spending time all alone at a palatial estate with servants to see to her every need was a soft kind of hardship.

Julia watched out the window, enjoying the bright green of the spring countryside. They'd passed through the village of Lynton not too long before, which meant that they were on Gregory's lands now. They might have been traveling across them for quite some time, actually.

Julia smiled at her husband, the rakish and passionate duke, as he slept on the seat across from hers.

She didn't have to steal her glances now, and took her time to appraise every inch of him. Asleep, he exhibited a sensuous charm she had previously missed. Though she supposed Gregory had more charm in reserve than most men possessed in their entire beings.

His head had tilted back against the seat, allowing a perfect curl of dark hair to sweep across his eyes. Julia had no idea how anyone could be so devastatingly masculine and beautiful at the same time. The hard, square jaw and the sculpted lines of his body suggested a man capable of action, someone who'd be difficult to defeat in a brawl or on the battlefield. But he had an artist's touch when it came to love, the little Julia had experienced of his prowess. Or perhaps a musician's talent. She imagined he knew just how to play with a woman's body, to get the most exhilarated sounds out of her.

She wasn't one for blushing, but she could feel the heat on her cheeks.

"Your Grace?" Julia cleared her throat. "We should be arriving soon."

"Hmmph." Gregory startled awake, blinking rapidly as he sat up straighter. "Julia. I must have closed my eyes for a moment."

"Do most moments constitute an hour and a half?" She bestowed upon him a most charming smirk, if she said so herself.

"Impertinence is a terrible feature in a wife." He came and sat beside her upon the bench. Julia suppressed a shiver of delight. "I must strive to make you more obedient."

"You'll have to work very hard, I'm afraid."

"Normally I detest labor." He kissed her. "However, I feel invigorated by the challenge."

Julia could think of nothing to say immediately, as his kisses tended to have a seismic effect upon her.

"I think it will be nice to have some time in the country. Just the two of us."

"Yes. It should be just the two of us." The way he phrased it was odd, but before Julia could inquire further her husband gestured to the window. "Take a look, duchess. Does it meet with your approval?"

Julia looked outside and became frozen with amazement.

Her family's seat, Pennington Hall, was considered a fine country manor, and she'd always been proud of it. But Lynton Park eclipsed every single aristocrat's estate she had ever glimpsed before.

The carriage drove past a small pond fringed by willow trees and emerged into sunlight that shimmered across acres of pure green lawn in both directions. Far ahead stood an enormous house in the classical style. It was made of a fine, warm stone, three stories tall, with Grecian columns decorating the facade and a grand triangular frieze atop. The frieze displayed the Ashworth crest carved in stone, a stag and a lion flanking a shield. Sunlight glittered across the endless display of windows.

"I told you," Gregory murmured in her ear. "Size does matter."

The house sprawled, forming a sort of L shape against the brilliant emerald lawn. They rode past a fountain and expertly gardened sections of roses, tulips, and daffodils.

This was Julia's new home.

"I'm ever so glad I lost my shoe at the Weatherford ball."

"Glad you lost your head as well?" Gregory traced his thumb up and down her back, making Julia warm with delight.

"I'd never lose something that precious. I

merely left it unsupervised for a moment."

Julia felt an odd contentment. She remained ensconced in this carriage, secure within her husband's embrace. For today, at least, and perhaps tomorrow as well, he was hers. She couldn't grow used to him, but she could enjoy him while their time lasted.

"I'm interested to see the interior of a house belonging to the greatest lover in England or on the Continent."

"What do you think it resembles?" Gregory sounded amused. "A brothel? A temple to my own handsomeness?"

"Something in between, perhaps."

Julia had her own ideas. Ashworth was a man who lived for physical pleasure and novelty, and she doubted there'd be anything in his estate that didn't please him in some manner. She envisioned red velvet drapery and silken bedspreads, along with the finest crystal and tasteful yet erotic art hanging upon the walls, mixed up with landscapes and still lifes as camouflage for unsuspecting guests.

He was a man of sin, so she almost feared what she'd find at the end of this drive.

"There they are." Gregory smiled as their carriage pulled up to the front steps of the house. An army of liveried footmen and maids awaited, ready to greet their new mistress. Gregory got out and handed Julia down, then led her to a middle-aged woman with a warm countenance.

"Mrs. Sheffield. Good to see you again." Gregory nodded to the woman in greeting. "It's been far too long."

"Nearly eighteen months, Your Grace. We are so glad to have you back at Lynton Park." The housekeeper gave her curtsy and seemed sincere in everything she said. All the servants looked composed, but Julia sensed that every single one of them was happy to see Gregory, from the housekeeper to the scullery maid. The duke must make a good employer.

Julia felt proud of that idea. To her, nobility who treated their servants like property were the worst sorts.

"Allow me to present my new wife, the Duchess of Ashworth." Gregory placed his hand upon Julia's lower back, sending little thrills throughout her body.

"Your Grace." Mrs. Sheffield beamed as she curtsied. "Welcome to Lynton Park. I trust you'll find everything to your satisfaction."

"I'm sure I shall," Julia replied.

She believed she'd like this woman, and all the servants for that matter. Gregory took her by the arm.

"If you don't mind, I'd like to take my wife on a small tour of the house. I want to show her the gardens, the library, the parlors…" He leaned nearer to Julia's ear. "There's the most marvelous view of the lake from the duke's bedchamber."

Julia's heart sped up. She'd been able to think of little else on the drive up here, and a long carriage ride with Gregory so near had left Julia with a pang in her stomach. She was hungry. Starving, actually.

If she was to make this house of depravity her home, better to do it at once.

"Oh! Shall I have Miss Winslow bring Felicity later to meet with Your Graces?" Mrs. Sheffield asked.

Felicity? Julia glanced at Gregory in puzzlement.

"Miss Winslow and Felicity are in residence?" He sounded amazed.

"They left early for one of Miss Winslow's natural expeditions. She's created something of a botanist in Felicity." The housekeeper sounded proud.

Before Julia could politely ask what they were talking about, the euphoric cry of a little girl came bounding across the lawn.

"Your Grace! Hullo!"

A girl of ten or eleven came racing up the steps to greet Gregory. The child latched onto him with enthusiasm, another shocking thing to see. Even beloved children learned from an early age never to throw themselves into an adult's conversation, or to paw at their parent. Or guardian, in this case? Julia wasn't so certain.

The child had a tangle of black hair and grass-green eyes set in an impish face. Her clothes were smart but the entire front was muddied, as if she'd taken a flying leap into a patch of wet earth.

"Hello, my girl." Ashworth's whole countenance warmed. It wasn't fire, as Julia had seen so often, but clear sunlight. "Where's your governess?"

"Beg pardon, Your Grace!"

A woman hurried up to them, moving with both speed and elegance. She wore a dark gown, befitting a governess, but didn't keep her head lowered and her eyes downcast the way most women of her station might in the presence of nobility. The woman stopped at the top of the steps and curtsied to Gregory, then hastily did the same for Julia.

"Hello, Your Graces. Please excuse Felicity's current state. We didn't expect you home until this afternoon."

"We made better time than I'd anticipated." Gregory cleared his throat. "Julia, this is Miss Viola Winslow. She attempts to govern my ward." He gave a fond smile to the girl at his side. "Which brings us to Felicity Berridge, the chit herself. Now curtsy properly, Felicity, and show my new wife some of the polish I've struggled to give you."

But there was no coldness in Gregory's voice or demeanor. The child obeyed with great cheer.

"Hello, Your Grace." The girl giggled. Julia liked her at once.

"Hello, Felicity."

Julia maintained her composure, but she felt rather dizzy with the surprise. There was nothing in the least wrong with Gregory taking in a ward, but no one had mentioned a word about the girl. Laura hadn't, and she knew everything to do with society and those who moved in it. Felicity Berridge was a well-kept secret, which led Julia to the possibility that Felicity was not Gregory's ward, but his daughter. An illegitimate one, of course.

Though there was no physical resemblance between them, that didn't mean they weren't related. The idea that Felicity was Gregory's by-blow did not upset Julia; rather, it was the idea that he'd fathered a child on a woman and then evidently refused to marry her, or to give his own daughter the position she deserved in society.

Based upon everything she'd seen of the man thus far, it felt wrong to suppose something that awful. But Felicity presented quite a mystery, and until she understood the facts Julia would feel ill at ease.

"Are you well, Your Grace?" Miss Winslow appeared concerned.

"Quite well. Only tired from the journey."

Julia could not allow Felicity to think her hesitation had anything to do with the child's presence, so she petted her hair. Felicity beamed, revealing that one of her front teeth was missing. Julia laughed.

"I thought you both would've been sea bathing in Cornwall by now. It is the time for your usual holiday, isn't it?" Gregory asked Miss Winslow.

"I'd a cold last week. It's started to finally clear up." Miss Winslow sounded apologetic, which was absurd. A person couldn't control illnesses, after all. "We could be off tomorrow, if His Grace would prefer some privacy."

"Oh, can't we stay?" Felicity tugged at Miss Winslow's arm. She was a headstrong little thing, only increasing Julia's approval. "I've not seen the duke in ever so long, and I want to know the duchess better!"

"Do stay." Julia wasn't sure why the words came tumbling out of her mouth, as a child scampering around the house was the last thing a newly married couple might want. But if Felicity was Gregory's ward, then Lynton Park was her home and she shouldn't be evicted from it.

And if she were more than his ward, well, then Julia would have several pointed questions for her new husband.

"Are you sure, Julia?" Gregory appeared surprised.

"The house seems rather large," she drawled. Quite an understatement. "I'm certain we can find a spot of privacy here or there."

"You'd think that, wouldn't you?" Miss Winslow sounded fond, and also tired. Then she paled and lowered her head. "Sorry, Your Grace. I shouldn't have spoken so familiarly."

Miss Winslow appeared to be about Julia's age. The sight of her fearful subservience only made Julia recall being under Constance's thumb.

"I'd like a little familiarity, Miss Winslow." Julia needed new friends and allies. Besides, any woman who let a girl romp around in the mud was doing something right. Felicity deserved a release for her high spirits.

"Very good, ma'am." The governess seemed quite relieved.

"I'll see you both later, but for now I'd like some time with my new bride." Gregory stole Julia away with ease, finally leaving the servants and the girl and governess behind. Julia strode through the entryway into the house's front hall.

Again, she met with surprise, because it wasn't the voluptuous bordello she'd been expecting. She'd anticipated Gregory's tastes would run to the baroque, the more lavishly opulent the better. But the space was bright and airy, with the customary oil portraits and landscapes decorating the wall. Lynton Park was elegant. Tasteful.

"Come. I want to show you around." Gregory stood before Julia. "What would you like to see first? Upstairs, perhaps?" Where the bedrooms were, undoubtedly.

"Is there a portrait gallery? Some of these are so fine." She turned around to admire the art and gave him her back.

Until she had a few questions answered regarding Felicity, he wasn't sneaking her off anywhere for passionate, conjugal purposes.

"You'd like to look at art?" He sounded a bit disbelieving. "If you wish to examine some sculpture, there's a masterpiece of male nudity waiting only upstairs, in the eastern wing." He was at her back, and his nearness almost caused Julia's knees to weaken. Wretched man, he could overpower her will so easily.

"Would this devastating statue be housed in the duke's bedchamber?"

"I only unveil it on special occasions."

The man was so arrogant, so certain of his own appeal. Worst of all, he was right to be so sure. Julia began to tilt backward into his embrace but forbade herself to tilt one inch more. They needed a frank conversation.

"Mmm. I think a bit of family history first, if

you please."

Gregory made a low, almost bestial noise. "Are you certain you're not out to drive me stark raving mad?"

"The thought had occurred to me."

"The title's three hundred years old. Naturally there's a gallery." Gregory sounded frustrated, but he didn't badger her. Julia's new husband took her arm. Even when she was this uncertain of everything, his touch still managed to shake her to the foundation.

They wandered to the western wing of the house, past salons and the door to Lynton Park's grand ballroom. Julia imagined hosting her own events here, being regarded as one of the great ladies of the area. It was a dizzying thought.

The family portrait gallery occupied a wing of its own in one of the older parts of the estate. The mullioned stained-glass windows let in horizontal slats of colored light as Gregory led Julia past one painting after the next.

"Godfrey Carter, the first duke." He pointed out a man in an Elizabethan ruff. "He was supposed to have been a rather fine statesman, but I always thought it looked like that ruff was devouring his head. Not terribly dignified."

Julia walked past the portrait to a woman dressed in clothes of the mid eighteenth century, and thought she detected something of Gregory in the lady's face. Julia was trying to find the right way to bring up Felicity, but she became a bit spellbound by the abundance of history. She'd always enjoyed studying family portraits, namely because she liked trying to piece people together. Gregory seemed to have a mind like Godfrey's, but a smile like Claudia, his grandmother. There was something mischievous and willful in the cast of both their eyes.

She thought of Felicity, and how mischief might well run in the family.

"You seem distant."

Gregory sounded much more formal now, his patience for this mystery at an end. Julia knew that she must speak her mind.

"Felicity's a very dear girl." She meant it.

"Indeed. She's a wonder."

"Because she's so wonderful, I was curious why you'd never mentioned her before."

"I'm not much involved with her upbringing, so it didn't seem urgent." Already, he sounded on his guard.

"Not even to your wife?"

"I'd have told you eventually."

"Also, why does no one in London seem to know of her existence?"

"Are you accusing me of something, Julia?"

All the mirth had departed Gregory's face and voice. Her husband stood beneath a portrait of some military ancestor of his, and Julia was caught off guard by the striking resemblance. Both men appeared crafted from iron, their powerful bodies radiating challenge to any who dared oppose them.

"There's no shame in making a little girl your ward." Julia decided to dare. "But hiding her away suggests covering up a great secret."

"I don't like when you play games." He had some audacity to stand there and judge *her*, considering her suspicions.

"If Felicity's your daughter, treating her like a stain to be covered up is cruel. Just tell me, is she yours or not?"

After all, how could Julia respect a man who went eighteen months without seeing his own child? Felicity didn't appear maladjusted but calling her father "Your Grace" instead of Papa was much too formal.

Gregory took slow, powerful steps toward her. While Julia had no fear of him, she had to stay firm.

"That's what you think, then?" He sounded maddeningly neutral.

"I'm only asking a question. It's not that farfetched, all things considered."

"You believe I would sire a child, allow her to remain illegitimate, then conceal her from society out of shame?"

Julia realized she had made a mistake. A grave one, even. All of Gregory's humor and sly seduction had vanished, so that only fury remained. Due to his rakish reputation and his eternally confident demeanor, she'd never imagined he could be insulted, but she'd been so bloody wrong. Julia had struck him right at the core, and she couldn't even tell why.

So much for understanding the man at all.

"I'm sorry," she began.

"Save your apologies." The duke turned his back on her and strode away, passing through the beams of sunlight. She paced after him.

"Erm. Perhaps I jumped to conclusions."

"Catapulted might be the better term." He sounded angry, which only made *her* angry. It was a flaw of hers, to grow irritated when she knew she was in the wrong.

"What was I supposed to think?" she snapped.

"You were supposed to think better of me."

Damn everything, he was right. Why *had* Julia brought it up in such a way? Because she was tired? Or, in a guilty pocket of her soul, perhaps it was because seeing little Felicity had been a sharp, painful reminder that Julia herself would never be a mother. That her arrangement with Gregory meant she would have security and status, but never the love of a family. If Felicity were Gregory's, then it would be one more daily reminder of what Julia could never have.

"If you say she's not yours, I believe you! You don't need to say anything more. Isn't the fact I take you as a man of your word enough?"

Gregory turned, bringing Julia to a fast halt.

"Perhaps it should be. But I'd hoped you knew me better than to even think all that."

"I hardly know you at all."

Once again, Julia's mouth moved before her mind could advise caution, but it was true. She knew the man before her as intelligent, bold, a good-natured rake. That would be enough to entice eager women to become his lover, but his wife? Even a marriage in name only required some deeper understanding of one's partner.

"That's true. We don't know each other," he

said. Even though the sun was bright, Gregory's storming mood seemed to darken the gallery. "Well, you're correct that you need an explanation."

"I told you I'll take you at your word."

"No. I want to explain this. I didn't think I'd have to do it today, as I expected Felicity and her governess to be gone."

They'd stopped, Julia noticed, beneath a portrait of the late duke, Gregory's father. There was a physical resemblance between the pair of them but also a gulf of difference. The other duke had been painted with hawkish intensity. The man appraised the world as if judging whether or not it was worthy of him.

Gregory, she realized, did not judge others. He did not ask them to be flawless specimens worthy of his attention.

"Go on. Tell me," she said.

"Felicity's illegitimate. You're right about that." Gregory leaned a hand upon the wall. "But she is not mine."

"Oh. Then whose is she?"

Why had Gregory taken her in? It was good, to be certain, but even though she believed him to be a good man it was still a grand gesture.

"She's the Earl of Rockford's bastard." He said the word without apology, though uttering "bastard" before a lady would elicit many gasps from good society.

"Are you and the earl friends?"

He scoffed. "Hardly."

"Then I fail to see why you took Felicity on."

"You believe I shouldn't have done such a thing?" Now he looked as if Julia were the monster.

"No! Only I can't understand why or how you became involved in the first place."

Julia felt lightheaded beneath Gregory's appraisal. She'd seen him serious, but only in the throes of passion when his intent was anything but pure. The Carter Club had no clue about the man beneath the sensual, charming facade. Laura didn't know, either. Perhaps the man was not the one-note libertine she'd envisioned. The notion did more than shock her; it frightened her. If she'd misjudged him so severely, what must he think of her now?

"Ten years ago, I was attending a house party at the earl's estate up in Derbyshire. It was a weekend of frivolity and debauchery, much like any other. The countess preferred to stay in town, allowing her husband all the libidinous activities he desired." Gregory began to walk the gallery again, rather like a great jungle cat surveying its domain. Julia followed, intently listening. "I noticed some commotion to the side of the ballroom—something to do with the servants. But such matters were beneath our attention, particularly with gambling and loose women to entice us."

Julia shook her head.

"At least I wasn't mistaken that you were a rake," she said. It was meant to lightly tease, but Gregory flinched.

"'Were' being the operative word, my dear."

Julia decided not to press him about that distinction. She didn't like the strange surge of hope she felt. As they walked, Gregory continued his tale.

"At three in the morning, I awoke to knocking. There was a maid at my door, a mere chambermaid. Anna. She risked her job and perhaps a good deal more to disturb a duke in the middle of the night."

Indeed. Most other members of the *ton* would have berated Anna, or even physically struck her, and all without consequence. The idea made Julia sick to her core.

"Why did she wake you?"

"Because one of the servants had delivered a baby girl and then died. That was the cause of the minor commotion I'd noticed earlier in the evening."

Julia did not need to be told who had fathered the baby.

"Didn't the earl know she was expecting his child?"

"No, and he was beside himself with rage. Apparently, the girl had managed to hide her condition."

Julia wasn't certain how that could work, but she knew from experience that women in desperate situations tended to be resourceful.

"Rockford wanted to send the child to a workhouse." Gregory's joviality had vanished, and in its place, Julia found a smoldering, volcanic rage. Not at her, but directed toward the events of that night ten years ago. "He was prepared to abandon her to poverty. It's almost certain she'd have died before she was one year old."

That an earl had been willing to cast aside his own child, illegitimate or not, the moment she was born was so hideous that Julia felt the urge to get back in the carriage, ride to Derbyshire, locate the man, and bash him right in the nose. The worst part was that Rockford would have gotten away with it, too. Society might secretly condemn him for his actions, but no one would ever challenge an earl.

Except, perhaps, a duke.

"Anna told you because she believed you'd intervene, didn't she?" Julia asked. Then, before she could stop herself, blurted out, "Why?"

Damn her. That had been abominably rude. But it brought some of Gregory's warmth back, and his laughter.

"I asked her the same. She merely said she believed I'd do the right thing. I said she must not know me very well."

"Or perhaps she did." Julia hadn't thought this man could do more to surprise her, but he'd proven her wrong.

"Perhaps," Gregory replied. "She vanished after that, and while I knew I ought to go back to bed, somehow I found myself asking Rockford to let me take on the baby." He blinked, as if still stunned by his own actions. "Can't say what possessed me to do it. Well. Perhaps I can't abide a man who tosses a child away as if it's worthless."

Julia had always prided herself on her perceptiveness, but she had missed this side of her husband entirely. Perhaps she was not as observant as she'd thought? Or was Gregory a master of controlling what side of him people saw?

If that were true, how much more of him remained undiscovered?

"I agreed to bring up Felicity quietly, at least until she was ready to make her debut. Even then, I couldn't allow anyone to know her parentage. Most of the *ton* will think as you did, that she's my by-blow, but I shan't mind." Finally, his rakish smile returned. "It would only confirm my terrible reputation. I've worked so hard to maintain it, I should hate to see it disappear now I'm married and respectable."

"Yet you told me the truth," Julia murmured.

"Well. You're my wife, aren't you?"

Julia's heart beat faster to hear the words "my wife" on his lips, and realized how much she loved the sound. For much of the past month, she'd dreamed of Gregory's eyes and mouth, and of the mysteries of his body. Passion had sparked between them from the moment they laid eyes upon each other.

But this was something else, perhaps even more shocking than love. Julia *liked* this man, impossible as he could be.

Though could one honorable deed compensate for all the debauchery of his past? She did not know, and not knowing something rather terrified her.

All she knew for certain was that she wanted to spend as much time with this man as she could before he was gone from her life forever.

"Thank you for telling me." She licked her lips, the next words sticking in her throat. "I apologize for doubting you."

"An apology from the Duchess of Ashworth?" Gregory pretended shock. "Lord. The end of days is surely upon us."

"How dare you?" But Julia laughed as she walked the gallery at his side. "You don't know very much about me yet, Your Grace."

"Indeed. But I hope to rectify that problem immediately."

Julia left the corridor on the duke's arm, but she couldn't stop the wild course of her thoughts. Because she did like him far too much for comfort. She liked him, Julia realized, more than any other man she had ever met. Including the man who'd broken her heart ten years prior. To want Gregory was one thing; to want to *be with him*, that was different. When he left her after they came together, would she be able to smile and carry on with her life?

Or had Julia set herself up for the greatest heartache she'd yet known?

CHAPTER FIFTEEN

What was Gregory to do with this woman? He sat upon the picnic blanket with Miss Winslow and watched as Julia chased after Felicity, both of them laughing breathlessly. Felicity was out to capture a frog; Gregory wished now he hadn't agreed to have their picnic near the creek. Why the child had such a love of mud and reptiles and other grubby creatures he didn't know, but he could at least excuse her madness due to her youth. Whereas Julia? Well.

"You have to be quiet when you sneak up on them." She had removed her shoes and stockings, the daring minx, in order to better teach Felicity the finer points of frog catching. "And bend down low, ready to snatch them in an instant."

"How'd you get so good at frogs, Your Grace?" Felicity giggled again, happy as a frog-catching lark.

"My papa taught me at our country estate in Kent." Julia brightened with the memory. "He loved the natural world. He also taught me to fish, but never to hunt game. He didn't believe in it."

"He sounds like an awfully nice man." Felicity then scrunched up her face and tried valiantly to be silent as she crept up on an unsuspecting frog.

"I'm glad the duchess and Felicity have taken to one another," Gregory muttered as Miss Winslow set out some sandwiches from the wicker picnic basket. "However, I don't love this bloody reptile-catching business."

"Amphibians," Miss Winslow replied, neatening the sandwiches on the plate. "Frogs are amphibians, Your Grace."

Even though Gregory was her employer, Miss Winslow had practically raised Felicity from the time she was four years old. Since his visits to Lynton Park were rare, the woman ran the household as well. She had become almost a governess to Gregory himself over the years, and he didn't half mind it. Though now he was married, having two different women to keep him in line might be difficult.

"Either way. It's a dirty business." Gregory gazed after Julia again, who clapped her hands and cheered when Felicity nabbed a frog. They were both delighted. Lord, how disgusting.

Though when he fixated upon Julia, the word disgusting was the last word that sprang to mind.

Her golden hair had lost the tightness of its artificial curl, reverting to its more natural and loose state. Gregory preferred her that way, the goddess of nature. The sunlight glistened upon her skin in a way he'd never noticed before. Not only that, but the bloom in her cheeks was radiant. Julia loved the country air, he saw that now.

After they'd returned from the gallery, the tension between them seemed to have lifted but Felicity had bounded over, dragging them both into her plans for the morning. Miss Winslow had tried to keep a handle on the girl, but there was little in this world more willful than Miss Felicity

Berridge. Besides, Julia had been happy to go on a picnic and explore the creek.

Gregory had groaned and complained about the further interruptions, but he was secretly almost relieved. The longer they put off consummation of this marriage, the more time he had to spend with Julia. To listen to her laughter, to see the beauty of her in motion.

Gregory ate a strawberry, his body still ravenous for her touch. There was no doubt in his mind that she wanted him badly, maybe even as badly as he wanted her. But there was a difference between them: Julia wanted him once, and then never again. Whereas Gregory was growing evermore certain that once he'd had her, he'd want her again. And again. And once more for good measure.

He teetered back and forth between wanting to make love to her now and dreading the moment that their bargain would be completed. He watched as Julia laughed and bounded after Felicity, her hair glistening in the sun, and he felt his body stir with desire. Though Gregory had never been with a virgin before, he was confident that he'd make the experience as blissful for his wife as possible. God, how he wanted to slide deep inside of her and claim her as his. He wanted her to shiver beneath and around him as he took her, melded into the softness of her body.

He'd never waited this long for any lover before, but he'd also never wanted anyone this badly. More than that, he'd never *liked* anyone this much.

When was the last time Gregory had bothered to get to know anybody? Not just a woman, but another human being? For most relationships, you didn't need more than a surface understanding of the other person, but this was no ordinary relationship. Even between a man and a wife, he could swear this had the charge of something unusual.

Really, he ought to be grateful that Julia and he would only come together once, and never again. If they remained virtual strangers, Gregory would not have to wait for her to find out all his most wretched qualities and be repulsed by them. She'd learned far too many of his secrets already; he couldn't seem to keep her at emotional arm's length like every other woman he'd ever known. Then again, when he'd told her of Felicity, he'd seen the most extraordinary change come over her. She'd always looked at him with interest and amusement. This had been different.

She'd looked at him as if she might respect him.

If she does, she's a bloody fool. He'd taken in Felicity, but only out of spite for the type of parents who'd raised him. Gregory hated seeing a child tossed aside as not being good enough. He knew that pain himself only too well. Still, raising a child out of spite for people who were long dead wasn't the act of a good man. Goodness had been incidental.

Perhaps Julia thought he was someone else, and the idea that he'd disappoint her further only fueled his anger.

"Your Grace! Look!" Felicity capered over and knelt beside him on the picnic blanket. "I've named him Sir Percival. Isn't that a grand name for a frog?"

The child hoisted a slimy amphibian into his face, and Gregory pulled away.

"Felicity, put it back." He couldn't hide the shortness in his voice. Damn it.

"Come along. Let's put Sir Percival back together." Miss Winslow coaxed the young girl to follow her to the creek. Felicity appeared a bit downcast, making Gregory feel like even more of a bastard. His mood was blacker than pitch at this point, so Julia sitting beside him with her bare feet and ankles on display, tantalizing bits of flesh that he couldn't touch here in public, only served to make him fouler.

"You didn't need to snap at her like that." His wife sounded disapproving, which made him clench his jaw.

"The girl could stand to learn some decorum. I don't know what I pay the bloody governess for, if not for that."

"Then perhaps you ought to spend more time with her." Julia slipped her stockings and shoes back on, then ate a sandwich. "It's clear she adores you."

"Hmmph. Women always have done," he grumbled.

"I've seen how you are with her." Julia's tone softened, which only set Gregory's defenses up further. If this woman thought him the kind of rake who yearned to be reformed, she didn't know what she'd married. "Why don't you spend more time here at Lynton Park? I can tell Felicity would adore it."

"And would you adore it, too?" He spoke with casual ease, but Gregory's heart picked up the pace. What if Julia were hinting that she wanted him to remain, even after they'd made love?

"Oh no." His wife rolled her eyes. "I believe we'd drive each other mad soon enough. We might trade places, though. I should take myself off to southern Europe on a honeymoon and leave *you* here."

"Has that been your plan all along? Intolerable chit," he teased. Gregory wrestled with quiet disappointment, making certain not to show how he felt. She wanted this business concluded and him gone; like a fool, he was trying to find desire that wasn't there.

When Julia laughed at his words, she stirred something within his soul. No, not his soul. His body, naturally. That's all this woman was to him, a delightful bedroom escapade. Nothing more. She could be nothing more, because Gregory had been rejected once by those he loved. Never again.

"Who are you calling a chit, my lord?" But Julia sounded pleased as she selected a strawberry and nibbled at it. Gregory fisted the blanket beneath him; God, what a ravishing mouth she had. He leaned nearer to her, breathing in the clean lavender and linen scent of her. He whispered in her ear.

"If you wish to discuss this further, we might

take our argument indoors."

If he could only enjoy her once, he intended to enjoy her thoroughly.

"A private tussle, you mean?"

She sounded delighted by the idea, which fed the fire in his blood. If it weren't for the innocent child gamboling about, he'd have kissed the wench. Perhaps he might instruct Miss Winslow to see Felicity somewhere else. Into town, maybe. Or to France. China must be particularly nice this time of year.

"I must ask you something." Julia gazed up at him with those blue eyes of hers, catching Gregory in their depths like a wolf in a snare. He had to be careful not to become too trapped by her.

"What, my dear?"

Julia sat up farther, robbing them of the splendid intimacy of the moment.

"Why don't you show this aspect of yourself to society?" She seemed puzzled.

"I've told you before, Felicity must remain secreted away until she turns eighteen. That was part of my understanding with Rockford."

"Not that. The man you are up here is so different from the one I met at the Weatherford ball. Surely if the *ton* knew the real you, you'd never have been caught up in so many duels."

"They *do* see me for exactly what I am." A pounding in his temples began, and all his headaches these days had to do with the spirited woman he'd made his bride. A woman like Julia was brilliant, more so than most men he'd known, but she was also frustratingly naive. "I told you when we first met that I mocked doting husbands and ruined wives. I've fought so many duels, it's a bloody miracle I'm still breathing. Rescuing one child doesn't alter what I am."

"Forgive me, Gregory, but that is a load of codswallop and you know it."

"So now you're to tell me all about myself, hmm? You've known me a matter of weeks, madam. I assure you, the past thirty-two years I've gotten to know myself rather well, and I am no woman's ideal of chivalry or courtesy."

Julia didn't grow incensed. Rather, she appraised him with those clear eyes, her mouth set in a line that said she would not budge.

"What happened to you?" she whispered.

"Nothing. I am myself, and that's all." The world was turning much too bright around Gregory, and he wished to scream to the heavens like a beast. Why was she so determined to rouse fury and passion within him? Why was she so bloody good at it? As if to mimic his roiling emotions, dark gray clouds began to roll in from the west. Already, the wind was picking up, lifting the corners of the picnic blanket to flutter about. "We'd best go inside. Miss Winslow! Get rid of that frog and take Felicity in at once."

"What in the devil has got into you?" Julia snapped. No coyness or misdirection with this one. No, Julia charged straight at the problem.

"I'd rather not be drenched in a downpour. Isn't it rather obvious?"

"Oh, you're impossible." Julia's cheeks colored

with frustration. "You're a bloody impossible fool!"

"You bloody impossible little fool."

Gregory's father loomed over him, looking down upon his son with contempt. Gregory was only eight, and to his mind the Duke of Ashworth was the most fearsome giant in the world.

"Please, Papa," Gregory whispered. "I just thought they looked hungry."

A group of Irish travelers had camped down near the river, not one mile from Lynton Park. Gregory had come to see if there were children to play with, and when he learned that his new friends hadn't enough to eat, he'd snuck down to the kitchens to get them some bread and cheese. Gregory had returned to the camp with the food, unaware that his father was watching and following him.

The traveler children looked terrified, their cheeks bulging with the stolen bread.

"I want you gone," the duke said icily to the children. "You and the rest of your filthy kindred must leave my lands, or I'll have you shot."

"No!" Gregory began crying, which only served to deepen his father's disdain. "Papa, it wasn't their fault. It was mine! I, I just wanted to be friends."

"You are the Marquess of Kerrick." His father curled his lip. "A future duke. You do not have 'friends' among such people." The duke shook his head slowly. "Yet again, Gregory, you are an utter disappointment to me."

It was as if he'd gone back in time, thrust right into the middle of that horrid moment. He'd disappointed his friends and his family and had ended up with neither. Even when he tried to do good, he got innocent people hurt. Gregory was the most useless bastard on the planet.

"Gregory?" Julia's voice gentled. She had noticed the sudden change in him. "Please talk to me."

Talk was the last thing he wanted from her now. He didn't want to talk or to think. He didn't want to continue to hate himself in front of the one person he was beginning to adore. Gregory didn't speak the truth. Instead, he lashed out with a lie.

"Very well, if you must know. I'm tired of waiting for our bargain to be completed." He practically growled the words as he turned to her, and Julia shrank back in surprise. "If you're not interested in your duties as a wife, then say so and I'll be on my way. But your indecision has interfered with my plans, so either return to the house and find your way into my bed, Your Grace, or bid me farewell."

Julia never spoke, only watched calmly as Gregory finished and rose, tromping off to collect his ward. Felicity was still hopping near the creek, gleefully squealing whenever Miss Winslow attempted to get her under control.

"Felicity!" he shouted. That got the child's attention. "Put your shoes on and return to the house at once—"

"Your Grace?" Miss Winslow kept one hand to her bonnet, trying to stop the wind from snatching it away, and pointed at something behind him. "The duchess is leaving."

Gregory whirled around in shock and saw that the governess was right. Julia had taken her horse and was currently riding it in the exact opposite direction of the house. She cantered farther ahead, into the heart of the storm as the clouds burst open and rain began to pound the country-side. Dear God, she'd be soaked and catch her death, or else thrown from her horse in the storm and break her neck.

"Damn everything to hell," Gregory snapped. He raced for his own horse, saddled up, and rode hard after his errant wife.

CHAPTER SIXTEEN

Julia didn't care that she was soaked to the skin as she galloped across the field. Her bonnet had gone flying a mile back, and her shoes were sodden, but she felt no cold or fear as she charged ahead. All she wanted was to put as much distance between herself and her husband as she possibly could.

During all the time she believed they'd been getting to know one another, Gregory had been merely impatient to press his rights as a husband. He was probably weary of her presence, tired of trying again and again to have her and then depart. Well let him depart, then. She'd risk the threat of annulment rather than submit herself to a bastard like him.

The rain pattered against her face, her tears melding with the drops. Another man had left her crying in the rain. She should have guessed this was how it would turn out.

Julia screamed when lightning streaked across the heavens and her horse reared up in terror. She was a capable horsewoman, but riding sidesaddle was not the easiest way to keep a seat, and she went flying as her mount bucked her off its back. Julia landed, crying out when her ankle twisted to the left. Breathless, she lay upon her side in the tall grass and watched her horse toss its head and gallop in the direction of the stables.

"Come back!" she shouted, obviously to no effect. How could she be such a damn fool? When Julia became too angry, she allowed common sense to run away from her. No sane person would have ridden a horse farther into a storm, away from shelter.

"Well. Gregory can return to the house and have a nice hot bath and meal by himself. Then he'll be sorry," she grumbled, getting to her feet and limping toward a wide-branched tree. "Indeed. He's the one who'll truly suffer."

If she'd been in the mood to laugh, she'd have laughed at herself. Julia collapsed beneath the tree, where she pulled off a shoe and rolled down a muddy stocking. She wasn't much of a physician, but she didn't think she'd broken the bone. It didn't even hurt that much now; all she needed was to sit here and wait for the rain to die down. Perhaps Gregory would send a search party. After all, allowing his new bride to perish in a storm would look like criminal carelessness to the *ton*.

"Or they'd think him the cleverest man in England." Julia sighed. "Why am I talking to myself?"

Her head lifted as she heard the thud of cantering hoofbeats coming her way. Had the horse turned back for her? She got unsteadily to her feet and discovered another rider on another horse.

Even though he was still far away, she recognized the wild tangle of dark hair and the incensed expression. So. Her husband had come looking for her after all.

Julia merely sat down and continued massaging her ankle as Gregory pulled up on his horse. The animal snorted, its breath steaming in the rain as Gregory climbed down.

"The devil were you thinking?" he roared. When the duke's silken charm and good humor evaporated, he rather resembled a furious beast. He yanked on his horse's reins, guiding the creature under the sheltering branches. "Get on. I won't have you catch your death out here."

"No, indeed. After all, you must be paid for your investment in me, mustn't you?" Julia had no intention of going anywhere with him. If he thought he could speak that way to her and have her meekly obey him, he'd married the wrong woman. "If I allowed you to marry me with all that pomp and expense, I'd better do my wifely duties. What else am I good for, if not for that?" she snapped.

"Look. Don't be a stubborn fool about this."

"I'm afraid obstinacy is one of my marked characteristics." Julia lifted her chin in defiance. "Besides, we shouldn't go anywhere until the weather's cleared a bit."

She could barely hear herself over the pounding rain, and Gregory conceded the point. Grumbling, he tied his horse's reins to a branch, then sat beside her. Julia shrugged away when her husband attempted to lay his coat upon her shoulders.

"It's wet," she said.

"But it's warm. You're in only a damn muslin gown, your shawl's missing, and so's your bonnet. You may be stubborn, my dear, but I hope I didn't marry a stupid woman."

Julia didn't want to give in to him, but if she refused he'd be proven right. Only a fool would ignore the peril she'd placed herself in, and so Julia begrudgingly snatched the coat and wrapped it around herself. Lord, her husband's coat was gloriously warm; his entire body was wonderfully warm, as she recalled. Even when she was this angry at him, Julia recalled their wedding night when he'd lain atop her and she blushed.

"How shall we pass the time?" Gregory looked up at the sky, water running in rivulets down his chiseled features. She pretended to ignore the exquisite picture it created.

"Stoic silence is always welcome."

He scoffed. "I doubt you've gone five minutes without giving an opinion your entire life."

"That's not true." Julia's temper flared at once. So much for stoicism. "I'm perfectly capable of keeping thoughts to myself."

"I shall count the minutes," he drawled. "I doubt there'll be many of them."

Odious man. Hateful, despicable, mockingly attractive bastard. Julia stewed in the insults for a moment or two before she opened her mouth to give them voice.

"There." Gregory appeared triumphant. "Forty-nine seconds."

"It was longer than that!"

"I assure you, I know how to count." Gregory drew nearer, and Julia couldn't find it within herself to tell him to go away. "How badly are you hurt?"

"I don't think it's terribly sprained." Her throat felt dry as cotton as he lifted the hem of her skirt to just beneath her knee. Gregory ran his palm along her calf, causing Julia to bite her lip. But his hand cupped her ankle, and with amazing strength yet gentleness he began to move her foot, brow furrowed in concentration as he worked. "What are you doing?" she whispered.

"Ascertaining if there's a break," he replied. "I've dealt with injuries before."

"Oh." All her smart words failed as Gregory continued to touch her. The man made her want to be defiant one moment, then unsure of herself the next.

"There." He breathed out in evident relief. "Nothing's broken."

"As I said." She snatched her foot away and rolled down her skirts. "Don't touch me more than is necessary, sir."

"You can be a damnably rude chit, did you know that?"

"I've often heard that like attracts like."

"First time I've ever been called a chit," he said. "I rather enjoy it." But Gregory didn't pull away from her. Rather, he took her in his arms, and Julia wondered if she should struggle free.

"You can't just have your way with me in the middle of a field!"

"You're shivering, Julia. As I said, I'd rather you didn't catch pneumonia and die. Not until after our first anniversary, at least."

She was indeed trembling in his embrace, though perhaps not due to the cold. Julia allowed

herself to rest her cheek against the warm slope
of Gregory's shoulder. His body sheltered her as
nicely as the tree. If she allowed herself to grow
too comfortable, she might nod off to sleep. How
he'd mock her then.

"I've not yet forgiven you," she said. Gregory
sighed.

"I didn't mean those things, you understand.
I'm tired from the journey."

"That's a long-winded way of saying 'I'm sorry.'"

"I *did* apologize," he muttered. Honestly, men
were impossible creatures. Julia noticed that the
rain was beginning to lessen. Hopefully soon the
mist would clear and they could ride out. Her
husband gave a deep, beleaguered sigh.
"Returning to Lynton Park dredges up all sorts of
memories. Most of them are unpleasant," he muttered. "I'm afraid I stumbled upon one of them
and snapped at you as a result."

"Oh. Well." She cleared her throat. "I suppose
I understand what that's like. Pennington Hall's
been ruined for me since my father's death."

"So I'm forgiven, then?" he asked. There was
warmth at the edge of his voice now, and it made
her smile almost against her will.

"I imagine riding out after me in the rain was a
grand enough gesture."

"I'm pleased to hear it." He tilted her chin up,
and his lips ghosted against hers. Julia felt the
most delicious heat flooding her limbs and unfurl-
ing itself in the space between her hips. Somehow,
she wanted him even more after an argument.

Gregory seemed to sense it, and chuckled. "We might take advantage of this opportunity," he whispered, kissing her neck and wringing a gasp from her lips. "There's no one around to see us, and you're half undressed already."

It was likely meant to tease, but Julia thought of lying beneath him for a few heavenly moments and then watching him vanish before her eyes. He'd be gone for Spain, and she'd be left behind with her own sad memories. She flinched and pulled out of his embrace. Gregory didn't press her; he only gazed on her with real concern.

"Tell me what's wrong, Julia."

"What?" She was about to tell him that nothing was wrong, but he cut her off.

"I'm not an idiot. Something's got you frightened, and we'll get nowhere until you bloody tell me. Are you frightened of the pain? Are you frightened of *me*?"

"No." The answer came naturally to her, because she did not fear him. He excited and frustrated her, but she never worried he'd physically harm her. The damage would all be to her heart.

"What is it?"

I'm afraid that I like you too bloody much, and that once our business is concluded I'll lose you forever. There. Now you know. But of course the words didn't pass her lips.

"Nothing," Julia replied. "Nothing is wrong."

"I doubt that's true," he said. Gregory sounded tired now, almost as if he knew this was pointless. He didn't press her, only embraced her in order to shelter her from the storm. Julia laid there in his arms and felt the fierce beat of his heart against her body. She wanted to feel every inch of him, of his arms and his skin, the rest of his devastating physique. Perhaps it was the way she hungered for him, or the way the rain reminded her of that morning at Pennington Hall. If she couldn't tell Gregory how much she feared losing him, Julia could at least explain some of her hesitation.

"I was engaged once before, when I was seventeen years old," she said quietly. Gregory didn't respond, only allowed her the space to continue. "It was the first and last time I went to London during the Season. I met a young man named Mr. Lucas Campbell at Lady Weatherford's engagement party. I'd never been so captivated by anyone before. We hardly spoke to another person throughout the entire affair. After that, we met however and whenever we could. He made certain to gain an invitation to every ball I frequented, and every time I attended the opera he was also there. I had more fun with him than anyone else I've known."

At least, anyone until Gregory. The duke had been the first man since to delight Julia with his presence, which was half the problem itself.

"And?" Gregory murmured.

"Three weeks after we'd met, he proposed to me. Constance panicked and made immediate plans to take me away from London. But Lucas... that is, Mr. Campbell told me he'd come and fetch me. That we could elope to Gretna Green and be married inside of a week. We agreed to a place and a time; he'd come to Pennington Hall under cover of night and take me away. I remember packing that morning, ready to burst out of my skin with the excitement. I couldn't have cared less that he had no fortune or title. All I wanted was to be with him."

Julia had snuck out of the house around midnight, waiting near the front gate for Lucas to fetch her. She'd wondered if he'd have a carriage, or if he'd come only on horseback. She hadn't cared either way.

Midnight came and went. Then a quarter past. By the time the clocks struck one, she'd begun to shiver. But she'd stood there, knowing that Lucas was only detained and that he'd come. Even when the rain began at five o'clock, she stood there.

Even when it was six and she knew he was never coming, she'd stood another half hour because she couldn't bear the thought of trudging back inside of the Hall and facing Constance.

"I don't know why he never came for me," Julia said. Her voice sounded dull. "But I fear Constance may be right; he probably realized that I wasn't worth the trouble."

"Then he was the greatest fool in the fucking world," Gregory said.

He surprised her by lifting her chin and brushing a thumb along her cheek to catch a tear. Julia hadn't even realized she'd begun crying. How embarrassing.

"I suppose that's one reason why I'm afraid of our union. If afraid's the proper word."

"I feel like even more of a bloody fool than

before. I'm sorry, Julia, for those things I said," he whispered.

"I imagine I could forgive you." She couldn't help smiling. Gregory pressed his forehead to hers, and she felt so warm and sheltered in that moment that the rain simply vanished around them.

"Then I suppose we'll have to take our time with this." Gregory gave a growl of impatience, but she felt no pressure from it. "I won't have that imbecile sully another moment of your life."

"He wasn't an imbecile." Why should Julia defend such a man? "I only mean that he was rather intelligent. Very witty."

"Wit doesn't matter if a man is weak." Gregory made her face him, and Julia saw gray fire in his eyes. Though the rain had stopped and she was warm with his coat around her shoulders, she began to shiver. He held her tight, as if he would never let her go. She couldn't recall ever feeling so secure. "I don't care if he ran off with an heiress or got eaten by a bear on his way to claim you. The man was a bloody idiot, and I'm only grateful he didn't succeed in making you his wife. Wretched though that makes me, I can't help myself." The duke kissed her once, a kiss that almost caused her to lose balance. "I don't care how long it takes to possess you. I'm pleased with our arrangement, Julia."

The words themselves shouldn't have sounded passionate, but the way he said them conveyed a depth of feeling that she'd never imagined him capable of.

"Gregory," she whispered.

"Oi! Hello there!"

A male voice shouted at them from out of the mist, and soon after a man drove toward them in an open cart, a pair of horses before him.

"Woolen. How are you?" Gregory helped Julia to stand.

"Fine, Yer Grace. Miss Winslow came upon me an' said you and Her Grace was stranded in the storm. Came to find you, I did. Ma'am, are ye well?"

"Quite well. Thank you."

Julia felt dizzy as Gregory and Mr. Woolen helped her into the cart and settled her comfortably. She forced Gregory to take his coat back, as there was a blanket tucked beneath sacks of grain she could use. Her husband mounted his horse, and they returned to the house as quickly as could be.

But as they drove, Julia couldn't tear her eyes from the duke.

I'm pleased with our arrangement, Julia.

He'd listened to her story and not deemed her pathetic. Rather, he'd seemed more impressed with her than before. Julia looked up as the sky began to clear, and a hint of blue revealed itself after the storm.

CHAPTER SEVENTEEN

Julia soaked in the tub for nearly an hour, desperate to get warmth into her bones. She lounged against the porcelain back, her eyes gently shutting as she breathed in the jasmine bath oil that perfumed the water. Gregory, after learning of Julia's wretched past, had allowed her privacy and time. When Julia finally climbed out of her bath, the sun was already on its way toward the horizon.

One of the housemaids assisted her dressing. Julia wore another of Mrs. Maxwell's splendid creations, a gown of rich blue satin. She had the girl dress her hair especially nice, tightening the curls so that they framed her face. Julia finished with a spray of lilac scent and wore her teardrop diamond earbobs. She wanted to appear as lovely as possible when she spoke with Gregory—as a way of maintaining her own dignity, of course.

She hated that she'd appeared so helpless to him this afternoon. To think she'd been sprawled out in the rain with a bruised ankle, telling him the story of Lucas Campbell. What a wretch she must have appeared.

Yet he'd kissed her. *I'm satisfied with our arrangement.*

When Julia was prepared, she went next door to find Gregory's chamber empty. She rang for a servant, who told her the duke had ridden out soon after the rain stopped. To where? No one knew.

Julia might have explored the rest of the house, but standing in the doorway of Gregory's chamber once again, she could think of nowhere else she wanted to be. She touched the dark blue of his silken bedspread, and then sat upon it. The mattress was comfortable; imagine spending the entire evening here.

With her husband.

Julia knew that it was a violation of privacy, but she wanted to know this man as he truly was. A person's possessions told the truth in a way the person himself rarely could. Julia studied the wardrobe filled with clothes of the finest cuts, all with Gregory's own particular scent of cleanliness and something undeniably masculine clinging to them.

The clothes were handsome and expensive; the soaps and tonics in his washroom were the same. His taste was not as excessive as Julia would have imagined. While everything was luxurious and comfortable, there was no ostentatious design. Nothing too voluptuous. Nothing that a famous seducer of women might typically wish for.

She hesitated at his desk, holding several pieces of his correspondence in her hands. Julia finally decided that she was being far too invasive and shoved the letters back into place. However, one letter floated out of her grasp and lay half open upon the desk. It was in Spanish, a language she could not read, but she noticed that the woman who had written to Gregory signed herself *Señora*

Guzmán. Julia's stomach clenched; perhaps this woman was the reason Gregory had picked Spain as his first "honeymoon" destination. Given his reputation, a Spanish mistress was not an unreasonable conclusion to draw.

But having spent time with him now, and particularly after their moment together in the rain, Julia felt it was far too simple an explanation.

As night approached, she found she didn't want dinner. Julia was growing impatient for her husband's presence. She sat upon Gregory's bed and finally lay down, her arms spread out to her sides.

Julia's hand passed beneath a pillow, and her fingers made contact with what felt like a book. She sat up, taking the volume out from its resting, or rather, hiding place. The cover was well worn, and the pages were yellowing. A few of them were dog-eared; the book had clearly been well-loved, read and reread.

The Complete Sonnets of William Shakespeare was embossed in fading gold leaf on the cover. Julia gaped in surprise as she turned the pages. She knew that Gregory was well educated, but most men did not keep volumes of poetry close by as they slept.

Julia instantly flipped to sonnet 116, her very favorite. It was one of the pages Gregory had marked as special.

Let me not to the marriage of true minds admit impediments.
Love is not love which alters when it alteration finds,
Or bends with the remover to remove.

To Julia's surprise, she discovered Gregory had underlined certain words and sentences. In fact, he'd written some musings in the margins of the work. Of the line *It is the star to every wand'ring bark/ Whose worth's unknown although his height be taken* Gregory had written "What if you know your own worth? Or lack of it? What then?"

Julia imagined his voice saying those words, the soothing tones laced with bitterness. For the first time, she felt she'd gotten an uninhibited glimpse of the man behind the handsome facade, the grand estates, the witticisms. Gregory wrote his truths in the margins of sonnets, unable to speak them aloud to another living soul.

A lack of worth? Was that truly how Gregory thought of himself?

"What the devil are you doing?" he snapped.

Julia shut the book as the duke glared at her from the doorway. She placed the sonnets aside.

"I wanted to find you, and I happened upon this." Julia felt strangely shy in his presence now, as if she'd seen him exposed. "Is...is sonnet 116 your favorite? It's mine."

"Yes." He was curt as he snatched the book from her and placed it in a drawer. "You should go down to dinner. You had a fall this afternoon, and you need your strength."

"Why are you cross with me?"

"I'm not." He punctuated the sentence with the sharp closing of a drawer. "I merely don't appreciate you skulking around my personal effects."

Julia wondered if she ought to discuss Señora

Guzmán; he'd probably like that even less.

"You're welcome to search my chambers if you like." Julia moved behind him. "I've nothing to hide. Not anymore."

"Yes, now the tale of the deplorable Mr. Campbell has been revealed." Gregory did not turn, but she could feel the tension radiating from the straight line of his back. "I said this afternoon that we should take our time with intimacy. I meant that, for your sake. Time is necessary."

"'Love's not time's fool, though rosy lips and cheeks within his bending sickle's compass come,'" Julia murmured, speaking a line from the sonnet.

"Ha. It shouldn't shock me that one's your favorite." Gregory finally faced her, though he kept rigid and out of her reach. The man was a surly wall, impossible to tear down. He would not bend to Julia. "The most idiotically romantic of them all."

"Yet it's also your favorite," she said.

Gregory's jaw tightened, and the line of his elegant mouth grew firmer still. "I appreciate the irony. In my experience, love is the opposite of immovable in the face of destruction. The lightest rift in a marriage causes many a wife to flee into the arms of distraction."

"Then it's not love," Julia said firmly.

"What do you know about it?" Gregory shut his eyes. "Forgive me, I'm being blunt again."

"It's true that I don't know what it is to be a distracted wife. Not like the women you've known in London." Julia felt a bit ill but ventured ahead anyway. "Or in Spain. Señora Guzmán, for instance?"

Gregory appeared incredulous. "You've been poking about my correspondence?"

"I realized I was being silly and put the letters away. But I couldn't help seeing her name. I couldn't read the letter, of course." Julia took a deep breath. Her heart was going much too fast. "Is she the reason you're headed to Spain?"

"Yes," Gregory snapped. "She is."

"Very well. Thank you for your honesty." Julia wouldn't let him see her wince with the pain of that revelation.

"Señora Guzmán oversees a home for orphaned children in Madrid," he said. "She and her husband do good work but are in constant need of funds."

Julia's spirits lifted. She could scarce contain her delight.

"You're happy to supply those funds?" she whispered.

"If you must know, overseeing the development of decent housing for destitute children has taken up the bulk of my energy while I've been abroad." Gregory didn't sound proud; he looked rather irritated, in fact. It was like he hated having to tell her of his good qualities. "Even rakes get tired of raking after a while. Doing something worthwhile with my fortune provided a nice change of pace." Gregory huffed, all impatience as he ran a hand through his dark hair. "Don't look at me like that. This changes nothing."

"You're wrong." She fought against tears of

relief. "This changes a great deal, Gregory. You're not the man I thought. You're the opposite, in many ways."

"You know nothing about me, or any of it. You're an innocent." Gregory sounded cross as he shouldered past her, headed for the door.

"You're right. I am." Julia shut her eyes. "And I'm tired of that innocence." She could feel his hesitation on the threshold of his escape. Gregory watched her like a wary hawk as she came up beside him and shut the door. Julia pressed her back to the solid wood, and her eyes sought his. She wet her lips, both nervous and burning with excitement. "I want you. Even if it's for just the one night, I want you."

She couldn't force him to stay with her, but she couldn't deny herself the overwhelming need to be his for a second longer. If the price of making love to him was to lose him forever, so be it.

"Julia." He sounded shocked, but not horrified. Gregory did not instantly kiss her back when her mouth found his, but Julia melted against him nonetheless. She tasted his lips as he slowly responded, both of them sharing each other's breath as they embraced. Julia sighed as her mouth opened and her husband's tongue touched lightly against hers. "I won't force this. If you're unsure—"

"For the first time in my life, I am gloriously certain." She kissed the side of his neck, brushed her lips along the hard line of his jaw. The duke gripped her, pressed her to his body so that she could feel his growing arousal. Every kiss left her more famished than the one before. "I want this. Gregory, please."

"You want all of this?" he growled, kissing hungrily down her neck. Julia reclined in his arms, gasping with joy at the feel of his lips on the swell of her breasts. She turned, begging him to undo her gown. Gregory moved swiftly, his motions assured.

When her gown pooled at her feet, Julia leaned back in her husband's embrace. She groaned softly as his hands roamed across her body. He cupped her breasts through the thin silk of her chemise, squeezed them until she saw pinpricks of light dancing about the room. Her body ached with want; Julia could feel how sore she was between her legs. She made short work of her stays, and then turned back into Gregory's embrace. He growled as he removed her chemise, until Julia was standing before him entirely bare save her stockings.

She kept a hand pressed to his clothed chest, feeling the wild pummel of his heart. She quivered as his hands touched her once again, touched all of her. He worshipped her with his fingers and palms, rolling a thumb around and around a nipple until it hardened into a sensitive bud. When Gregory slipped one hand between her thighs, Julia clenched tightly around him. She shivered, but not from cold or fear.

"You like this, then?" He groaned to feel her beneath his hand, and then around his finger as it slipped inside of her. Julia felt how engorged and sensitive her wet flesh was.

She was not afraid now. He had seen her, and she had seen him. She knew how good he was, even if he was also deliciously wicked. Even if this was their one and only night, they understood each other.

"Take me now." The sultry voice was not hers; the confidence could not be hers. But Julia wasn't herself any longer. She was his. She let him carry her to the bed, where he unrolled her stockings and spread her out before him. Gregory wore the expression of a great predator enjoying his moment before the kill.

"Lie still, Your Grace." His breath was a hot kiss on her inner thigh. "I'll hear your screams yet."

Julia shrieked in surprise when she felt Gregory's tongue between her legs. When she jerked, his hands held her firm. Gradually, she allowed herself to close her eyes and accepted the immediate strangeness of his mouth upon her sex. But it was strange for a mere moment; soon after, the way his tongue flicked across her sensitive, swollen bud caused her to writhe and to moan.

How could anyone experience this much pleasure? Julia once again felt herself lifting off the earth and into heaven as he kissed and sucked at the most exquisitely sensitive spot on her body. She began to chant his name again and again, as if she were praying to him. When Gregory lavished attention on the very center of her bud, Julia erupted. The world became light and heat around her, and she wailed out in ecstatic triumph as she shuddered in her climax.

"Beautiful," Gregory rasped. Julia watched through her half-lidded gaze as the duke undressed himself. Layer upon layer fell away, until he knelt above her on the bed in all his chiseled and masculine glory.

And finally, she became acquainted with the full, throbbing length of his masculinity.

"Oh my God." Julia's voice was high and breathless. She sat up, her eyes running along his member. Soon, unable to stop herself, she played her fingers down his cock. She gasped at the warm, velvet feel of it as she cupped him in her hands.

"That's good," Gregory whispered as Julia trailed her fingertips along the length of him. When she touched the swollen crown of his member, he tilted his head back and groaned to the ceiling. "Fuck, this has been worth every blasted second of waiting."

Julia shivered as she realized this was how they'd be joined, but she wanted it more than she feared it.

Gently, she lay back upon the bed and allowed Gregory to cover her with his body. They kissed, and he lavished his attention upon her breasts for a few heart-stopping minutes. "I want you to be ready for me," he rasped, the tip of his tongue circling her nipple before he bit down upon it.

The sensation of his mouth on her breasts nearly sped Julia to another climax. She begged him for release. For all of him.

Julia tasted herself upon his lips as Gregory kissed her and once again aligned their bodies.

She felt his immense girth nudging at the opening between her legs.

"I'll go slow," her husband promised.

She clung to his shoulders as he began. Julia winced as he opened her, his cock so damnably large that she worried it would split her apart. But whenever she moaned in pain, he slowed as he'd promised. Finally, when Julia was stretched as far as she believed she could go, Gregory gave one fast thrust of his hips and slid all the way inside of her.

There was a moment of sharp pain, but it wasn't as horrible as she'd been expecting. She buried her face against his neck and let out a few wrenching gasps.

"Are you all right?" he whispered in her ear.

"Yes." She clenched around him once, delighted when he groaned in satisfaction. "Please, Gregory."

Julia wrapped her legs around the duke's waist on instinct as he began to thrust. At first the movements were gentle and fluid, giving her time to grow accustomed to the strangeness of having him inside of her. God, he was extraordinary. Julia panted as Gregory began to ride her harder, his hips jerking at a greater pace than before.

"Push against me. That's it," he moaned as Julia's body united with his own. Julia gripped a fistful of his hair as she leaned her forehead against his shoulder, amazed at the extraordinary feeling of the man inside of her. Already she could sense the climax approaching again, but she wanted to enjoy this union as much as possible first.

She slid one hand down Gregory's back, her fingertips playing upon the dimples at the base of his spine. She relished the feel of his body moving in and out of hers, claiming her. Making them as one.

"Julia." His voice was tight now, almost wild with abandon. "You're perfect. Fuck, this is so good."

"Gregory." His name was the only word she could remember as they rode each other toward their end. Her body tensed beneath and around his as her heart raced faster with pleasure. "Oh God."

"Come with my name on your lips." He claimed her mouth in one last fierce, almost painful kiss. "Julia. Come for me."

She did, the exquisite feeling shattering and remaking her from one instant to the next. As she finally lay spent beneath him, Gregory snarled as he pulled out of her body and, with one quick stroke of his hand, came upon her stomach. Julia lay there and felt the warm patter of his seed, and then shut her eyes in post-coital bliss as her husband stretched out beside her, his heavy breathing a delight to listen to. She gazed at his flushed face, the sheen of sweat upon his body, the curls of his hair damp with the exertion.

When they'd both caught their breath, Gregory wet a cloth and helped to clean her. Julia lay back in bed, pleasantly sore between her legs.

"It seems our union has been well and truly consummated," Gregory murmured as he lay back down beside her.

"Indeed." Julia grinned. "I've decided to give you excellent marks for effort."

"Oh? Effort, but not technique? You intolerable minx."

He kissed her as if still ravenous for her touch. Julia was pleased to discover her husband's whole body became more and more excited as they embraced.

"I can only appreciate your technique with more experience," she whispered.

"Then there's only one thing to do," he replied. Gregory laid himself back atop her. "You must be worked hard, my lady. You said it yourself today. Our union was bought at great expense, and I'm a man who gets his money's worth."

Julia believed in paying her debts in full.

CHAPTER EIGHTEEN

Gregory had never slept so well as he did with his wife's naked body warming his arms. Come the next morning, he awoke groggily to find the bed beside him empty. Julia had vanished, though the sheets were still warm from her body. Still warm from their frantic exertions throughout the night.

Gregory rolled onto his back and passed a hand down his face. He'd a reputation for being a lover with stamina, but even he'd been amazed at his own insatiability. He could not enjoy her body enough times; he could not hear her whimper or shriek her climaxes enough to fully satisfy himself. Even after last night, his body stirred with the aching desire to make her his once more.

Where the devil was she?

Julia wasn't in her room. When he rang for his valet, he learned the lady had dressed and gone for a walk in the gardens. Tomkins had been surprised to find his master voluntarily awake and dressing at eight in the morning.

"Is something wrong, Your Grace?"

"Nothing at all," Gregory said as his valet helped him with his coat.

Nothing except the temptress that he'd married, that is. Gregory walked downstairs, foregoing the thought of tea or breakfast as he hastened to the gardens. Gravel crunched beneath his boots as he strode out into the chill morning air to find his wife.

Gregory stopped when he was halfway to the rose garden. His wife.

Julia was now truly his wife in every way. Their marriage was consummated, and she was safely the Duchess of Ashworth. Their bargain had been completed.

Would she now wish him to depart and leave her in peace?

After last night, he didn't want to believe such a possibility. She'd been jealous about Señora Guzmán, though she'd tried to hide it. Julia had loved all the varieties of bedsport to which he'd introduced her. Surely she wanted him to remain with her.

The hell was he thinking? He truly *did* have business to attend on the Continent. He needed to make for Madrid, to replenish the Guzmáns funds and help himself to some of that excellent Spanish wine while he was about it.

But there wasn't enough wine in the world to make him forget Julia, not after the ecstasy of last night. Gregory's senses sharpened as he set off in pursuit of her once again. He had to know if she wanted him gone. If he was to be rejected, better to get it bloody well over with. He would not inconvenience her if she wanted him away. Gregory was a proud man, much too proud to pine for his own damned wife from the shadows of his estate.

"Good morning, Your Grace."

Julia's voice floated over to him, stopping the duke in his tracks. His bride was seated upon a stone bench beside a primrose bush. The morning light painted her in tones of cream and gold, and she was dressed in a soft gown of white muslin. Her hair curled becomingly around her face, and her blue eyes seemed to brighten with mirth. She was the most radiant creature he'd ever espied.

Fuck. Gregory had stumbled into a damnable snare. If he tried to turn away from her, he'd only be drawn back closer than before.

"Morning," he said. Julia frowned and stood. She held a rosebud she'd snipped from one of the bushes and played it thoughtfully upon her chin.

"You seem distant," she said. Was he mad, or did she look a bit shy? "Was there something you wanted?"

Yes. There was. He wanted no distance between them, and no clothes, either. Gregory was not going to mince about and hope for a signal; he would take action.

"You left our bedchamber, my dear. I find that quite rude," he replied. She responded with a teasing smile, one that made him think of the delicious ways to employ that mouth of hers. What a heavenly prospect.

"Surely a little fresh air and exercise are crucial to a happy marriage."

"I'm afraid those are precisely the things a honeymoon doesn't require."

Julia went into his arms very willingly, and her kiss matched his in passion. Thank God, she didn't seem to want him to leave. He still gave her pleasure enough that she craved more of him. Would she wish him gone tomorrow? The next day? He didn't know or care. For now, Gregory was going to enjoy himself. Thoroughly.

Julia dropped her rosebud as Gregory hoisted her up and carried her out of the garden.

"Your Grace, what will the servants think?" she asked breathlessly.

"They may think whatever they like, so long as we're not disturbed."

...

They were not disturbed for the next several days. Even Miss Winslow managed to wrangle Felicity out of their way, though Julia did insist upon seeing the child at tea or for a walk or a picnic. Though Gregory would have been glad to remain naked and locked in his bedchamber with her, he could refuse her nothing.

Especially because she refused him nothing in return.

Had Gregory ever planned to leave Lynton Park, or Julia? The memories of booking passage to Spain felt like some bizarre dream, laughable whenever he awoke beside his new wife and made love to her again. He wrote to his bank and told them to send funds to Madrid, as much money as was required. He'd give the Guzmáns his entire fortune if it meant he could remain in Julia's arms.

She relished their lovemaking as much as he did. They came to know the duke and duchess's bedrooms very well. They didn't remain in only the bedchambers, either. Gregory and his new duchess christened the study, the eastern parlor, and the library as well.

The library provided especial opportunities for

pleasure. Julia came up with the most delicious idea as she took another volume of bloody Shakespeare from off the shelf.

"Can you recite sonnet sixteen perfectly from memory?" she asked him coyly.

"Am I a performing monkey for Her Grace?" Gregory took the book from Julia's hands and laid her out upon a settee. "All beasts deserve reward for their endeavors."

"Then let me amend my request. Recite sonnet sixteen perfectly," Julia said, her hands beginning to undo his trousers. "So long as you don't make a mistake, I won't stop."

"You're a diabolical harridan," Gregory said, his eyes closing in bliss as she wrapped her hand around his throbbing member.

"That's not how the sonnet begins, Your Grace."

"Fine." He hissed as he felt the quiver of her lips upon his manhood, and then the velvet slip of her tongue. "'But wherefore do you not a mightier way make war upon this bloody tyrant, Time?'"

Julia hummed as she worked, which almost caused him to spend straightaway. "You certainly know your Shakespeare, my dear."

"He's only the finest poet known to the English tongue," he replied.

Julia gave ample demonstration of how talented her own tongue was. It's a miracle she didn't finish him off right then.

Gregory continued his recitation, groaning inwardly as his wife's golden head bobbed on his cock. When he was on the precipice of release, he fumbled a line by mistake and almost had a heart attack when she stopped her ministrations and adopted a coy smile upon seeing his discomfort.

"Intolerable hussy," Gregory snarled.

"Shakespeare never wrote those words."

Oh, she was a marvel, this woman. Gregory found his way back to the poem and uttered the last line—"And you must live, drawn by your own sweet skill"—just as Julia took him as deep into her mouth as she could. His hips surged as he finished, and he was weak with enjoyment as he felt her drink deeply of him.

"Mostly excellent, Your Grace," she purred. Gregory had her lounge back upon the settee while he pushed her skirts up to her waist.

"I'm afraid we'll need to test your own skill now, duchess. Sonnet twenty-nine, if you please."

"That's hardly a challenge," she replied, clear eyes flashing with glee as Gregory bent his head, caressing her inner thigh with his lips. "'When in disgrace with fortune and men'—*Oh!*" she shrieked when he began.

"Careful. That wasn't correct," he whispered, smiling to hear her moans of frustration and bliss as he continued.

Gregory could not think of anywhere else in England or on this planet he would rather be than with Julia. In bed with her, their naked bodies pressed close; beneath the outspread branches of a tree outside, enjoying the natural splendor with no one for miles to reprimand them for their obscene behavior. Even when fully clothed, he loved dining with her and listening to her laughter and opinions on everything from the state of modern Parliament to poetry. She was also a woman who didn't believe in wasting time. Even while on her honeymoon, she visited the town of Lynton and looked in on the dame school, which she found less than satisfactory. Apparently, Gregory had not paid enough attention to how the village children were educated, which Julia would fix straightaway. He felt the most intense pride in watching his duchess throw herself into her duty with determined enthusiasm, insisting that any and all tenants under her protection would receive the best of everything.

She was wonderful. She was beautiful, and brilliant, and charitable, and exquisite in bed, but more than that she was in every way a delight to his senses.

He'd never before known what it was like to want someone by his side at every moment of every day. To think of something funny and want instantly to tell it so he could hear the sound of her laughter. And so far, through all of this, she hadn't yet grown tired of him.

Gregory was certain that eventually the ecstasy of their lovemaking would fade, as it always did. Then they'd part, surely. It would be easy, and without pain.

So that night, after he and Julia had finished another breathless round of lovemaking, she surprised him with a rather forward idea.

"Do you think we might continue on like this?" She laid her head upon his chest as she spoke.

"Hmm? Are you in an uncomfortable position?" He frowned.

"I don't mean physically laying upon you." She sounded as though she were rolling her eyes. Gregory would have to exact delicious punishment on her for that. "I mean, Your Grace, would it be possible to continue as we are?"

"As we are?" he echoed, still not certain he understood, though Julia's ever-deepening blush suggested something momentous.

"We seem to do well together, don't we?" she asked. They did far better than well, and she had to know it. "Perhaps you don't need to go abroad. We might return to London together next month for the close of the Season."

"And after the Season?" He could scarcely feel her in his arms now; his whole body seemed to have gone numb from the shock. She couldn't mean what he thought she meant. Could she?

"After the Season we might return home, to Lynton Park. Or go abroad ourselves. Together."

"You mean for this marriage to be a true one?" Gregory was shocked by the suggestion, even though they *were* literally married.

"It's unimportant." Julia began to turn from him, but Gregory held her close.

It was against everything they had planned, this suggestion. Before they'd made love, he would have adamantly refused even the possibility. Gregory had prepared for the pain of letting her go, but he could never have known the joy she would bring him until he experienced it firsthand. And as one day led to the next and Julia still did not ask him to leave, he began to feel at home. At Lynton Park, with her, with the servants and Felicity, with everything he'd sworn he would never have. A life of commitment to one other person, and all that entailed.

If he had adored her less, he would have felt the fear more. But as it stood, Gregory found himself agreeing with Julia's suggestion.

"Perhaps," he said. He was amazed at his own words. "Perhaps that could work."

"Truly?" Her eyes lit up. She was gorgeous when she was happy. He wanted to keep her that gorgeous always.

"After all, some time spent flaunting my bride before the *ton* would suit me nicely."

Julia sighed in seeming exasperation. "Of course. You must be admired wherever you go."

Gregory pressed his lips to the crown of her head. "I meant I should like to be the envy of every man in town with you on my arm."

"Oh." God, he loved making her blush. "Well. I'm more than some possession, you know."

But Julia smiled as he kissed her.

"Believe me, my dear. I know that only too well."

As they returned to kissing, and everything that kissing led to, Gregory thought of this brave new world he was heading toward. A true marriage. A true husband and wife. The thought no longer terrified him; now he felt himself straining eagerly toward such a union.

He would make no firm decision now. He would wait until at least the end of the Season before coming to any conclusions. But if all this remained as good as it was now, then perhaps...

Well. Perhaps this rake truly *had* been redeemed.

• • •

"I've never known the duke to spend so much time at Lynton Park before. You are an excellent influence on him, Your Grace."

Miss Winslow and Julia were seated upon a blanket, watching as Gregory showed Felicity how to properly wield a croquet mallet. Julia appreciated the duke's agile, muscular form as he demonstrated a perfect technique.

"We've been in residence here nearly two weeks. That's unusual?" she asked Miss Winslow.

"Oh yes, Your Grace. The duke rarely stays more than a week, if that."

"I think it's good for Felicity to have him about," Julia said thoughtfully. After all, the child needed someone she could view as a father.

"If I may say so, I think it's good for His Grace to have *you* around, ma'am."

"Yes. I suppose I rein him in a bit." Julia smiled. "Or at least tire him out."

Julia laughed, and Miss Winslow joined in. Julia had never felt so relaxed, seated beneath the dappled shade of a tree and watching Gregory enjoy himself. Her eyes were innately drawn to wherever her husband happened to be; she'd seek him out even when she was thinking of something else. Then again, these days she rarely thought about anything else. Thank God for her little school project in the village of Lynton, or she really would have been happy to remain in bed with her husband for days on end.

Every morning that she woke beside him was better than the last. Julia hadn't known that the married act between a man and a woman could be so heavenly. Every part of Gregory thrilled her, from the strength of his body to the fire of his intelligence and the ease of his charm. Every day Julia spent with him, she wanted only one thing: more. More of this, of them together.

And he'd agreed, hadn't he? Two nights ago, he'd agreed that this marriage between them might become something true. Julia would not have only the title and wealth of the Duchess of Ashworth, but the duke as well. In truth, she'd come to feel that her title was nothing without Gregory.

He was the most devastatingly wonderful lover she could have hoped for. And she liked him, more than she probably should.

But maybe they really could make this marriage a true one. If he believed it was possible, then perhaps Julia could have some faith.

"I wonder who that is?" Miss Winslow frowned as a horse and rider appeared on the edge of the park, cantering rather quickly toward the picnickers.

"Is he a messenger?" Julia squinted, trying to make the man out. "Ah. Doubtful, if the fine cut of his clothes is any indication. I didn't realize Ashworth had neighbors; the estate seems so quiet."

"Oh." Miss Winslow put a hand to her mouth,

and to Julia's surprise went quite pale. That is, until two pink spots appeared on the woman's cheeks.

"Who is it?" Julia asked.

"It may be His Grace, the Duke of Huntington." Miss Winslow instantly cast her eyes down and began to neaten the edge of the blanket again and again. "He owns a smaller estate not five miles from here. The Duke of Ashworth and His Grace are quite friendly. So I believe," the governess added quickly.

"Indeed." Julia watched the woman carefully, but Miss Winslow became coolheaded again upon the instant.

"Huntington!" Gregory roared, laying aside his croquet mallet as the duke cantered up and stopped his horse. "The devil are you doing here?"

Julia went quickly to the men as the duke climbed down from his horse and made her a hasty bow in greeting.

"Your Grace? Your servant," the man said, bending politely over her hand.

"The Duke of Huntington, is it?" Julia made a quick curtsy. She'd heard of the Duke of Huntington before but had never seen him. He hadn't even been at their wedding, and nearly everyone in the *ton* had attended.

"Yes. My apologies for our not meeting until now. I've been in France, and this fiend you've married *would* decide to wed while I was away." Huntington grinned as Ashworth slapped him on the back.

"Hunt's an old friend, Julia." Gregory

appeared delighted. "Hopefully you've come to stay to dinner, you bastard."

Julia laughed, pleased when her husband waived formality in front of her.

"You seem to have chosen the proper bride, Ashworth." Huntington bowed again to Julia in a complimentary manner. She could at least understand Miss Winslow's fluttery excitement upon seeing him. The man was even taller than Gregory, perhaps all of six and a half feet, with hair that was a brilliant blond and eyes of sky blue. To Julia, Gregory remained the most handsome man alive, but this duke certainly gave him fine competition.

"Come along. We'll have Miss Winslow take Felicity up to the schoolroom," Gregory said.

"You'll also want to begin packing," Huntington replied as they began to return to the house.

"I beg pardon?" Julia couldn't help her surprise.

"Forgive me, but this isn't a mere social call on an old friend and his new wife," Huntington said. "I've come to you with a message, Ashworth. From Her Majesty."

"The queen?" Gregory and Julia exchanged bewildered glances. "What the devil does the queen want with me?"

"She wants to see you and Her Grace at once." Huntington grinned. "The Duke and Duchess of Ashworth are being summoned back to London with all due haste."

CHAPTER NINETEEN

That evening, the two dukes played billiards after supper, while Gregory tried to understand precisely what his damned friend was telling him about the queen's strange request.

"I still don't see why Her Majesty needs us to return to town."

"Call it a queen's romantic whimsy." Huntington chalked up a cue. "I only arrived back in town last week, and I've been unable to avoid talk of your relationship. Every gossip sheet in London called yours a fairytale romance from the moment you proposed to the duchess. Since your marriage, the *ton* has grown even more insatiable for news of this Cinderella and her duke. You have no idea how wise you were to leave the city. Your wife's managed to eclipse every debutante this Season, and Her Majesty's taken note. You and Her Grace have captured the queen's imagination to such an extent that she's decided to host the final ball of the Season at the palace. Its very theme is inspired by you and the duchess." Huntington gave a wicked grin as he made an elegant shot, sinking two balls at once. "The queen wants a costume ball, with fairy stories and folktales as its theme."

"And Her Majesty wants the actual Cinderella and her rakish prince in attendance," Gregory muttered.

"It will make her ball a true triumph."

Gregory knew he couldn't refuse, but the idea caused his mood to sour. He'd planned to return to London with Julia at the tail end of the Season, hoping to take their place in society without much commotion. But if they were to be feted by the *ton*, the attention would be exhausting. Still, the Season would only last a few more weeks. During that time, he'd allow this marriage to continue to bloom, as glorious as it was terrifying. And if August came and their union remained strong, then he and Julia might be off to the Mediterranean together, a land of sunlight, crystalline waters, and relaxed standards as regards to public nudity. A fairytale ending indeed.

"If Her Majesty wants a performance, then I suppose a change of costume will be in order," Gregory said, though he remained a bit irritated. After all, a man went on honeymoon only once in his life, and now he'd be required to perform for good society. He took his shot and cursed when he missed by a wide margin.

"It's difficult to believe you're the same Ashworth as three short months ago," Huntington said drily. "The man I knew would never miss a shot with only a couple of glasses of port in him."

"This is what happens when a man marries. His tolerance for liquor and dissolute society begins to fade."

"Thank you for the compliment," Huntington replied, "but my dissolution was never as marked as yours. A rake's quality is far more important than the quantity of his conquests."

"When we were at Oxford, you were never so selective."

"Compared to you, I was practically chaste." Huntington took another shot and added more chalk to his cue. "Care to know the sharpest difference between the man I knew and the one I see now?"

"Even better hair?" Gregory sank a ball into a corner pocket, pleased with himself.

"You seem contented." Huntington leaned upon his cue, looking as if he were enjoying Gregory's discomfort.

"Julia's the sort of woman who satisfies a man easily," he replied. Gregory, though, had to admit the truth: that these last few weeks had been the best of his life. "If you're going to laud the institution of marriage, Hunt, you might focus on finding your own duchess. The woman won't fall out of the sky and into your lap, though I'd wager many would happily catapult themselves at you if it increased their chances of success." Huntington was one of the few members of the *ton* whose estate made Gregory's appear almost modest.

"Moorcliff Castle needs the correct mistress." That was always the duke's answer whenever called upon to marry. "Besides, we're not talking of my happiness, but of yours."

"I would be a happier man if I wasn't required to strut about London like a peacock on display for royal approval."

"You've never been a man who loathed public attention." Huntington laughed.

No, indeed. At the beginning of this mad

adventure, Gregory had been only too delighted to flaunt his sham of an engagement, eager to send away the lust-filled dames of London and their trigger-happy husbands. What the queen demanded was only a repeat of that same performance, so why should he hate the very notion?

If anyone were to look closely at this marriage, they would find nothing odd or false about it. Perhaps that was the very problem; Gregory finally had something that he wanted to keep all to himself, away from the prying eyes of the *ton*.

But it was only for a few more weeks, and then he and Julia would finally be released from this nonsense.

Yes. Only a little longer, and they'd both be free of society's gawking. When he lined up his cue and took another shot, he was once again in rare form.

• • •

When Julia returned to Carter House, she discovered a veritable treasure trove of fashionable calling cards. She didn't know how to go about returning all of them *and* being fitted for her ball gown at Mrs. Maxwell's. Fortunately, Lady Weatherford and Susannah paid a call within an hour of Julia's arrival.

"You simply won't believe it," Susannah said by way of greeting after Julia had embraced her stepsister. The young woman handed Julia a gossip sheet, her eyes practically aglow with delight.

Julia had to sit down when she read over *Mrs. Babbington's Babble*, the most renowned gossip column in London.

Rumor has it that the Duke of Ashworth has returned to town alongside his new bride, cutting short their wedding trip to attend Her Majesty's grand ball as guests of honor. The new duchess will find herself with nary a free moment for the rest of the Season, if the hordes of society matrons and hopeful debutantes descending upon Carter House this week are any indication.

"Why should anyone be so invested in my marriage?" Julia shook her head as she folded up the *Babble* and laid it aside. "It's true that a new *ton* bride always receives a fair bit of attention, but this sort of mania is supposed to die down after the wedding!"

"Blame it on the duke." Laura smiled over her teacup. "It was his idea to flaunt your Cinderella romance before all society. The pair of you did such an excellent job that they now wish you to continue playing your parts, at least until the middle of July."

"Still. Why would the queen herself become so invested?" Surely monarchs had better and more important things to do than speculate about Julia's marriage and husband.

"You know how royalty are," Laura replied. "Sometimes they grow weary of fox hunting and wish for more interesting prey."

"You know how to make all this sound as unterrifying as possible," Julia drawled.

Over the next several days, she scarcely had

time to feel nervous, or even to think. Julia's every waking moment that wasn't spent in Gregory's arms was consumed by preparations for the queen's ball. Mrs. Maxwell had declared that, as the guest of honor, Julia's gown must outshine every other woman's in the room. The modiste had decided to embrace the Cinderella romance, turning Julia into a fairytale heroine for the ages. The gown was to be white satin trimmed with silver, and a pair of slippers frosted with crystal beads, to give off the shine of glass.

The preparations were not all that society required of Julia. As one of its new and most fashionable leaders, she received calls from half of the *ton* in the morning, and then had to pay afternoon calls upon the other half who'd called yesterday morning. She had invitations to literary salons and dinner parties, along with access to all the most pernicious gossip imaginable. If she had to listen to Lady Mountridge tell Mrs. Simpson's most scandalous and debauched secrets one more time, Julia would force every fashionable lady in London to swallow her own bonnet.

Even the Society of Ladies for the Expansion of Female Literacy proved impossible. At Julia's luncheon to celebrate being named chairwoman, she'd been eager to discuss plans for outreach to the more rural areas of England. Instead, all the members wanted to discuss was her costume for the upcoming ball.

For years, she'd dreamed of being in society and taking her place amongst the married women of the *ton*. Julia had never imagined that life as a duchess could be so bloody draining.

She'd married Gregory to gain access to this world, but Julia had discovered that society was not the great prize she'd coveted. Her husband, however, filled the best part of her days. She'd never anticipated anything like it.

And when she casually mentioned the possibility of traveling with him to Portugal or Spain in the autumn, he didn't try to change the subject, nor did he appear uncomfortable. He seemed to be growing increasingly attached to the idea.

And as the days passed and the duke showed no sign of tiring of her, Julia allowed herself to hope that this honeymoon period might last the rest of her life. The more she saw of him, the more Julia liked him. The more she experienced his prowess in the bedroom, the more she craved him. She was now convinced there was nothing she could learn about the Duke of Ashworth that would cool her burgeoning affection for him.

So when Mrs. Woodhouse invited Julia to a tea hosted in her honor by the Carter Club, Julia found herself unable to refuse.

CHAPTER TWENTY

Gregory was less than thrilled at the idea of his wife parading into a society tea with an assortment of his former conquests.

"Of all the perverse women I've known in my life, you rank at least in the upper five." He practically growled his disapproval as Julia finished dressing for the Carter Club tea, and it gave her pleasure to see him so surly. The more she irritated him, the more passionately he forced her to repent her waywardness. When she returned home from the outing, she imagined Gregory would be so apoplectic that he'd be ready to tie her up in literal knots. Speaking of…

"Lady Clifton mentioned a Neapolitan Knot when we last met." Julia added a dab of lavender oil to her wrists, completing her toilette while her husband prowled behind her. She watched him in the mirror, enjoying her show.

"If you go to this blasted tea, you won't be receiving any special treatment. In fact, I swear I'll never touch you again."

Julia bit back some laughter as she stood and smoothed her frock once. That was a vow they both knew bloody well he'd never be able to keep.

"I doubt we'll speak of you at all, Your Grace. The ladies seem desperate to know more about me, the woman who tamed you."

"Just tell me you aren't walking into this lionesses' den alone."

"Of course not. Lady Weatherford will accompany me." Gregory knew Laura would never let any harm come to her, and relaxed.

"A wife should bend to her husband's will on this," he muttered. But the duke took her into his arms as he spoke, probably hoping to entice Julia into a deeper embrace. Which would lead to an afternoon spent in bed. Which would leave her no time at all for tea. Tempting as the thought was, Julia kissed her husband and stepped out of his arms. A bloody difficult business, that.

"I'm afraid I rather like bending to my own will." Julia kissed him once more, forcing herself not to capitulate any further. "But I shall be home soon."

"And I shall have to think of ways to make you more obedient," he said. "Perhaps tying you to the bed *would* be the correct way to start."

"I look forward to your endeavors." Julia smiled.

• • •

The Carter Club gathered at Elizabeth Woodhouse's home in Hanover Square, and Julia was relieved to see that most of them were not dressed in mourning anymore. There were about fifteen women present, not including Julia and Laura, all of them aged somewhere between five-and-twenty and forty. The women greeted one another warmly, and were in positive raptures when Julia was presented to them.

"My dear friends, allow me to introduce the Duchess of Ashworth." Elizabeth tittered and waved everyone to their seats. A circle of chairs had been placed in the drawing room, with trays of sandwiches and tea resting upon nearby tables. "I daresay she's accomplished what most would have believed impossible."

"You're a hero, my lady." A younger woman nearly swooned as she took a cup of tea. "You must have such stories to tell us."

"If they're of a more carnal nature, please don't." Laura spoke to Julia from behind her teacup. "There are some mental images of Ashworth I do not require."

"I think I should like to know more about all of you," Julia said evenly, surveying the room filled with delighted faces. "Er, about your interests and pursuits, that is. Those that aren't related to my husband, if that's all right."

To her relief, the women laughed.

"I shall start," Elizabeth said. "Not only am I hostess of this little gathering, but I'm the original founder of the Carter Club."

"Indeed?" Julia worried that this might prove an uncomfortable few minutes, but Elizabeth Woodhouse proudly gestured to the paintings hung upon the eastern wall, right between the windows.

"Most here will tell you a similar story, Your Grace. We lost ourselves in marriage. Some of us love our husbands dearly, you understand, but women in our society are raised with only one purpose in mind our entire lives: to be wed. When we attain that goal, well…" Elizabeth sighed as she stood and made her way over to the artwork. "I for one realized I'd no concept of who I truly was, or what I desired. Such realizations can make for a very bleak life indeed."

Murmurs of agreement rippled through the gathering. Julia noticed Lady Clifton wipe away a tear with the corner of her handkerchief. Mrs. Pankhurst had got into the biscuits again, and ate one with sadness.

"I understand," Julia said.

"You see, that's why we all cherished our time with the duke so highly. The man is a sensational lover, to be certain." Elizabeth heaved a sigh, echoed by the rest of the women save Julia and Laura. "But he ignited other passions beyond the physical in many of us. For instance, look!" She gestured to the paintings. "I was so transformed by our time together that I began to paint scenes inspired by erotic myth. Women are expected to sketch flowers and trees, or to make watercolor portraits of their children's pets. But now I've learned to love my art! It inspires me with so much joy. Observe, if you will, my own rendition of Cupid and Psyche!"

Julia stood and more closely inspected the painting, which was actually quite a handsome image. A young woman held a candle and leaned over the gorgeous, naked figure of a sleeping man.

"My, but Cupid looks rather like…" *Oh dear*. "The duke. Doesn't he?"

"I'm afraid that all my heroes are modeled

after His Grace." Elizabeth clucked her tongue. "What can I say? Inspiration is a potent drug."

"Indeed." Julia surveyed the next portrait, Lancelot and Guinevere locked in an embrace. Lancelot, of course, looked rather like Gregory. She had to admit, Elizabeth was a talented artist. "May I ask, what does your husband think of your newfound calling?" She couldn't imagine the man loved his wife painting romantic pictures of a former lover.

"At first, he didn't think much of it," Elizabeth said. "But eventually my paintings fanned the flames of his own carnal imagination. We are ever so much closer now as husband and wife."

"In truth, most of us have improved our marriages," Lady Clifton added. "Ashworth showed us what we were missing in the bedchamber, but as Elizabeth has said, he gave us further inspiration!"

"I've begun a charitable institution that instructs disadvantaged young women in various trades," Mrs. Pankhurst offered.

"My husband and I now breed bloodhounds," one of the older women said. "It's finally given us something to talk about other than the children!"

"My husband and I host weekend-long parties of general debauchery at our estate." One of the younger women sighed with pleasure. "We've learned our marriage is ever so much happier with more people in it!"

"Oh my God," Laura whispered.

Julia was shocked as well, but also strangely proud of Gregory. At first, she'd thought him nothing more than a man who used and discarded women and made husbands furious. But how many *ton* marriages had he also repaired, not only with his talents as a lover, but with his passion for living?

"The duke has a great deal of spirit," she said. "Whoever he's with benefits from it."

"Indeed!" Elizabeth beamed. "Oh, and I've also begun to expand my artistic talents into sculpture. I'm told it's wrong for a lady to work with her hands in such a manner, but I find I can't help myself. Look! Here's my attempt at Adonis." She gestured to a smaller statue upon a table to the back.

"I can't look." Laura moaned, quickly turning her head away.

"It's an...exact likeness." Julia found every chiseled detail of her husband's form in the entirely naked work of art.

More and more of the women offered up their own stories. One had begun writing poetry, while another wished to begin a philosophical salon. Another lady had thrown herself fully into motherhood, while another was making plans to set sail for the West Indies. Above all else, they were in positive raptures about the physical happiness Gregory had inspired in them, and in their husbands, too.

"You needn't be so shocked, Lady Weatherford." Elizabeth offered her a sugared almond biscuit. "We are all married ladies here. No one should be scandalized!"

Laura was doing her best to conceal her horror, which Julia greatly appreciated.

"You can look at this one," Julia said, luring her friend over to admire another of Elizabeth's paintings. "Gregory, I mean, Romeo is fully clothed in this one."

Laura groaned and found a spot where she might sit down a minute. Well, she *was* pregnant.

"I hope this hasn't been too unusual an afternoon, Your Grace." Elizabeth wandered over to Julia and sat beside her. She quickly refreshed Julia's cup. "I can only imagine how this appears from an outside perspective, but please believe that everyone in this room is delighted to have you."

"I admit I had my doubts," Julia said. "But meeting you all has been an unexpected pleasure. In fact, it's only made me esteem my husband more."

"I can tell you are both a splendid match." The woman beamed and sipped her tea.

"How long ago were you acquainted with the duke?" Julia asked. Lord, but what a strange question for a wife to ask a former mistress.

"We saw one another for two months when I was up in Edinburgh visiting a cousin. That would have been almost five years ago now."

"There are Woodhouses in Edinburgh?"

"Oh no. Woodhouse, naturally, is my husband's family. My maiden name is Campbell."

"Campbell?"

Julia frowned as she studied Elizabeth's features once more. There was still something about her that seemed so familiar, and now the name only heightened that feeling.

"This will sound odd, but we've never met

before, have we?" Julia asked. "Before you came to call upon me at Carter House, that is."

"Oh no. I'm certain I'd have recalled meeting you, Your Grace."

Elizabeth was all sincerity and kindness, but Julia couldn't shake the ugly feeling growing in the pit of her stomach. Now that she looked more closely, she noticed that Elizabeth's strong nose and large, heavy-lidded blue eyes reminded her of someone else. Someone she'd not seen in ten years. Sickness began to knot at the pit of her stomach with the realization.

"Mrs. Woodhouse, do you have any brothers?"

"Sadly no. Three younger sisters."

Julia's heart slowed with her relief, but only for a moment.

"I do have a cousin, though, who might as well be a brother. We grew up together in Northumberland. He's staying with us for the Season, as it happens."

Julia could not stop herself from speaking the name.

"Mr. Lucas Campbell?"

"Oh! Have you met before?" Elizabeth appeared delighted by the thought.

Julia felt as if the ground was cracking open beneath her feet. She needed to behave well; she couldn't afford for anyone to gossip.

"We met years ago." Thankfully, she kept her voice light. "Now I know where I thought I'd seen you before. The two of you bear such a strong resemblance." Julia smiled even as she began to scream deep down inside. Thankfully, tea should be almost finished. It would not appear strange for her to make an exit now. Julia set her cup down and rose slowly. "Thank you so much, Mrs. Woodhouse. This has been a most, er, memorable afternoon."

"Oh, must you leave so soon, Your Grace?" Elizabeth appeared disheartened, but the risk of running into Lucas was worse than a slight breach of etiquette.

"It's on my account, I'm afraid." Laura was only too happy to leave the rather strange gathering. "My doctor says I must not overexert myself these next few months."

Julia could have kissed the woman. She and Laura made a polite farewell and left. As the steward showed them to the door, Julia glanced around but saw no trace of Lucas. When the front door shut behind the women, Laura tilted her face to the London sky and exhaled in relief.

"I'm only delighted Mrs. Woodhouse hasn't taken to crocheting erotic tea cozies of your husband. Julia? My dear, whatever's the matter?"

Laura did not know about Lucas Campbell. No one except for Constance, Susannah, and the servants at Pennington Hall knew. And now Gregory, of course. For years, Julia had nursed the pain of that experience in private, too ashamed to let anyone else know. Even now, as the Duchess of Ashworth, she found it too difficult to tell her dearest friend.

But if Lucas Campbell was in London for the Season, then Julia knew she must tell her husband.

CHAPTER TWENTY-ONE

Gregory hated to lose at billiards, but his wife had rather consumed the better part of his thinking. Percy and Huntington noted his wandering mind at their club, happy to take a small fortune off of him in winnings, but Gregory hadn't any time for them. He hadn't been worried when Julia went off to that accursed tea—if anything, he'd found it perversely amusing. He'd much to be guilty of in his life, but the Carter Club was not, he believed, one of those things. A man and woman choosing to engage in pleasure was hardly a crime.

But he found he couldn't stand the idea of losing the respect he saw in Julia's eyes. Somehow, this woman still enjoyed his company as much as she did his talents in the bedroom.

He could not wait for this cursed Season to finally be at an end. He wanted to be alone with Julia. He could abscond with his bride to anywhere they chose on the Continent, or maybe even farther. He'd never seen India, and had always meant to go. Perhaps into the steppes of bloody Mongolia, where no one spoke a word of English. Yes. Then no one could interrupt Gregory's preoccupation with his new wife.

Though getting good service might be a chore...

"Ashworth. Where the hell is your head?" Percy asked.

"Mmm. Delightful," Gregory muttered, not listening to a word his friend spoke.

When he returned home, Peele informed him that Julia was in the library. Gregory went to her, wicked thoughts circling through his mind. She always chose the library when she was feeling especially amorous and creative. Perhaps he might test her Italian, have her recite perfect sections from Dante while bending her across the desk.

His duchess was standing against the far wall, the afternoon sun highlighting her against the window. Gregory felt himself stir at the mere sight of her. Julia was a vision in an afternoon dress of rose silk; he knew she'd look even more beautiful without the garment.

"Did the lionesses behave themselves?" he asked.

Julia startled and slammed her book shut. Odd behavior, especially when she gave him a nervous glance. Now Gregory's nascent fears began to take real form. She must have been shocked and disgusted by what she'd learned at that damned tea.

"Julia?"

"They were delightful. Truly. Though Lady Weatherford may never recover after seeing Mrs. Woodhouse's, er, art gallery."

"Indeed. I haven't seen any of the portraits myself, but I hear they're an excellent likeness." Damn everything, the tea must have truly unsettled her. "Come here."

He rarely gave orders, and Julia rarely capitulated without another word. She crossed the space and obediently wrapped herself in his arms. Gregory delighted in the faint floral scent of her perfume, and the way her lips trembled against his. There was still overwhelming passion in her kiss. That, at least, hadn't been harmed.

"Gregory, I need to tell you something."

"What is it?" He sounded collected, but he felt the true creep of dread shiver along his spine. Would she tell him that her discoveries at the blasted Carter Club had killed her admiration for him? Even if Julia gave her body to him willingly, the potential loss of her mind and soul pierced him like a dagger.

"I learned Mrs. Woodhouse's maiden name."

Gregory blinked; this was not the torrid secret he'd anticipated.

"Excellent work. With such a talent for extracting information, you really must become a Bow Street runner."

She wrinkled her nose at him, the playful expression that quickened his blood and gladdened his heart. Perhaps this hesitancy had nothing to do with him after all.

"It's Campbell. I discovered she's Lucas Campbell's cousin. And…" Julia sighed. "Though I didn't see the man, she told me that he's staying with her in town for the Season."

"Ah."

The most baffling mixture of emotions crowded him in an instant. First, he wanted to find this Lucas Campbell and beat the man bloody for the pain he'd caused Julia. Second, he felt a stab of almost bitter jealousy.

Julia was quivering in his arms at mere mention of the bastard's name. Lucas Campbell still held a powerful fascination for his wife all these years later. Even if Julia hated the man, the fact remained that the mere promise of potentially seeing him again had unmoored her.

Women didn't experience such emotional devastation if feelings didn't remain in even their smallest form.

"Is that all you can say? Ah?" Julia frowned.

Oh, was she growing indignant now?

"Would you like me to call the man out? Fight a duel on your behalf over ten years after he betrayed your trust?" Gregory felt Julia leave his arms, but he couldn't stop the horrific spin of his thoughts. "Or are you afraid we'll see him before the end of the Season?"

"Obviously the latter!"

"Why? Are you afraid he'll slip a bag over your head and make away with you as his helpless captive?"

"As if a bag would render me helpless." She sounded so insulted by the idea that Gregory laughed. Immediately, all the tension fled his body. God, what was he on about? Julia was not the type of woman to sit and simper for a man who'd rejected her, especially after all these years. If anything, Gregory would have to intervene and protect bloody Lucas Campbell from the Duchess of Ashworth's molten wrath.

Julia's eyes still blazed with fury and fire, even as a smile tugged at her lips. Those very delectable, very kissable lips.

"Your Grace, jealousy does not become you," she said.

"Hard to believe. Nearly everything does."

"I don't find vanity an especially attractive quality." Yet Julia did not resist when he embraced and kissed her. In fact, she was the one who specifically bid him lock the door and take her on the desk.

He was the one who insisted on reciting Dante.

• • •

Julia knew that much of polite society regarded the Vauxhall pleasure gardens as second-tier amusement. The gardens were open to the public, after all, and therefore a rather vulgar form of entertainment, but she'd missed them in the ten years she'd been absent from London. Gregory should have preferred to spend the evening at the Carnahan ball or the opera, but upon her insistence he'd been unable to refuse her the trip.

"The way they've strung the lanterns," Julia marveled, strolling along the graveled path with her arm through her husband's. "Look! Some are designed to suggest the constellations."

"Why do I have the sinking suspicion you know the lot of them?" her husband mused.

"I believe that is Ursa Major." Julia delighted in showing off her knowledge, because she knew how it pleased Gregory. He might pretend to the contrary, but the man found her mind an aphrodisiac. It was one of his most intoxicating qualities, the way he appreciated her wit. "The greater she-bear."

"Hmm. I'm assuming there's a greatest as well. I've only interest in the truly spectacular, my dear, as you well know."

Oh, she had an inkling. This afternoon, they hadn't left the library until it was almost nightfall and he'd performed at what he considered his highest ability. Julia had been happy to work toward that pinnacle.

"I say. This is a pleasant sight." The Duke of Huntington approached them from out of the crowds, bowing slightly to Julia. "You seem far more present than you did this afternoon, Ashworth. Has your mind finally stopped its wandering?"

"A mind as formidably quick as mine needs space to ramble," Gregory drawled.

"Or perhaps thought of Her Grace was a distraction. As it should be."

Julia shook her head. Huntington was a charming rascal indeed. Her thoughts flitted back to Miss Winslow, and the way she'd blushed and stammered at the man's appearance.

"You took enough of my money this afternoon, you bastard. Buy me a drink to make amends," Gregory said.

The men laughed and wanted to head for the refreshments, but Julia wasn't done studying the beautiful orbs of colored glass that lit the night. She bade the gentlemen leave her for a moment to secure their ale; after all, she was a capable woman surrounded by good society. She could well manage herself. As Ashworth and Huntington went in search of a drink, Julia wandered along the pathway, admiring the shimmering lanterns as they swayed in the breeze. She quickly noticed a copy of the constellation of Orion and paused to inspect it.

"Your Grace! What a pleasant surprise."

Julia looked up in shock at Elizabeth Woodhouse's voice. The other woman approached her, beaming upon the arm of a man.

A man Julia knew quite well.

Run away. It was the first panicked thought that went through her head as Lucas Campbell approached her. She wanted to flee, partly out of shock, partly from shame, and more than partly because she felt she'd break the man's nose if she didn't leave. Catching sight of him again forced Julia to relive the agony of waiting in the rain on that long-ago night. Honestly, she was now so angry she could kill the fellow.

But his cousin was here, and Elizabeth could not be allowed to know the full extent of Julia's past.

"Hello, Mrs. Woodhouse." She accepted the lady's curtsy, all while her heartbeat quickened. Julia glanced around the crowds. Where the devil was Gregory?

"I told my cousin, Lucas, of our club gathering this afternoon. When I mentioned your connection, he was most adamant about seeing you again! Though we'd no idea you'd be here tonight. What serendipity!"

"Indeed." Campbell's voice was as deep and smooth as it had ever been, and he sketched Julia a bow that would have been thoroughly charming had it not come from him. "Somehow, Her Grace remains completely unchanged after all this time."

"I could not say the same for you, Mr. Campbell." Julia struggled to keep her tone friendly, but the more she looked upon the man she'd once loved—or believed she'd loved—the greater the urge to strike him became. Julia recognized the younger man she'd adored at once. Campbell had been and still was an attractive man, over six feet tall with a strong build, blond hair, and classically handsome features. But now, the smile she had once thought sensuous resembled a smirk. His eyes, which she'd once compared to the blue of a summer sky, appeared flat and empty as a snake's.

Quickly, Julia judged every bit of him against every bit of Ashworth, and in every possible way Lucas Campbell came up wanting.

"Indeed? Have I changed so much?" Campbell seemed puzzled, and Julia needed to remain polite.

"I only meant that it's been so long since we saw one another. Memory plays tricks on us all."

"Oh, I see my husband wants me. I shall leave you two a moment!" Elizabeth bustled away with a cheerful air. Julia wondered if the woman had meant for this to be an awkward meeting, but she seemed too unconcerned for that. She was a well-intentioned lady, if remarkably unperceptive.

Right now, Julia wished for Gregory. The last thing she wanted was a stroll through the gardens with Campbell.

"It's wonderful to see you, Julia." He looked at

her as though it'd been mere days since they parted, rather than a decade. Julia realized that he still felt entitled to her attention and to informality.

"If you don't mind, I'm married now. Your Grace is the better form of address." Julia made certain to keep her tone frosty.

Campbell smirked, unbothered by her animosity. "I never knew you to be such a snob."

If it hadn't been so public here, Julia might have struck him in the shin. Or perhaps in a higher, more sensitive point on his body.

"Snobbery and propriety are hardly the same thing." Damn it, her temper was already beginning to show itself. "Are you acquainted with my husband?"

"No, I haven't been to London these past ten years. I've been up in Edinburgh."

"Have you married?"

"Why do you ask?"

She didn't care, truly. In fact, Julia found she couldn't care less, which was a delight.

"It's a polite question."

"I never knew you to be this cold before, Ju— Your Grace."

Julia didn't want the whole *ton* to bear witness to the increasingly heated argument, so she ambled toward a hedgerow trimmed in multiple sharp, geometric shapes. Farther away from prying eyes, she spoke low.

"You've either forgotten what happened ten years ago, or you don't care about the events. If the former, perhaps you need to see a physician and have your head examined. If the latter, you ought to be horsewhipped through Regent's Park."

"There is a third option," Campbell said quietly. He loomed above her, drew nearer than she wanted him. "I didn't broach the subject because I wanted to shield you from embarrassment in front of my cousin."

"How thoughtful. And with that, Mr. Campbell, I need to find and rejoin my husband."

Julia turned to go, but he shifted his body so that he blocked her way with ease. It was a movement done with subtle grace, so that it would not attract the attention of passersby.

"Wouldn't you like me to explain what happened?" he whispered.

"If there was a choice between hearing your explanation and flinging myself into the Thames, I'd happily go for a swim."

But he wasn't budging, and Julia didn't want to attract attention with a squabble. She couldn't risk open gossip.

"Not a day has gone by that you've been far from my thoughts, Julia." He sounded as he had so long ago, full of promise and softness. His hand reached to touch her, but he pulled back when she flinched. "I rode to Kent prepared to lift you upon the saddle in front of me and travel to Scotland all night if that's what it took."

"And what? You lost your way in the dark? You experienced a convenient round of amnesia? You were abducted by the faeries?"

"I stopped at an inn not three miles from

Pennington Hall to rest my horse and discovered I hadn't even enough money for a pint of ale. That was when I realized I had to protect you."

"From what? A trip to Scotland without ale?"

"A life without money. I'd no inheritance, and no real prospects. If I had taken you away then and married you, I'd have consigned you to a life of poverty." He looked pleadingly at her, his every expression and gesture filled with remorse. "I couldn't face you to tell you; I knew if I rode up and found you then, I wouldn't be strong enough to send you home. I'd have married you anyway and hated myself for it forever. So I left and made my way north to find a career. I wanted to be able to support you before I sent for you."

It sounded tragically romantic, a man sacrificing his own happiness for the sake of the one he loved. Like something out of a mediocre novel.

"And you would have sent for me?" she asked. "Then why did you never write to tell me all of this?"

"It wouldn't have been proper. And, I confess, I feared you hating me. In fact, I came to London this Season with the express hope that I'd find you. I prayed that you hadn't married, and that we might finally be together. My darling, I've dreamed of you nightly for ten long years. How could fate be so cruel as to now keep us apart like this?"

He spoke those honeyed words with real pathos and reached for her hand again.

"You came to town to find me, did you?" Julia asked.

"Please. Is there some private place we can go? A time we can meet? I've so much to say to you." The charming young man she'd known ten years ago had returned.

But Julia didn't give him her hand. She was thinking.

"You came to find me, yet you're still staying with your cousin for the Season." She took a step away from him.

"What's that got to do with anything?" Campbell frowned.

"Surely a man with enough money to support a wife could find fashionable bachelor lodgings for himself. What *is* your profession, anyway?"

"I've studied to go into the law." His tone was much more even now, and all the ardor in his gaze had dimmed.

"Studied, but you're not practicing. Are you?" All the pieces of this insipid puzzle came together for her, and Julia forced herself not to laugh. "You never spoke a word about money when we first met. You told me of all the wonderful places on the Continent we'd go when we married." She saw it fully. "Because you thought I'd a large enough inheritance to support you in the manner you wished to live."

"That's not true." But his eyes told a different story.

"Of course. One of Lady Beaumont's daughters is a real heiress; it's been *ton* gossip since my dear father was laid to rest. But you didn't realize it was my stepsister's fortune, not mine, until after we agreed to wed. Isn't that right, Mr. Campbell?

And now that I'm a married woman of great fortune, you'd like nothing better than to grow close again and take whatever crumbs you can charm from me. Perhaps you fancied a risqué arrangement between us."

"Your husband *is* the Duke of Ashworth, after all. Fidelity is hardly a virtue to him."

"Interesting. I thought you knew nothing of my husband."

Julia felt as if she'd been let out of a cage in which she'd been sitting for ten long years. Every instant she spent with Campbell made him appear smaller and lesser in her eyes. How could a man like this, who broke promises and used people, compare to the man she'd thought he was? Or to the man she'd married.

Like a thunderclap, the realization struck Julia down to her marrow. She could shake off her infatuation with Lucas Campbell so easily because now she'd known real love.

She loved her husband. She loved him passionately. Julia could have laughed with the knowledge, giddy as a child. What was she still doing with this nothing of a man in front of her, when she could be with Gregory?

"Julia. Listen to me," Campbell pleaded. But she saw the hollow man that he was now, and she walked away from him with confidence. Let society talk if they noticed her abrupt departure; what did their gossip matter? Julia knew what was true, and what she had.

There he was, directly in her path. She nearly crashed into her husband, who stood before her as tall and imposing as ever.

"Gregory!"

But Julia's bliss soon evaporated in the face of the duke's cold, neutral expression.

"Huntington told me the identity of your conversational partner." He squared his jaw. "Lucas Campbell, hmm? How extraordinary to run into him here, of all places."

CHAPTER TWENTY-TWO

He should have bloody well known this would happen. After all, Gregory had written the damned book on libidinous, forbidden passions. When Julia had first told him of Lucas Campbell all those weeks ago, Gregory had thought nothing of the man himself. What were the odds the bastard would ever show his face again? Gregory should have known that life would never pass up an opportunity for absurd comedy.

Yes, this afternoon he'd felt a flare of jealousy in the library, but Julia had quickly driven those disquieting thoughts from his mind. She'd trembled because the pain and the trauma of her past had unmoored her, not because of any lingering desire she felt. Gregory had believed that.

But he'd returned with Huntington to find his wife locked in a passionate discussion with another man. Gregory had come to know every slight gesture of his wife's body and the tiniest expression on her face. The rest of the *ton*, perhaps, was fooled by her performance, but Gregory had seen how she blazed with passion.

How that other man loomed over her, drew nearer to her.

How even when she shied away from him, that furious energy still connected them, an invisible tether.

During his hedonistic days as a womanizing

rake, Gregory had engaged in blazing rows with his lovers. All had been born out of passion, infernal lust, furious regret. Usually a spat preceded an epic session of lovemaking; sometimes he believed his paramours picked fights in order to facilitate heated reconciliations.

Gregory could recognize the muted passion that glinted like sparks in his wife's eyes.

"Who is that man?" he'd asked Huntington, praying the duke did not know. But, of course, Gregory could not be so blessed.

"Mr. Lucas Campbell. His family home's not far from mine in Northumberland," Huntington had replied. Whatever else the duke said, Gregory couldn't bloody recall.

It was simply too much of a coincidence that the man his wife had tearfully discussed this afternoon should be at Vauxhall tonight. Perhaps that was why Julia had been so adamant about making a trip to the gardens when they could have been at the Carnahan ball.

In all his years as a rake, Gregory had pitied the husbands who shared their wives' attentions with him. Was this what they had felt? No wonder they'd wanted to kill him.

"Gregory!" Julia approached him, but paused. Her smile vanished, the surest sign of guilt.

"Lucas Campbell, hmm?" Gregory wanted to call the man out on the spot, but talking to a lady in a public space was hardly a punishable offense. "How extraordinary to run into him here, of all places."

"What precisely do you mean?"

"It was an observation, my dear. If you read more into it, perhaps ask yourself why."

Two spots of color bloomed upon her cheeks; he'd roused her passions. Julia's passions were easy to rouse. Gregory had learned that only too well today.

"Your Grace. A pleasure to meet you," Campbell said, walking over to Gregory and giving a polite bow. "The duchess and I are old friends, and she was just speaking so highly of you."

"Given your *friendly* history with my wife, you'll forgive me if I harbor my doubts." Gregory's vision pulsated with rage, and he couldn't stop the briefest fluttering of his imagination. He pictured Campbell lying in a field, having been laid low by the duke's gun.

"Nothing has happened," Julia said. For fuck's sake, if anyone overheard her, they'd believe the exact opposite to be true.

"I shouldn't think that it had. Mr. Campbell, you'll have to excuse us, but my wife has had rather a tiring day. It's best we return home now."

The irony of it all would've been delicious if he hadn't been so furious. Here he was, Gregory Carter, the greatest rake in London, now playing the part of a jealous husband. If only he didn't know the truth of marriage and husbands and wives so bitterly well. If he were a normal man, he wouldn't suspect Julia of anything. He might even believe this all to be a coincidence. But if he were a normal man, he'd be a mere cuckold and laughingstock. The thought made him want to rip all the blown glass constellations out of the trees and smash them underfoot on the earth.

"I hope to see you both again soon," Campbell said smoothly. The bastard. If Gregory hadn't wanted to avoid a scene, maybe he would've struck the fellow on the jaw right now. For what reason, he did not know. He'd make one up.

"What the devil's got into you?" Julia snapped as they bid a quick farewell to Huntington and hurried along the path toward the boats. Gregory kept her arm tight through his.

"Do you truly want to cause a scene?" was his only response. That at least silenced her until they were into the boat. Julia attempted conversation on a couple further occasions, both in the boat and in the carriage afterward, but Gregory would not acknowledge her words. He couldn't look at her.

He should have bloody well known better.

Finally, they had returned to Carter House and gone upstairs, marching alongside one another as rigidly as enemy soldiers waiting for an opportunity to draw.

"If I may be so bold as to inquire," Julia said when they were shut away in the duchess's chambers, "why are you acting as though the devil himself spat in your porridge?"

"Ah yes. A sampling of your finest country aristocrat wit." Gregory made certain to stand as far from her as he could, because even now he could barely resist her. Julia angry was perhaps more erotic than Julia at any other time, or filled with any other emotion. His loins ached at the mere thought of her hot, furious mouth against his, of her moans as he entered her and as they rode one another to several heated climaxes in an effort to burn away the rage.

He was addicted to this woman, and it must stop. She'd scrambled his wits, but she would not make a fool of him. He would not allow that to happen.

"I'm perfectly delighted you looked as though you wished to murder Campbell, but I fail to see why *I* should bear the brunt of your displeasure!"

"You're clever, my dear, but if you believed I wouldn't see through the machinations behind your serendipitous little rendezvous, then you're not half as clever as I first believed," Gregory snapped. He started toward the door that divided their bedchambers, planning to lock it behind him, but Julia flung herself into his path. Her color was high, meaning that he was closer to the truth than he knew. She would never be ashamed otherwise, surely.

"And if you believe this little story that you've obviously concocted, then you're as great a dunce as I once believed you to be!" she cried.

This would normally be the time to trade barbs with her, to test his wits against hers while they made quick work of their clothes. But this was different; this was war, not a mere skirmish.

Because in his most secret heart, Gregory had always known that she would not be his forever. Not because Julia herself was a wretched woman; no, she was and remained a damned goddess. But Gregory's great curse remained, his inability to be enough. He could give her pleasure, he could lavish her with gifts, but he couldn't inspire her with eternal fidelity. He just didn't have it in him to be loved so completely.

This was my fault. I let this game go on for far too long.

"Talk to me!" His wife pleaded with him, her hands pressed to his chest in supplication. That was a far nicer sensation than her strangling him, though she might attempt that next if he didn't cease infuriating her. "You must know that I didn't arrange any secret meeting with Campbell. Good Lord, I'd have to be the thickest adulteress in the world if I told you he was in town while planning to meet him!"

Gregory shut his eyes, because of course that was the truth. Julia was many things, but not a coward or a liar. None of this was her fault. She did not yet know that she could still feel erotic passion for a man who'd jilted her, just as she did not yet know that Gregory could not hold her fascination forever. Even though Gregory was right to see the futility of their situation, he'd been wrong to accuse her of anything. Damnably wrong.

"Yes. You're right," he murmured. "I was a prat to say such things, my dear."

"So! You damnable fool." But this time the words were delivered like a caress, and Julia cradled his face in her hands. Gregory could feel himself losing the will to continue fighting already, so great was her spell over him. All he wanted was to fold her into his arms and bury himself inside of her sweetness, her passion.

But it would only delay the inevitable.

"I know you're telling the truth," he said. "But I saw how you looked at him, Julia."

"I beg pardon? Then surely you noted my expression of incandescent rage."

"After ten years without him, was it only anger that you felt? Or did you experience a reawakening of any other feelings?"

This time, his wife drew away looking as if he'd struck her, and Gregory felt like the greatest cad alive. But no, better to do this now.

Better to walk away while they both still had some dignity remaining.

"How dare you ask me that, after everything I told you?" she said softly.

"I've known women to curse a man's name one instant and rush into his arms the next. I've seen my share of longing looks from thwarted lovers, many of whom said they wished me dead and in hell. Every one of those women came back with a word or a glance from me. There's no such thing as hate without love. Though, in truth, I doubt the very existence of love itself."

Or rather, I do not believe I'm capable of such a thing. But if he said that, it might make her want to challenge him and prove to him that he was wrong. Gregory couldn't put Julia through this kind of madness one more night.

"Well. At least hate itself is quite real," Julia snapped, though he saw something he could scarcely believe: tears stood out in her eyes, and one slipped down her cheek. His wife turned her face away in order to calm herself. "This is an absurd situation."

"I agree entirely. Which is why, after the queen's ball in seven days' time, we should follow through on our original plan and lead separate lives. Happy ones."

"Is that what you want?" Julia sat down on the bed, almost as if she were dizzy. He'd made her miserable, but it would have happened sooner or later. In time, she would welcome the next dashing rake into her heart and bed. Gregory's vacant spot would be snapped up by some younger man eager to gain notorious experience, and Gregory himself would travel to the Continent and stay well out of the way. Perhaps he'd return to his old womanizing ways, though at the moment he couldn't picture such a thing. But he couldn't stand to watch Julia grow tired of him and find other conquests in the hunting grounds of Grosvenor Square. He knew he'd challenge any man to a duel, and he'd had enough of staring down the barrel of a gun.

Gregory didn't want to be away from her for a second, but he saw now the horror he'd inflict upon her if he remained in her life. He couldn't look at Lucas Campbell without seeing a potential competitor for her affections. He was too warped by his lifetime of debauchery to be the husband Julia needed. His jealousy would wear his duchess down until she broke, or until she broke *him*.

He'd either drive her away from him with his jealousy, or she'd lose interest in him naturally over time. It all led to the same unhappy end unless they did the smart thing now.

"What I want is to live in peace. I want your happiness." God, but he meant it. "This is the way to achieve both those outcomes, my dear."

"There has to be another way," Julia began.

"Enough." He held up his hand. "Please, enough."

She stopped then, almost shocked by the weight of his tone. Gregory could not give her another chance to argue with him, or another opportunity to tempt him into making the wrong decision, so he left and shut the door behind him. Gregory locked it, and waited in the center of his room. He waited to hear her footfall, or the sound of her trying the knob.

But his wife made no attempt to come after him.

CHAPTER TWENTY-THREE

Three days passed, and Julia felt as if she were haunting her own life, going through the motions of living without feeling any of them. Gregory, who preferred to sleep well into the middle of the morning, was always up and dressed and gone before she herself awoke, no matter how early she arose. Julia continued her round of fittings for the ball, her morning and afternoon calls, and a nightly routine of suppers and parties, but none of it mattered. Even when she and her husband were together, she felt the rift between them.

Gregory made certain never to be alone with her. Julia's anger had burned itself out, but she couldn't allow herself to go numb. She patently refused to accept this ridiculous fate.

Still, in her darker moments she worried that the duke understood what she could not. Perhaps Gregory was only being realistic about his own shortcomings. After all, if he believed that Julia could ever again want that wretched Lucas Campbell after what the man had done to her, then she'd married a fool.

The duke either didn't know Julia at all, or he knew himself too well. Neither was a promising option.

Julia sat and stewed in her unhappiness during tea with Susannah and Constance. Her misery had one good function, at least. She barely felt the barbs of her stepmother's words.

"I fail to see why Her Majesty should choose a fancy dress party as the grand sendoff of the Season." Constance *tsk*ed as she nibbled an almond biscuit. "And a fairy tale theme? Really, I feel terribly sorry for the queen and the *ton*. To think they've all been led astray by a story that wouldn't make a sufficient plot for a bad novel."

"I assume you're speaking of my marriage, Constance, dear." Julia knew that her smiling placidity only piqued her stepmother's rage. It was one of her few pleasures left. "At any rate, I wouldn't place too much stock in your tastes in fiction. I know you've a difficult time comprehending a story that doesn't come with many pictures."

Susannah cleared her throat pointedly before sipping her tea. Julia knew the girl hoped to keep this from devolving into an argument. Alas, poor Susannah's wish would not come true today.

"A rise in station has turned you even more uncouth, Julia." Her stepmother glowered.

"Well. You are the expert in that phenomenon." Julia smiled sweetly.

"Oh, please. I so wanted this to be a nice tea." Susannah put her cup down and seemed to droop. Ashamed, Julia recalled that she and Constance were the only family Susannah truly had. She didn't want to make the girl choose between her stepsister and her mother.

"Lord Cheltham asked after you last night," she said. Susannah gave a thin, tired smile. "Do you not like him? I hear he's a regular caller."

"He's also a mere baron," Constance said with a slight laugh. "My Susannah can do better than that. If *you* can achieve the rank of a duchess, I doubt my darling girl will settle for anything less than a duke herself. Or perhaps she might even aim for royalty."

"At the moment, most princes are eighty, married, or both," Julia said. "Happy hunting."

"Besides, I don't know that I want to marry my first Season." Susannah appeared agitated, almost as if she'd had this exact conversation before. Constance ignored her daughter completely.

"What of Ashworth's friend, the Duke of Huntington?" Constance leaned slightly across the table, almost upsetting the tea things. "He's titled, vastly wealthy, and as young and handsome as a man can be. Would he not be a perfect match for our dear Susannah?"

"I see now why you allowed Susannah to have me to tea," Julia drawled. "Unfortunately, I doubt Ashworth would encourage you to start targeting his closest friends. The Duke of Huntington is a particular man. He's extremely amiable, so if he wished to pursue Susannah I'd have no objections. But I won't try to force the matter."

"And the duke doesn't want to pursue me anyway," Susannah added quickly. How interesting. Most young girls would be prepared to sell their souls if it meant possible marriage to a handsome duke. Had Susannah someone else already in mind?

"You might discuss it with your husband," Constance said.

"He wouldn't consider it."

"He might if you asked him." Constance stirred her tea, relishing Julia's discomfort. "Unless you are not both so close as you pretend."

"Our marriage is perfectly happy." Julia hated to lie, but she hated Constance's satisfaction more.

"My dear girl, this childish pretense is wearying. You accomplished the great dream of womankind: you tricked your way into a position of rank and influence through marriage. If you'd only accept that as enough, I could respect it. Instead, you struggle to maintain this ridiculous charade."

"Tricked?" Julia thought of her father in that moment. Sir Arthur had mourned the death of Julia's mother bitterly for years. He'd told Julia frequently she was his solace, the one gift her mother had left for him to cherish. When he'd met Constance, Julia recalled the joyful spark she'd seen in his eyes. He'd wanted to give Julia a mother, but she also knew he'd wanted a wife again. He and her mother had been so blissfully happy, according to him and to the servants. He'd wanted that happiness again. "And you tricked my father into marriage, then? To raise your own position?"

"It's no differently than I did with Susannah's." Constance seemed outright puzzled.

"Mamma!" Susannah paled.

"If I'd looked for love, I'd have ended up a shopkeeper's daughter and wife the same as my mother." Constance displayed no embarrassment at her admission. If anything, she appeared proud of herself. "You two ladies have only ever known position and privilege. You can't imagine how grim the world appears without those two things."

Maybe the woman had a point, but Julia still felt revolted at the idea.

"My father married you because he loved you!"

"Please, my dear girl. He married me out of love for *you*." Constance's smile soured. "You were all he ever spoke of. He married me to provide you with a mother and a sister in Susannah. We were both only useful objects to him."

"That's not true," Susannah said.

"You were five years old when he left us, Susannah. How could you possibly know? Sir Arthur wanted a family for his daughter, and I wanted a title. We both got what we wanted out of the other, and that was enough. That's all men and women are to each other, Julia. Useful objects. At your age, such appalling sentimentality should be well behind you. I'm certain you only embarrass yourself with the duke." Constance shook her head as she selected a cream-filled pastry. "No wonder he's booked passage on a ship for Spain."

"How on earth do you know that?" Julia asked. She felt suddenly ill. Gregory had said they would be parting after the end of the Season, but to think he'd already booked passage and that *Constance* of all people knew that fact before his own wife was like a stab to the gut.

Julia's stepmother appeared victorious, as if her deepest suspicions had been confirmed.

"The word is already spreading across London that the duke is leaving the country the day after the queen's ball."

Julia had to salvage this.

"Of course, it slipped my mind entirely. Ashworth is off on business to the Continent for a few weeks. He'll return to Lynton Park as soon as he's finished. Thank you for letting me know of the *ton* gossip, dear stepmother. What silly creatures, chattering about affairs that don't concern them in the least. One would think these women had other, more important things to discuss. But I suppose for a certain kind of person, gossip relieves the tedium of an empty life."

Constance narrowed her eyes. "Your ruse is unraveling quickly, Julia. Pray you don't provide Her Majesty any mortification. If she discovers your grand romance to be a farce after all the expense she's gone to for this ball, well. You and Ashworth both may have to flee the country in disgrace. Separately, of course."

"Will the two of you stop?" Susannah shoved away from the tea table, tears of frustration on her cheeks. "I don't know why everyone in this city must be so horrid to one another. I wish I'd never debuted at all! I'm sick to death of society!"

"Darling." Julia rose to comfort her stepsister, but Susannah fled the room.

"Look what you've done now." Constance glared as she stood. "You should leave, Your *Grace*. I must see to my daughter."

Though Julia outranked Constance, Beaumont House was not her home any longer. She'd been reduced to the role of a guest here. Julia stiffly took her leave and walked out into the London streets. As she entered her carriage, she believed she could feel eyes upon her from every direction. Julia wondered if people were whispering about the silly duchess and her fraudulent marriage.

The worst part was that if they were, they would be perfectly right.

· · ·

"Tell me it isn't true." Percy sat down alongside Gregory, obliterating the duke's attempt at peaceful dissolution. He was on his second ale, and the sting of life was beginning to grow fuzzy at long last.

"What would you like me to deny? I'm afraid that if you're waiting for me to dismantle Kepler's laws of planetary motion, you're out of luck. The man's reasoning is remarkably sound, and I'm a tad drunk at the moment."

They were at their gentleman's club, the air around them currently filled with cigar smoke and inebriated laughter. Gregory had taken to a corner, intent on brooding and counting the minutes until he could depart this cursed city. His coming flight, incidentally, was what bothered Percy as well.

"The news is spreading about London like the plague. They say you've booked passage on a ship bound for Spain the day after the queen's ball. And they say that you are not taking the duchess with you."

"I can't stop the bored matrons of the *ton* from saying whatever they please, but I must admit I thought you had more on your mind than they do, Perce. Next you'll have very firm opinions on which brand of button is decidedly unfashionable."

"Why are you fleeing from us and from your wife?" Percy seemed shocked into disbelief, which only infuriated Gregory. Men like Percy could never understand people like him. Rotten, unsympathetic people with only the basest human instincts.

"Julia will be returning to Lynton Park. She's much she needs to learn as mistress of a large estate. And I have business abroad."

"Please. You've never gone abroad for business in your life."

"You don't know that," Gregory snapped. There was so much even his closest friends didn't know about him, his charitable endeavors included. But Gregory didn't want to tell Percy about all that; the man might argue that he should stay with Julia, which would be all too tempting.

"I confess I have no idea who you are anymore," Percy snapped.

"Marriage changes a man," Gregory muttered.

"Evidently not well enough. How could you open your wife to the possibility of gossip like this?"

"When you're furious, Perce, you tend toward a ruddy complexion. Rather like a bruised tomato. It gives one ideas for all the least flattering insults." Gregory swallowed the rest of his ale quickly, planning a hasty exit. If his oldest friend was happy to berate him publicly, then Gregory wasn't going to give the rest of the *ton* added ammunition for gossip. "Besides, how the devil was I to know someone would learn of my plans?"

"Because you are now part of the most talked-about couple in London."

When Gregory had married Julia, he'd thought himself a genius for performing their love in a most public manner. After all, he'd gotten those society wives and husbands to leave him alone. He now saw the flaw in that particular plan. These women no longer wanted a night in his bed, but they were positively fascinated by what went on in it between the duke and his damned wife.

"We can't lose the queen's favor," Gregory muttered. The ale had started to loosen his tongue. "I'll have to cancel my plans yet a-bloody-gain and find a slyer way to the Continent. I might have to disguise myself as a sailor. Or swim the Channel. Whichever proves more amusing."

"I've often pitied you, Ashworth, but I've never been ashamed of you before," Percy said.

The blood all rushed to Gregory's head, and he just managed to keep from tackling his oldest friend and punching him repeatedly out of sheer frustration. What man could possibly pity him? What had Gregory ever lacked? He had wealth, charm, and the most perfect woman in England to call his wife. That he was currently trying to get away from her was his issue, not hers.

"Why should I be ashamed of knowing my own foibles?" Gregory stood and walked away from the table, though Percy insisted upon trailing behind him.

"I've never seen you lie to yourself before."

"I can be accused of many despicable qualities, my dear friend. I'm a seducer of married women, a destroyer of happy homes, and I've never once cried at the opera. But one charge nobody could ever level at me is the charge of being a liar."

The two men passed out into the summer afternoon, and Gregory signaled for his carriage at once. He hoped Percy would take the hint and leave, but that would have made his life far too easy.

"Why can't you simply confess it to yourself?" his friend demanded as Gregory's coach finally arrived. "I can see how miserable this is making you."

"Your conversation? You may have a point there."

Gregory climbed inside and shut the door, but Percy stuck his face in the window.

"It's not a sin to fall in love with your own wife, Your Grace." Percy's voice was laden with all the scorn a man might muster. He then turned on his heel and walked back into the club.

"Take me home." Gregory gave the order, and then sat back. He rattled through the city streets while Percy's parting words rattled about in his own skull. To fall in love with one's own wife...

Gregory almost wanted to laugh. He nearly had the coachman turn around and take him back to the club, all so Gregory could go interrupt Percy at billiards and shout at the man, "I love her! I know that I love her, you sanctimonious dolt! That's why I have to leave her."

But he didn't believe Percy—or anyone else—would understand that reasoning.

When he arrived back at Carter House, Gregory made straight for his chambers. He'd change and then take Huntington up on his offer of dinner. He'd go anywhere, so long as he didn't have to face Julia.

Of course, when the duke entered his bedchamber he found his wife serenely perched at the edge of the bed and waiting for him.

"Damn it all," he muttered. Being in the woman's presence itself was too strong a temptation. If Gregory hadn't been quite so firm in his convictions, he'd have taken her into his arms at once. But he hadn't done much right in his life, and he was determined not to be weak now. "Is something amiss? I need to hurry if I'm to keep my appointment."

"I just braved tea with Constance. Apparently the gossip is all over London that you're leaving for Spain the day after the queen's ball."

"Yes. I heard much the same from Percy down at our club." Gregory rang for Tomkins. "You needn't worry. I'll amend my plans at once to save you from the gossiping hordes."

"Thank you. I underestimated how much attention the *ton* would pay us once we were wed."

"I'm sorry." He meant it with all sincerity. "You shouldn't be subjected to ridiculous nattering."

"I prefer the scrutiny and gossip to life as Constance's wageless maid," she replied.

Wherever Gregory went in the room, he felt his wife's eyes follow after him. "Please talk to me. I can't believe that a chance encounter with Mr. Campbell demolished everything I thought we'd built together."

"None of this is your fault," Gregory said. What an absurd idea. Julia had every right to be furious with him, yet she remained calm and reasonable. The woman was a marvel he did not deserve. "Campbell reminded me of my own shortcomings, not yours."

"Why can't you allow us to be happy?"

Gregory could scarcely put his thoughts into words. He recalled his father going for more than a week without exchanging a single sentence with him. Gregory's mother had never written to him once when he was away at school, and the other boys had mocked him for the way he'd been abandoned by his own kin. It had gotten so desperate that Gregory eventually began writing his own letters to himself from his family. On the day that his parents' ship went down, he burned the whole of the fantasy life he'd concocted for all of them.

He'd been sick with his own relief at their death. Now he did not need to pretend any longer, nor did he need to be ashamed of his own inability to inspire affection.

He knew he ought to tell all this to Julia, because she might understand where no one else alive could. His wife had the most marvelous gift for intuition, but what could she say to this admission? That he was wrong? Or that she pitied him? The last idea was too intolerable to be borne.

"We could never be happy," he said. "Or rather, I could never continue to make you happy."

"Why?"

"Because you deserve what I can't give, and I'm not a strong enough man to watch you discover that fact on your own."

"What if you're wrong?" She was a stubborn minx.

"I'm never wrong about anything this important, unfortunately."

"Am I not enough to entice you to stay, then?"

"You bloody little fool," he growled. The duke was upon her in an instant, and Julia did not resist as he laid her upon the bed. The soft quiver of her mouth upon his was sheer paradise. "How many times must I demonstrate my desire for you?"

"Only until I'm fully satisfied."

"When will that be?"

"I've yet to find the limit of it."

He'd never find anything like this again—no other woman in this world would ever satisfy him. Only an idiot would give her up, and if he loved her less he'd keep her and enjoy her, let her grow to tire of him and ignore her displeasure in favor of his own delight.

But whatever shreds of decency resided within his breast wouldn't allow such a thing.

"That's precisely my point, Julia. I don't have what is required to fully satisfy you, and I never shall."

Once again, he was faced with the most startling sight: that of his wife struggling against tears.

"I think it's worthy of a chance," she said.

"I used to think I was a gambling man," the duke said. "But you are the one thing I won't risk."

And even though it broke something within him, he left her there.

CHAPTER TWENTY-FOUR

It was the day of the queen's ball, and Julia could not bloody wait for it to be over. When the sun rose tomorrow, she'd be in a carriage and bound for the west, headed for Lynton Park, where she could hide herself away from the prying eyes of society. But first, she had to finish with this ridiculous outfit.

"You shall be the most celebrated woman at the ball, Your Grace." Mrs. Maxwell beamed as she strutted around Julia, deploying one of her assistants to finish adjusting the waistline or the hem just so.

"I shall certainly be the most memorable," Julia muttered. The modiste had taken the challenge of outfitting the new, modern Cinderella, and she had bolted ahead with that challenge wedged firmly between her teeth. The white satin gown had been lavishly embroidered about the hem with whorls of silver thread, creating patterns of lush roses. Julia couldn't begin to imagine the expense, but that was her life now. As Duchess of Ashworth, cost meant nothing.

The gown was merely the first step. Julia didn't know where Mrs. Maxwell had come by or created the pelisse of sheer silver lace, but it created an almost ghostly effect when Julia slipped it on over the gleaming gown. In addition, Julia would wear a lavish collar of diamonds, with a diamond tiara and loose diamonds threaded artfully through her hair as well.

When Mrs. Maxwell had shown Julia the pinnacle of the outfit—a pair of lightly heeled shoes covered in shapes of glittering glass—Julia had almost laughed.

She'd never felt so conspicuous in her life. Though she'd always been considered an attractive and engaging person, even Julia in the first bloom of her youth had never known the excitement, or the terror, of being the most talked-about person in any room. Now she was the focus of *every* room she entered.

It was the dream she'd nurtured for ten long years when she was trapped in Pennington Hall, the hope that one day she'd find her place in society. But now she had all that, she realized none of the attention mattered a whit if Gregory wasn't with her.

A brutal irony. The one thing she hadn't married him for—himself—was now the one thing she didn't wish to live without.

"*Voilà.* Beautiful, Your Grace." Mrs. Maxwell clapped her hands with giddiness as Julia's gorgeous monstrosity of a costume was finally complete.

"Indeed. You shall eclipse every debutante this Season," a familiar voice said.

"Lady Weatherford." Julia could have cried with relief when her friend entered the shop. She needed a kindly face to keep her from brooding over her marriage. "Are you here for your own gown?"

"No, mine was delivered two days ago. Lord Weatherford is less than pleased I've chosen Beauty and the Beast as our joint costume." Laura laughed, though it seemed slightly unnatural. Forced.

"Are you well?"

"Quite well, my dear. In truth, I'm here because Peele informed me that you'd come for your final fitting. I hoped we might find a moment for a private chat."

"Has something happened?"

"No. Not yet."

What a mysterious comment. Julia was curious, but Laura didn't want to speak any further until the women left the shop. The viscountess dismissed her own carriage and rode with Julia through the park. Promenading couples all watched the duchess's coach with interest as it passed. A couple of gentlemen rode by on their horses and tipped their hats.

"Your popularity continues to grow," Laura said.

"Bother them all, what's wrong?" Julia had never developed the well brought up lady's ability to feign disinterest and wait for the conversation to turn naturally to the subject she desired. Far as she saw it, men could keep their tactfulness. Women needed to get things done.

"Two nights ago, I was at the Leowenes' house for a concert. I saw Susannah there, and who should I meet but Mrs. Woodhouse with her husband and her cousin in tow."

Lucas. Julia was now damnably grateful she

had gone to the theatre instead.

"Did something happen?" she asked.

"I introduced Susannah, and Mr. Campbell took a decided interest in her. Particularly, I must admit, when I mentioned to Mrs. Woodhouse that the girl was your stepsister." Laura appeared slightly guilty. "I'm sorry. I should have been more bloody careful."

"Whatever happened wasn't your fault," Julia said at once, taking her friend's hand. She'd recently told Laura the whole ugly story of her botched elopement, and how Lucas Campbell had managed to reenter Julia's life and insert a wedge between her and her husband. "Tell me about Campbell. What kind of interest did he show?"

But already Julia's mind was spinning, concocting plausible scenarios. Ten years ago, Lucas had learned that Susannah, not Julia, was the heiress in the family. Now Susannah was of age, out in society, and Lucas was still in need of funds. Not only was Susannah vastly wealthy, she was also beautiful, agreeable, and if Lucas was of a vindictive nature then taking Julia's stepsister as his bride would prove an excellent manner of revenge.

"He danced with her twice, and yesterday he called and brought flowers."

"How do you know this?" Julia's heart was in her throat. How the hell did she herself not know?

"I dropped round for an afternoon call. Lady Beaumont mentioned it. She seemed pleased; Susannah's got a bevy of suitors, of course, but

Campbell seems unusually keen."

"Yes, because he requires an heiress," Julia snapped. Leave it to Constance to not have a thought in her head. "Is Susannah happy?"

"Absolutely not. When her mother left the room, she told me that Campbell has made certain to ferret out wherever she'll be these last few days. She feels as though he's hunting her."

"Wretched man." Julia had made her mistake with Campbell in the past, but only she should have to pay the price. Not her stepsister. "Would you mind terribly if I stopped at Beaumont House?"

"I'd be only too delighted," Laura replied.

Once there, Julia found Constance alone. Her stepmother looked up from her needlework as Julia was shown into the morning room.

"I'm afraid Susannah is out."

"I'm here on her behalf," Julia said. "How could you of all people allow Mr. Campbell anywhere near her?"

"You make everything so very dramatic. There is nothing wrong with Susannah receiving a caller, is there? After all, not every man in London can fling himself at your feet, Julia. Unless this is your wounded pride speaking?"

"Stop these petty little games for one minute and listen to me! I fear Campbell has designs upon Susannah. Serious ones."

"Come now. I've no intention of seeing him as my son-in-law, and Susannah shows no interest in him as a serious prospect. After all, he's no title and no fortune. But he's done nothing untoward."

"You know the kind of behavior he showed me ten years ago. He's a snake, Constance."

"He treated *you* in such a manner, my dear, not your stepsister. The more suitors that flock around Susannah, the better. After all, the more attention she receives, the better the odds that the Duke of Huntington will notice."

Constance truly lived in a world of titles and fantasy. She didn't even care if Susannah could fall in love with the duke or not. The woman viewed human relationships as if men and women were dolls to be mashed together, an endless nursery game.

"If you don't do a better job of protecting Susannah, there could be consequences that she'll have to live with the rest of her life. From now on, you must not allow Mr. Campbell entry to the house, and you must quietly insist he stop pursuing her."

"Thank you very much, but she is *my* family, not yours." Constance put her nose in the air, challenging Julia to disagree. "All you want is for Susannah to stay in your shadow forever. I know what's best for my daughter."

"I won't see Susannah pay for your thick-headedness," Julia said hotly.

"You're not half as clever as you think, Julia. All you really know of the world can be found in some insipid library. Ugh, such a waste of womanhood. Sitting around, endlessly translating boring old Greek in that cursed *Aeneid*."

"Virgil wrote the *Aeneid* in Latin," Julia said.

"Oh, that is precisely my point! You think you

know everything, but it would be best for all of us if you took yourself back to Lynton Park and focused upon becoming a proficient duchess. Leave Susannah to me."

There would be no reasoning with her, so Julia left and returned Laura home. Back at Carter House, Julia began the long and exasperating process of preparing herself for the queen's ball. She bathed and spent hours dressing her hair in an elaborate forest of ringlets. All while her maid primped Julia and applied cosmetics, she thought the scenario through.

She couldn't rely upon Gregory for help, painful as it was to admit. He'd made it abundantly clear that he wanted nothing to do with their shared life. Besides, she feared he'd take any excuse to challenge Campbell to a duel, and Julia was not ready to become a widow or the wife of a murderer. Not yet.

As the world outside began to darken, Julia dressed in the white satin gown and the shimmering lace pelisse. She slid her feet into the glass slippers and allowed her maid to affix the collar of diamonds around her throat.

She'd have to look after Susannah on her own tonight. Julia was accustomed to managing things on her own.

But she was so bloody tired of it.

• • •

"Why do monarchs love fancy dress parties so bloody much?" Gregory growled as Tomkins helped him into the embroidered waistcoat. "I look like a stuffed silver peacock."

"That's an arresting image, Your Grace." Tomkins cheerily brushed off the back of Gregory's coat. As Cinderella's handsome Prince, he was expected to look the part. He'd been outfitted in trousers of pale dove-gray silk, a silver vest and cravat, and a waistcoat of bright platinum satin that made him wince whenever he glimpsed it in a mirror. He looked like a preening fool.

At least he didn't have to dance with glass shoes on his feet. He left the hardest part of the night to Julia's effortless capability.

Gregory waited downstairs for his wife to finish her toilette and join him. Fashionable lateness could be excused in ordinary parts of high society, but Her Majesty would never allow such a snub, especially from arguably the two most important guests.

When his duchess emerged from her chamber and descended the staircase, all Gregory's irritation evaporated. His ability to breathe halted as well.

The woman had always been a goddess in his eyes, but now he swore the rest of the world would see her that same way. She glided down the staircase, her plethora of diamonds winking in the candlelight. When she lifted her skirt the tiniest bit, he caught the flash of glass slippers. Even if Gregory regretted having to play the part of a handsome prince, he acknowledged that Julia was made for the position of a Cinderella. A true shame he couldn't crown her an actual princess at the end of the night. She looked like royalty.

"Well." He felt too tongue-tied in her presence, and bowed. "The queen wanted you to outshine every debutante in the city this evening. I'd say you accomplished the feat."

"I could say the same for you." Julia's dimple appeared with her smile. Gregory could have lost himself within her if he had time.

Giving this woman up would be the greatest sacrifice he'd ever make.

The duke and duchess entered their coach and set off toward the palace. Gregory watched Julia in the semi-darkness of their carriage, noting how she clutched a fistful of her skirt in an anxious gesture.

"Are you nervous?" he asked. It was unlike his wife to shiver, or to sit so still. Normally Julia was a maelstrom of energy and opinion.

"Shouldn't I be? After all, we might be walking into humiliation." She couldn't look at him, choosing to stare out the window instead.

"How the devil do you mean?"

"The *ton* has been gossiping about the state of our marriage. I saw Mrs. Fulbright at the modiste today, and she made a few pointed remarks that I'm sure she believed were subtle."

"They're cowards to a man. Or woman. A little effort on our part will dispel the worst sorts of gossips and scolds."

"What kind of effort?" She finally glanced at him and canted her head to the side, at once teasing and inviting. For the moment, her nerves seemed to have vanished. Well, why not? For one final evening, Gregory could be spellbound by her. He took his place at her side as the carriage rocked its way through the London streets.

"I'm certain you remember all our lessons, my dear."

"Our library sessions, you mean?" The ghost of a smile traced her lips. "Only too well. Sadly, polite society won't allow such a public exhibition."

"Because of mere jealousy. The sight of you in this gown will inspire the envy of every woman present." Gregory tugged at the fingertips of Julia's right glove. Slowly, he slid the garment off her arm, allowing the fine, supple leather to caress her skin as it departed. "It will also fire the imagination of every man present, though I'm certain the dress will be a hindrance to their fantasies."

"Am I so desirable, then?"

"You are coy, madam. You must know your own worth."

Gregory turned her hand so that the palm was up. Even in the near darkness of the coach, he noticed the pale tracery of veins against the fine skin of her wrist. He bent his head and kissed her there, reveling in the light gasp he wrung from her lips. Julia's fingertips traced his cheek, leaving lines of heat behind as she explored. Her palm cupped his face, lifting Gregory's head to meet her own. He laid a kiss upon her neck as Julia leaned back against the velvet interior of the carriage.

"When we arrive," he whispered against her hair, "you will have such a bloom upon your cheeks that everyone will know precisely what we have done."

"You forget, Your Grace. We must have a care for public opinion." But Julia's voice broke as he took her delicate earlobe between his teeth. When Gregory put his hands upon her body, he found her shaking with anticipation. "If I look so freshly tumbled, it will be a scandal."

"I don't mean for you to appear disheveled. When a woman is satisfied, that satisfaction is evident upon every inch of her body. In the way she holds her head. In the health of her color. In the set of her shoulders."

His hand caressed her silken front, and then disappeared between her legs. Julia moaned as he slid the garment up to her stockinged knee, then cupped her calf. Her legs were gorgeous, as was the rest of her. When they wrapped around his waist in the full throes of passion, he became the luckiest devil in England.

"You shouldn't," Julia whispered as his hand trailed up and up, cupping her sex. One finger slid through the delicate curls covering her mound, and his wife exhaled as he parted her silken folds.

"Do you want me to stop, then?"

Gregory loved the power he had over her as she whimpered and rocked her hips back and forth against his hand. He took his time, savoring the feel of her sex, the velvet warmth of her. Julia was a formidable woman, but she gave herself up to him completely with his merest caress. He still possessed her soul and her body.

Both of which he must relinquish.

"Why are you such a tease?" She gasped the

words as his thumb traced the perfect spot between her thighs.

"I don't tease, madam. I simply enjoy myself."

She clenched around his fingers as he worked her harder, and Gregory felt his manhood stiffen almost painfully as Julia let out a low, breathy moan with her climax. He kissed and nibbled at her jawline while her hands fumbled against his chest, her fingers trembling upon the fall of his trousers. Though he hated to, he held her wrists.

"Unfortunately, we haven't the time." Indeed, the palace was drawing ever nearer through the dark. "The moment has come to play our part in this little fairy story."

"Yes." Julia leaned back against the seat in seeming resignation. "One last ball to get through, and then the fairy tale ends."

Too true. Gregory felt bitter regret sitting in his heart as he watched his wife lift her head, preparing her smile for society.

At the stroke of midnight, their spell would be broken.

CHAPTER TWENTY-FIVE

Julia followed on Gregory's arm into the ballroom. The majordomo stopped them at the top of the stairs and loudly announced the Duke and Duchess of Ashworth to the assembly. As she descended into the party, Julia felt every eye upon her. Her skin itched with the sensation.

She couldn't immediately tell who was who in the costumed crowd, which should have been a comfort. After all, Julia could pretend she was surrounded by knights and princesses, fauns and nymphs, and she could imagine that these fantastical creatures were as pure-hearted as they would be in a storybook.

Only upon closer inspection did one realize that the seemingly harmless woodcutter was a terrible old baron, or that the milkmaid was actually a dowager countess renowned for the strength of her spite.

Well. Bugger them all. Tonight, Julia had to keep a watch out for Susannah.

"Have you seen my stepsister?" she asked Gregory as they parted the sea of watchful nobility.

"Er, difficult question when everyone's dressed up. Do you know what costume she's supposed to be wearing?"

"Yes. She's the Sleeping Beauty tonight."

Susannah's gown was another of Mrs.

Maxwell's creations, a pale golden silk meant to evoke the dawn. Well, as the princess Aurora, it only made sense. Julia scanned the crowds, hoping to spot Susannah, but she was consistently thwarted by the partygoers.

"Ah, if it isn't Cinderella and her prince?" The Viscount Carlisle, dressed as a satyr in false horns and rather furry trousers, bowed to them. He smiled especially at Julia. "May I have the honor of a dance, Your Grace?"

"Of course." Julia wore her smile like a mask while she kept watch for Susannah. The viscount took her away from Gregory, escorting her to the center of the floor. Julia heard whispers from every direction as she went through the motions of the quadrille; every person had noticed her, and everyone was talking in hushed excitement.

Julia wished she could laugh with Gregory about all of this. He was the perfect partner in any conspiracy. The thought of tomorrow morning and the emptiness he'd leave behind him was a fist in the pit of her stomach.

All she had was this one last night. She didn't want to spend it dancing with the viscount or worrying over Susannah.

But that second one had to be her foremost priority. When the dance ended, Julia finally caught sight of a familiar flash of copper curls.

She asked the viscount to escort her in that direction and made her way to the side of the ballroom as carefully as possible.

"Susannah!" Finally, Julia arrived at her stepsister's side. Susannah wore a false smile as perfect as Julia's own, but the girl's eyes were tight and terrified.

"Ah. Your Grace," Lucas Campbell said, sketching Julia a bow. "Pleasure to see you again."

Julia's entire body tensed as she faced the odious man. He was dressed well in a suit of midnight blue, a short, black velvet cape slung over his shoulder. Though anyone would consider him handsome, Julia now thought him the ugliest man of her acquaintance. How strange that ten years ago, he had enthralled her. His voice had sounded so musical to her ear. Now, it set her teeth on edge.

"Indeed, Mr. Campbell. It is a pleasure for *you*." Julia glared him down. "I hope you won't mind if I take my stepsister elsewhere. I've much I need to discuss with her."

"Yes. I should go. Lovely seeing you again, sir." Susannah's voice practically quavered with gratitude for her rescue. Julia gave her stepsister's hand a squeeze.

"I certainly hope I may count on you for that waltz, Miss Fletcher." The man gave a confident smile, assuring the women that he heard the discomfort in Susannah's tone and did not care a whit. He would pursue her regardless of her own desires. If Julia had been a man, she'd have taken someone's toy sword and beaten him over the head with it.

"We shall have to see, won't we?" Julia looped her arm through her stepsister's and walked Susannah away. She could have laughed with relief; in some way, she'd feared Campbell would try abducting Susannah, throwing her in a sack and hurrying off to Gretna Green while the unsuspecting ball continued apace. "Lady Weatherford told me about your little problem."

"Julia, he won't leave me alone! I don't know what to do." Susannah's lip quivered, but she remained strong. Brave girl. "I remember what he did to you. I'd slap his face if I could."

"Ah, but society would never accept such a thing," Julia muttered. Only men were allowed to show their emotions in such a way, or to defend family honor. Women were allowed to cry, but anger was strictly forbidden. "We're almost away from him. It's the last ball of the Season. Stay close to me or to Ashworth for the rest of the evening, and all should be well. I'm sorry, though, for your loss of liberty. I wish you could enjoy tonight properly. Still, you must have made enough conquests." Come to think of it, Julia was surprised that Susannah hadn't received any marriage proposals yet. Constance surely would have crowed about them.

"Mamma insists that Ashworth must introduce me to the Duke of Huntington." Susannah rolled her eyes, an unusual action for her. Typically, she never openly disregarded anything that Constance said; she was far too polite a daughter. "It doesn't matter if the duke likes me or not. I'm not about to marry this year, I've made up my mind to it. Mamma thought I was wise to turn down Lord Cheltham's proposal, but only because she believes I'm angling for a superior offer."

"I beg pardon?" Julia almost tripped over her

own glass slippers. When she had been Susannah's age, she'd have committed murder for a proposal from an eligible baron. Anything to get her away from Constance. "You turned down his proposal?"

"I'm not in love with him. I refuse to marry without any kind of love. Besides…" Susannah fidgeted with her dance card as Julia secured them a spot by the side of the room.

"Besides what, darling?"

"Besides, I'm not certain I wish to marry a member of the *ton*."

Susannah said it with prim force, and it almost knocked Julia back. Women all over England would do anything to take Susannah's place—to be beautiful, young, and wealthy enough to attract a man with a title and estate. Dash it all, Julia herself would have happily traded spots with her stepsister a few months earlier. Even if that meant being related to Constance by blood.

"Oh." That was all Julia could think to say.

"All anyone here wishes to discuss is the weather, money, or one another. They think of music as something to listen to politely after dinner. There's no passion in any of them."

Julia had never heard her stepsister speak so forcefully before.

"Well, the pianoforte is a desirable skill for a young lady," she said.

"But I don't want to merely play as a *diversion*. There are conservatories on the Continent I could attend if I'd the freedom to do so."

Susannah's point was obvious: if she remained unmarried.

"You truly don't want to marry, do you?" Julia felt amazed. How could she not have known this about Susannah?

"Not now. Not before I've tried for something more with my life." Susannah sighed deeply. "But Mamma would faint if she heard me speak this way."

Of course Susannah's dream wasn't the same as Julia's. They were entirely different women, after all, but that didn't make the girl's desire any less worthy than Julia's had been.

"Let's get through tonight, and then we can discuss these conservatories. Do they even allow women?" Julia asked.

"Some do. There's one in Vienna, I believe." Susannah squeezed Julia's hand. "Oh, do you mean that? Would you take my side against Mamma?"

"Darling, you must know me well enough to realize I'd do almost anything to get a rise out of Constance."

Susannah laughed. "Tell me the truth. Do you think it would be a horrible mistake, giving up the certainty of marriage?"

"For me, it's the oddest thing in the world. But you aren't me, dearest, which is one of the reasons I like you so much." Julia patted her stepsister's arm.

"But you like being married, don't you?"

These last few weeks had been among the happiest of Julia's life. Even all the sadness of parting from Gregory didn't change that fact.

"It depends on the person, I suppose. If I'd

married Lord Cheltham, I believe my life would be quite different today." Julia glanced across the ballroom at the rest of "good" society and realized how damnably bored she was of all of them. "I'd rather you risk never marrying if it means finding the life that makes you truly happy. Marriage itself is as risky as any other proposition."

"Thank you, Julia."

Susannah looked soft with relief when a handsome young man came over to ask her for a dance. Julia watched the girl sail around the ballroom floor, attracting admiring eyes from every direction.

How strange life could be. A few months ago, she'd have told Susannah she was a fool to give up security in favor of the potential for happiness. Now, Julia knew better. She herself had married for safety, and she had found herself in the most wretched place imaginable: painfully in love with a man who could not love her in return. In many ways, life as a spinster had been safer than this.

It was far better to always wonder what you were missing. Having it and then losing it was the worst pain of all.

"I doubt Susannah will vanish if you take your eyes off of her."

Julia suppressed a shiver of longing as Gregory stopped at her side.

"When it comes to men, I think it's always better to remain vigilant."

"We're men, my dear, not lions on the savannah."

"Oh, I think it an apt metaphor. After all, I've read that male lions prefer to laze about all day while the lionesses do the hunting."

"Yes, but male lions have those impeccable manes to look after. You can't blame a man for being fastidious about his grooming."

She did love trading light verbal blows with him, as she loved being in his arms and underneath him in bed. The thought of his naked skin pressed against hers sent a spike of deep desire rippling throughout her body. Julia wished the night would never end; that way, he would always be with her.

"We seem to be playing our parts to perfection." Her husband regarded the rest of the ballroom with a satisfied eye. "The idle gossip has all but disappeared."

"I believe a dance should eradicate the last traces of scandal," Julia said.

"Is it not rather uncouth for a man to dance with his own wife?" Gregory made a mockery of sounding appalled.

"Only if he's in love with her."

Julia wasn't sure how that blurted out of her mouth, but she waited in frozen horror to see Gregory's reaction.

"Yes. That would be a pretty story, wouldn't it?" he said quietly.

Julia wrestled down her disappointment, trying to ignore the brief sting of tears. She'd told herself this same thing over and over, that he did not feel the same as she. He liked her, as he liked making love to her, but passion was not the same thing as romance or affection. She must not start blubbering now. Honestly, of all the things to weep over.

"Then let's give this story a thoroughly happy ending, shall we?" she asked as the music finished and the dancers applauded. "I believe the waltz is next."

Gregory did not speak, merely offered his hand and took hers. Julia's mention of love had pretty neatly killed the cheerful mood between them. Her own damn fault, that. Her husband escorted her to the floor, whispers trailing after them as the entire *ton* watched with rapt attention.

Julia realized with some shock that they had never waltzed together before. Gregory was a splendid dancer, but he did not enjoy it much. Their dances in full view of society were rare indeed, so this would prove a delicious treat for all assembled.

For Julia as well.

The music played, and Gregory swept her about the room with the utmost masculine ease and grace. Julia had never felt as light as when her husband guided her in a waltz, just as she had never felt so desirable as when his eyes were upon her face. Indeed, as they turned in time to the lilting music, she felt the intense heat of his fixation upon her.

"You're staring, Your Grace."

"I'm hardly alone in that. Every other man in this room is spellbound by you." He held her as close against him as he might dare in public. Julia's heart quickened with his nearness.

"We need to discuss our next steps. Now that you're not sailing for Spain tomorrow, that is."

"I've already arranged it with Peele," he said. "You shall be leaving tomorrow morning for Lynton Park."

"Oh." She was stunned by the simple declaration. "Won't that attract attention as well?"

"It's quite simple, really. You leave to oversee the estate while I remain in town a few extra days, seeing to our affairs. I'll leave early next week, ostensibly headed for home."

"Ah. But in secret you'll be off on your own journey." Julia found she didn't wish to be held quite so tightly any longer.

"It accomplishes what we need. Your leaving immediately after the Season to see to our estate is only to be expected. No one will pay attention to what I do once I've left London. Finally, we can put this whole charade behind us."

Julia had wanted to believe that there was a secret reason for her husband's pulling away. That some undiscovered pain had erupted, driving a wedge between them. That most of all, she could coax him toward her with enough time and energy.

But she saw now the idiocy of her own beliefs. From the first moment to the last, Gregory had seen their marriage as a charade, a ruse, as something useful. He'd enjoyed her, but had not wanted to risk the pain that a longer association would inevitably bring him. Their union had never been anything more to him; Julia herself had been the fool for creating this fantasy.

She'd allowed herself to believe the fairy tale was real.

"I'm starting to wish you'd been on your way directly after our union at Lynton Park." She wished she could simply walk away from him in the middle of the dance, but they were trapped in this ridiculous position until the musicians had finished. She was trapped looking like a fool to him, and most of all to herself. How could she have been such a bloody idiot? "Then you'd have been safely on the Continent, and we would never have needed to continue this farce in front of all London."

"Forgive me for being honest, my dear." There was no mockery in his voice or expression; rather, Gregory appeared exhausted by the recent events. "But I thought you the type of woman who appreciated honesty."

I thought so, too, would be a foolish thing to say, so she bit her tongue. Finally, mercifully, the dance was over. Julia remained calm as her husband escorted her back to the side of the room. The instant it was permissible, she walked away from him.

"Julia. Wait."

He had her by the wrist, and she turned into him. They could not cause a scene here.

"I need some air," she whispered. "Alone."

This time, he didn't pursue her. Julia walked leisurely until she exited onto the terrace. Thank God she was alone here, with the rest of the partygoers chattering away inside the ballroom. Julia stood before the stone railing and turned her face to the moonlight. She sucked in deep lungfuls of breath, trying to get her reeling thoughts into order.

Julia shut her eyes and fought against the urge to wail, or scream, or go back inside and kick someone in the shin. Preferably either Campbell or her husband. Julia was not a terribly choosy person.

She hung her head, the grief starting to gnaw at her. She had to let him go, then. There was no other way. She'd clung to the hope that this misalignment between them was down to a stubborn misunderstanding, but Julia realized that no misunderstanding had ever existed. The truth was plain, and always had been.

He didn't want her the way she needed him, and it tore her apart inside.

Julia was so entwined in her own misery, she scarcely noticed movement in the garden below. At first she thought it some ill-advised lovers playing with ruin before the eyes of all society. As she turned to go back inside, she heard a soft voice say one word:

"No."

Julia froze and looked back as the woman who'd spoken vanished into a hedge maze, a tall man in quick pursuit.

Julia recognized the man at once, and she would have known the woman's voice even if she hadn't spied the golden gown.

Lucas Campbell was in hot pursuit of Susannah.

CHAPTER TWENTY-SIX

Gregory didn't hear a word any of the partygoers said to him as he circled the ballroom, desperate for the clock to strike midnight so he could leave. Julia had all but begged for him to say he loved her, and in his weakness he'd nearly capitulated. But that would only have made her cling tighter to him than before, and then he could never leave. Leaving was essential to his plan. He had to protect her. He had to safeguard his own sanity.

"You seem to be without your Cinderella, Ashworth."

Huntington emerged from out of the crowd as multiple young ladies' heads turned in the wake of his passage. The duke had donned a version of a huntsman costume, though most rugged hunters did not wear capes of rich green velvet. More was the pity for them.

"And you're without your…whatever you are," Gregory replied.

"The woodsman from that story with the red-hooded girl."

"Interesting choice. Surprised you didn't elect to be someone's perfect prince." There were loads of princes in fairy stories, after all. Gregory thought that in the world of a fairy tale, a prince was more common than a really good baker, and far less necessary.

"There are plenty of wolves here tonight, both

in and out of costume," the duke drawled. "I prefer to keep the most despicable members of the *ton* nervous."

Gregory laughed as they watched the dancers turn about the ballroom. Huntington was a rare one, a man of high rank and wealth who despised society almost as much as Gregory himself did. If Julia were here, she'd be delighted by the duke's observations and probably make a few pointed ones of her own. But she was off with Susannah, probably, taking some air and wrestling her disappointment with the man she'd married.

"I know Percy already spoke with you," Huntington said.

"Then you know nothing will change my mind."

"Men like us are raised by society to be careless of what we own." The other duke charged valiantly ahead, nevertheless. "With good reason; almost everything we possess can be replicated again. A house can burn down, or a horse can die, and another can be bought or built. We can purchase more land, and we can all but pay to have any wife of our choosing delivered to us."

"Yes. Wealth does increase feminine ardor, in my experience," Gregory said. Now he wanted to get away from talking to his friend and find something more pleasant to do. Like drinking himself into oblivion.

"But you can't buy the love of an excellent woman." Huntington's gaze was particularly cutting. "Once you lose that, you may never find it again."

"Worry about finding and losing your own duchess, friend. My affairs are mine alone."

The two dukes had been at school and university together, and over the years Gregory had borne witness to Huntington's especially charmed life. His parents' marriage had been filled with love and joy, and they had lavished affection upon their son and his two sisters. The old duke's death seven years past had been painful for his friend, but Gregory saw the inheritance of a substantial dukedom as serious compensation. Even with all these gifts, Huntington preferred to remain aloof and uncatchable. He'd marry when he chose, probably to a woman of grace and beauty who loved him as he loved her.

Huntington, like Percy, had good intentions but no comprehension of the real issues at play. Even though Huntington knew of Gregory's struggles with his family, he'd never truly understand.

"You really are a damnably stubborn ass." Huntington sounded testy. "I've half a mind to call you to a duel this instant, just to shock some sense into you."

"Never threaten a duel in idleness, Hunt. Wait until you've a lovely young bride and I've debauched her. You'll be grateful you saved calling me out for just such a moment."

"Perhaps you need to be bashed around the ears a few times," Huntington growled. Gregory walked away, not caring a toss if it was rude or not. He stalked through the party, temples throbbing as he considered finding Julia and planting himself at her side for the rest of the night. At least then his friends wouldn't come up one by one to berate him for his failings as a husband. They'd too much tact for that, and Gregory had long believed that only fools valued tact.

"Oh! Your Grace?" A woman halted in front of him so suddenly that Gregory nearly bashed into her.

"May I help you?" He didn't know the lady for a moment, as she'd donned the most purple wig he'd ever seen. She was also outfitted in a pale lavender gown with a pair of bright gossamer wings attached. Within a moment, however, he recognized her as Lady Beaumont. As if the night hadn't been painful already. "I see. Playing the Fairy Godmother tonight, are we, my lady? Forgive me for saying so, but supernatural benefactor never seemed to be your role in this particular tale." But Lady Beaumont wasn't in the mood for his jests.

"Please. I need help locating my Susannah. It seems she's escaped from the ballroom; she really is the most headstrong girl." Lady Beaumont tittered, but the quick flap of her fan and the strain in her voice belied how confident she sounded. "I'm not concerned, you understand, only I do know how society loves to gossip. I should hate for her reputation to be in any way tarnished."

"Of course." Gregory smirked. "Then you wouldn't be able to use the girl as a grappling hook to climb the very pinnacles of society."

Lady Beaumont appeared horrified, the first truly authentic reaction Gregory had ever seen from her.

"We may not get on well, Your Grace, but I hope you don't think me the sort of mother who wants to see her daughter shunned and mocked. Susannah's a terribly gentle soul; it would wound her to her very core."

The woman might be a brittle fool, but Gregory couldn't deny that she loved Susannah. Gregory sighed, feeling a bit caddish now.

"Perhaps your daughter is with my wife. They are so close, after all," he said.

"The duchess is gone, too." Lady Beaumont's irritation was growing more pronounced.

"Then I should think they are together."

"Find her. Please, Your Grace? Please find Susannah." Lady Beaumont fluttered her fan so quickly it was a miracle she didn't knock herself back with a heavy gust of wind.

"Very well, madam. I'll do so at once."

He bowed and made a hasty departure. As Gregory prowled along the corners of the ballroom, searching everyone in the crowd, a rather unpleasant idea began to itch at the back of his brain. He surveyed the sea of faces once more, looking for a particular man. He didn't know what costume Mr. Campbell would be wearing, but Gregory doubted he'd have trouble recognizing the fellow. When you disliked someone so fiercely, you always seemed to know them at once.

Campbell wasn't present, either.

While there was no real connection to make between these three absences, Gregory began to grow suspicious. His instincts were nearly as good as his wits, and he had the awful feeling that something unpleasant was occurring. He did not allow his emotions to show. Instead, he made his way out of the ballroom as discreetly as possible.

• • •

Julia's damned shoes kept almost slipping from her feet as she dashed outside. Music floated on the wind overhead as she stole toward the queen's gardens, her ears pricked for the slightest noise. She couldn't very well go bashing around yelling for Susannah or Campbell. If anyone heard her calling for one or, God forbid, both of them, Susannah's reputation would be shredded in a matter of seconds.

Thankfully, no one else was about as Julia hunted through the mazes of the hedgerows. Most of the flower buds were closed up for the night, sleeping softly beneath the moon. They saw nothing that went on; if only the rest of the *ton* operated on the same principle.

Julia was about to make her way back to where she'd started when she heard a soft gasp nearby.

"Stop! Stop! I-I'll call for someone."

It was Susannah's voice, and despite its gentleness Julia could hear the panic laden within it. Even at her most volatile and angry, Susannah could never become truly threatening. She was too sweet for this viper's pit of a society.

Julia's heart knocked hard against her ribs. If anyone were to come this way, Susannah's reputation would be gone in an instant.

Julia had no time to find a polite, quiet way

around the dense row of bushes placed directly before her. She pushed through the vines, thankful that nothing caught at or ripped her frock.

Susannah gave a soft cry of despair as Julia appeared. The girl was caught in Campbell's arms, and he'd pinned her against his body. Julia's stepsister clearly did not welcome these advances. If anything, she was fighting the bastard off as valiantly as possible. She shoved against his shoulders, but couldn't break free from his grip. One of the cap sleeves of her gown slipped down her arm, and her carefully arranged hair had begun to come apart in tangles about her face.

"Oh. You," Campbell said, his triumphant smile vanishing when he realized the interloper was Julia instead of some random member of society.

"Julia!" Susannah gasped tearfully, finally breaking from Campbell's grip. Julia gathered the girl to her, and felt Susannah trembling in her embrace.

"What did you do to her, you bastard?" Julia snapped. All propriety was slipping away, and she didn't care. She'd swear at this terrible man all she wished, and then she might call him out to a duel on the spot. If he refused, Julia was more than happy to take one of Gregory's pistols and go after the man anyway. So what if she were hanged? So what if women didn't do that sort of thing? How dare he assault her stepsister's innocence like this?

"I've done nothing to Miss Fletcher. Not yet, at any rate." Campbell sounded utterly bored by her presence. "Come now, Julia. There's no ill intent here."

"That seems the opposite of what I saw." Julia kept a sharp lookout. Now that she was here Susannah was a bit safer, but if they were all discovered the gossip would still be too delicious. To save Susannah, she had to get the girl away from this man. Quickly.

"He followed me outside. He wouldn't stop hounding me." Susannah gulped, trying to stabilize her voice. "Then when I thought I'd lost him, he came out of nowhere and tried to…"

The poor girl couldn't bring herself to finish that sentence, but Julia more than understood.

"Was it not enough that you nearly ruined my life? Did you have to attempt to destroy Susannah's, too?"

"Any ruination would have been swift. She only needed to be compromised enough that she'd agree to a hasty marriage. Once we were wed, the *ton* would not have cared about premarital indiscretions."

"Except that she does not and never will love you! When I think you couldn't disgust me more, somehow you find a way."

Campbell never lost his infuriating smirk, though his shoulders tightened. Julia was aggravating him, something she loved to do to terrible men. But more than her own fate hung in the balance now.

"I need to marry an heiress," he said.

"Then find one!"

"But none of the other debutantes are as

beautiful or rich as Miss Fletcher. Besides which, none of them are related to you, Julia."

"And is that so important? You have to hound a woman who doesn't want you merely to tweak my nose?" Julia was astonished at the insipid pettiness of this man's mind.

"You'll have to suffer an indignity every time you imagine Susannah in my arms. I assure you, that will be a sheer delight for me to envision."

Julia's stomach curdled, revolted at the thought of Campbell taking Susannah. She hoped her disgust was evident beneath the moonlight.

"She's safe from you now," Julia snapped. "I'm taking her away."

"I'm afraid I can't allow that."

Susannah gasped as Campbell circled around them, blocking their exit. He was too large a man for Julia to successfully skirt past, especially if she had Susannah to look after.

"Then I shall scream!"

"Do it. I would like that very much, indeed."

"I'll tell them you've assaulted her. Frightened both of us! You'll be turned away from every respectable door in town." But Julia felt that her threats had no real weight behind them.

"That may be true, but it is also true that your stepsister will be compromised by the scandal. She will be an unmarriageable pariah as well."

"I can live with that!" Susannah said, but Julia paused. She was older and more world-wearied than her stepsister. Susannah said right now that marriage did not appeal to her, but Julia wanted her to have every option in the world. One stupid moment when she was eighteen shouldn't have a huge effect on the rest of her life, but it would if Julia did not protect her.

"You understand." Campbell smiled at Julia's evident frustration. "Enough with these pretenses."

"Yes. Enough, indeed."

Julia released Susannah and stepped toward Campbell with as much dignity as she could muster. Her stepsister cried out in horror at Julia's seeming acquiescence to the man.

"So? No screaming?" Campbell grinned with his mockery. Julia imagined he delighted at having her meek and broken before him. But she would do anything at all to protect Susannah, and the girl could not be found here with a man in such a disheveled state.

"I shan't scream, and neither will my stepsister."

"Good."

Julia peeked up at the man from beneath her eyelashes, a particularly feminine move that often worked in the novels she read. It seemed that the authors of garish romance knew their business; fire sparked in Campbell's gaze.

"I must admit, I was disappointed when I learned you had no fortune," he said to her. "I should have liked a wedding night with you."

"I've learned much since marrying," Julia admitted. "Including those spots most sensitive upon the male body."

Julia had always been a tall woman, and was now properly glad of the fact as she kicked upward and connected her slippered foot to the center of Lucas Campbell's trousers. She could not see much of his face in the semi-darkness, but what she did observe appeared twisted with agony. He bent over, breathing heavily, but then lunged at her. Julia kicked at him once again.

And this time, the glass slipper left her foot and went flying off into the darkness.

"Susannah! Go!" she hissed. Her petrified stepsister finally sprang into action and hurried off into the hedgerows. Julia could only hope the girl would have enough sense to stop and make herself presentable before she calmly returned to the party, but already her fears had lessened. Susannah would be safe now.

Unfortunately, Julia had to make her own escape while missing a shoe. There was no time to hunt for it as Lucas Campbell straightened himself and came at her like some furious bull.

"You damnable bitch! I *will* have satisfaction."

And to think, she'd once considered him a gentleman. Julia evaded him and hurried away.

"I believe you've had enough satisfaction for one night," she said over her shoulder. Julia realized that she'd become disheveled in their tussle, and began to furtively pat at her hair and tug at her clothes.

She stopped dead when a man appeared before her out of the garden.

"Julia." Gregory didn't seem horrified or furious, merely astonished to find her here. She winced as she heard Campbell come around the corner, knowing he'd be red-faced and excitable.

She had no doubt what conclusions her husband would draw from this. "What on earth is going on?"

She could tell him what had transpired. He might even believe her. But it wouldn't stop that little voice of self-congratulation he harbored. The part of him that would take this whole, awful ordeal as further proof that their marriage should end in all but name.

There was no way to fight against his certainty. With a frustrated cry, Julia simply rushed past him and out of the garden. She crossed the lawn, hoping she wouldn't be seen so that she could order the carriage and go. The duchess left behind both the men who'd broken her heart.

A fitting end to the false fairy tale, indeed.

CHAPTER TWENTY-SEVEN

I believe you've had enough satisfaction for one night. Gregory had caught those words clearly as his wife hurtled around the corner of the hedgerow. He'd found her in a rumpled state, her cheeks flushed with feeling, her hair wild from the hands of another. Without offering an explanation, the woman had gone past him with a wail, disappearing into the night.

In every way, she and Campbell made the perfect scene of a romantic tryst thwarted.

Except that Gregory knew his wife well enough to understand that she'd never run away in shame from a bad situation. Julia would stand her ground against anyone. She'd left in visible disgust. With him? Very likely.

But Gregory doubted that he was the only man who'd offended her tonight.

"What the devil were you doing to my wife?" he asked Campbell.

"Oh? Are you certain that's the question?" The odious man smirked as Gregory approached. "Perhaps you should consider what the duchess has done to me."

"If she boxed you around the ears, I'm sure it's no less than you deserved."

Campbell didn't enjoy the suggestion that a woman had bested him.

"You might ask yourself what a lovely creature

like Julia was doing alone with me in the gardens. We can only snatch a few moments here and there." Campbell gave a dry laugh. "Undoubtedly, she'll insist that I dragged her here, but that woman needs no encouragement to follow after me."

"The Duchess of Ashworth."

"Pardon?"

"You shall address my wife by her title, Campbell, or at least by Her Grace. If you do not, I shall enjoy the distinct pleasure of taking you apart piece by piece."

Not many in London had ever seen Gregory truly angry. Unlike most men, he didn't roar or swagger about when he was furious, puffing himself up in an attempt to appear impressive. He became quieter, and much more still. It was the instinct of a predator to conserve all energy possible when going in for the kill.

Campbell noticed the shift and grew distinctly nervous. Wonderful.

"Fine. Then you might return this to *the Duchess of Ashworth*." The man snagged something from the ground and proffered it to Gregory. Moonlight sparkled on shapes of glass. Julia's slipper. "We became so animated that she left without this."

"I'd sooner believe my wife lost it in a struggle trying to avoid you."

"Oh, I believe the *ton* will see it all my way." Campbell sneered, his anger rising as Gregory refused to be manipulated. "How the fairy story will be tarnished when they learn the Duchess of

Ashworth dallied with another man during the queen's ball. Shame will hang heavy over both your heads."

"Be careful what you threaten," Gregory growled.

"It is no threat. No one need learn of my escapade with Her Grace tonight. That is, so long as a financial arrangement can be made between us two men."

"My money will buy my wife's reputation. Is that it?" Gregory smiled, calm as ever. "Blackmail. What a charmingly common weapon of choice."

"Nothing common about it." Campbell practically spat the words. Apparently, the great seducer of women hated to have his pride poked at all. "There's no way to ensure my silence otherwise."

"Oh, there is. If I silenced you on the other end of a dueling field, for example."

"What?"

Gregory moved with expert speed and surety and clobbered Lucas Campbell across his left jaw. The other man dropped Julia's slipper with the shock. He staggered back a few steps, then came at Gregory with a muffled roar. Such boorish behavior matched the beast that he truly was.

Campbell was not a soft member of the idle elite. He knew how to shift his weight in a fight and how to jab, but Gregory had been involved in more than a few brawls during his time. He'd never fought with too much vigor before; after all, it wasn't like he had a reputation worth saving.

But this wasn't about him. It was for Julia.

He struck Campbell, ducked so that a blow

sailed over his head, and then gave a short, sharp jab to the other man's midsection. Campbell coughed and spluttered with the wind knocked out of him, sinking to the ground and bending over as Gregory stood above him.

"If you're threatening my wife's good name, then I must have satisfaction. We meet upon Hampstead Heath at dawn. We shall settle this as gentlemen."

"Y-You can't. Dueling's illegal," Campbell gasped.

"Believe me." Gregory smirked. "I've mastered the ins and outs of most illegal matters. Finagling one final duel shouldn't be too difficult." Gregory snagged Campbell by his lapels and pulled the bastard to his feet. The coward quailed as Gregory brought their gazes level. "My wife's honor is my business, you putrid sack of shit. If you've debauched her and are threatening to ruin her, there won't be a place in this country you can hide. You won't be able to evade me on the Continent, either. It doesn't matter if you go to Madrid or all the way to Moscow. I'll hunt you down, find you, and put a bullet through your small, shriveled heart."

"I didn't debauch her!" Campbell's voice was shrill with fear. Apparently, Gregory looked rather frightening at the moment. "I swear on my life I never touched her like that."

"Then what, pray tell, were you doing out here?"

"I was courting her stepsister." Campbell gave a furious cry as Gregory struck him, sending him to lie upon the grass.

"Courting? I doubt that very much."

"Fine. I was attempting to entrap the girl into marriage. Is that what you wished to hear?" Campbell managed to get to his feet and kept a careful distance from the duke, whose every current thought was bent toward bloody murder.

"Julia discovered you," Gregory said.

"She got the girl away from here and kicked me in the damn balls. She was leaving as you arrived. I didn't harm Miss Fletcher or the duchess. That means there's no need for a duel."

"Oh, but I think there still might be ample need. After all, a bastard like you would happily tell pretty lies to good society. It would be no trouble to invent all sorts of scandalous scenarios and whisper them into the *ton*'s collective ear."

"Never. I swear it." Campbell appeared a bit dewy with nervous sweat. How unappetizing.

"Allow me some certainty." Gregory stepped toward the other man, relishing it when Campbell almost fell down in terror. "By morning, I want you out of London and back to wherever you come from. If I learn that you're still in town, I shall pay you a visit and drag you to the dueling field if I must. If I learn that you have spoken to anyone about what transpired tonight, I'll follow wherever you run and force satisfaction."

"You'll be hanged!"

"It would be a trade of my life for my wife's honor. It's a bargain I'd gladly make."

He meant every word of it. So long as Julia lived a long and happy life, he would be satisfied.

He was leaving the woman he loved tomorrow so that she could find the peace she was so richly owed. Dueling some piece of pig shit in a nice suit was a small price to guarantee that tranquility.

"You're a madman," Campbell said.

Of course Gregory was mad. He was in love.

"Leave the ball now, leave town, and I shall never feel the need to call upon you. But if I see you in London ever again, you will rue the carriage that brought you to the city. Do you understand?"

Campbell glowered, but he did not protest or try to fight. He was too much of a weasel to stand against Gregory. He valued his own worthless hide over anything else. Truly, a pathetic fool.

"I shall accept your terms, Your Grace." Campbell gave a stiff and mocking bow. "But what assurance have I that you'll keep to your end of the bargain?"

"I have no wish to bring scandal upon the woman I love. I will protect her from any harm, which is something you would never do."

Fuck, but Gregory realized with a sudden flash of clarity the truth of his own words. He loved Julia. He'd known it for ages, of course, but he had not considered everything he'd been willing to throw away for her sake. His own life? Without question. His fortune, his reputation, everything that made him what he was? He'd do without any and all of it to protect her.

And he realized something else, as Lucas Campbell skulked away into the night. Gregory realized that he could not be away from her.

It wasn't only that he needed to protect her. He needed to hear her voice, be in her presence, look upon her face in order to keep his own sanity. A lifetime without her was misery, but he'd accept that misery if it was what she wanted.

But she didn't want it, did she? She'd told him over and over, but like a blasted fool he'd refused to listen, too wrapped up in his own idiotic certainty. For Gregory's entire life, he'd run from the possibility of love because he was too shattered by his own inadequacies.

But Julia loved him despite all of it, didn't she? Somehow, he had managed to win her heart, and then he'd run from her at the first sign of challenge.

Even after that colossal disappointment, she still seemed to care for him. Perhaps there was a path forward for them, because Gregory knew that he would never find contentment in this world without her at his side. If Julia could love a flawed, broken man, perhaps there was hope.

Gregory used to laugh at the insipid concept of hope, but he had changed. Julia had changed him.

He forgot about Campbell entirely after that, and returned to the party. He hunted through the crowd for his Cinderella, but the silver-and-diamond vision of her did not appear.

"It's almost midnight, Ashworth. Where's Her Grace?" someone asked, and it was all Gregory could do not to punch the bastard flat-out for interrupting his search.

Yes, midnight. Gregory swore inwardly. He and Julia would be expected to be present, the center of attention, but she seemed to have taken her cue early and run away. Cinderella was supposed to wait until the stroke of midnight.

But Julia never did what she was told, another thing he loved about her.

"Oh, bugger everyone," Gregory muttered. If the queen had him thrown out of England for ruining the climax of her big event, Gregory would accept his exile. Unfortunately, as he made his way for the exit the bells began striking the midnight hour. The partygoers noticed Gregory and formed a wall about him, trapping him within a circle. As the last bell tolled, he stood there with his wife's shoe in his hand and felt the baffled stares of all London high society on his body. Including, from her perch upon a nearby red velvet dais, the queen herself. Her Majesty fluttered a fan and lifted a plucked eyebrow, silently demanding that Gregory explain this botched finale.

Fuck. How was he to negotiate his way out of this one? Gregory stared at Julia's shoe and had the flash of an idea.

"Ladies and gentlemen, you must excuse me," the duke said. He lifted the glass slipper into the air so all could see it. "My Cinderella ran away before the end of the ball, leaving only this behind as a clue. I must see it safely returned to her."

Gregory could not have achieved a more perfect Cinderella moment if he'd tried. The queen smiled, nodding to him in congratulation. Laughter and wild applause chased him out of the ballroom. He made his way to the palace's entrance, where he learned that his wife had already summoned their carriage and left for home.

Her shoe in hand, Gregory returned to Carter House. His mind kept flooding with everything that he wished to say to her, with ideas on how to say it, with how to prove to her his own idiocy over Campbell had ended. Gregory's heart lightened as he made his way to the front door. Julia might be put out now, but when he revealed that he was leaving neither London nor her, he believed she'd soften.

"Peele. Where's Her Grace?" Gregory asked as the butler allowed him inside.

"Beg pardon, Your Grace. The duchess is gone." Peele appeared green as he extended an envelope to Gregory. "She asked I give you this."

Head buzzing, glass slipper still in hand, Gregory ripped open the envelope and read the letter.

Gregory,
Forgive me for my stubbornness. I see now you were in the right, and that our union is too fraught with conflict to ever be truly happy. Susannah has no wish to return home, so I have taken her with me to Lynton Park. You are free to travel the Continent and find the peace you crave. I hope you will pardon me for not giving you my decision in person. Forgive me, too, for missing the end of the ball. At least now our charade is well and truly done.
Julia

Gregory did not curse or crumple the paper into a ball or drop the letter. Her words had left him too numb for any kind of reaction. He merely walked silently upstairs, noting the family portrait on his way.

Tonight, it seemed as though his parents were smiling at him in vindication.

CHAPTER TWENTY-EIGHT

"Julia, you're not paying attention!" Susannah said.

"Hmm? Of course I am." Julia sat up straighter on the picnic blanket, cursing her wandering mind. "Everything Felicity did is simply splendid."

"Thank you, Your Grace!" Felicity giggled as she stood before Julia, her shoes and stockings gone, covered in mud from head to toe. Well, Julia wasn't sure exactly when she'd done *that*. "Then I may go back to the creek and conduct another experiment? Miss Winslow says that I must stop work on the toad catapult, but I felt certain you'd agree that it is important for science."

"Aha. Perhaps it's not good for a little girl to work so very hard. Why don't you go inside and wash up, dear? The sun will be going down soon."

"It's only three o'clock!"

"Time flies. Off you go."

Felicity grumbled as she went to Miss Winslow's side and walked back with the governess. Susannah nibbled another biscuit in thoughtful silence as Julia looked up. Buttery afternoon sunlight streamed through the tree branches, dappling the soft earth around them. She and Susannah had been at Lynton Park for three days now, and it had been a heavenly time. Susannah had adored Felicity at once, and Miss Winslow made for a delightful companion. The three women had a wonderful time wandering the grounds with Felicity frolicking ahead, or having interesting discussions over dinner. After all the anxiety of the London Season, absconding to a secluded haven felt like paradise.

But of course, one glaring omission remained. Every night when Julia went to bed, she laid in the dark all alone and stared at the ceiling. Should she write another letter? Should she send word to Gregory in London?

Julia cursed her stupidity at writing that first idiotic note just before leaving Carter House. But she'd been right to do it. Hadn't she?

"You must talk to me," Susannah said.

"I'm sorry I haven't been myself, darling. I suppose I'm tired after a few strange months." Julia began packing their things into the wicker picnic hamper, eager to return to the house. She usually would love nothing more than a chat with her stepsister, but Susannah often wanted to discuss Gregory when it was the two of them together.

"Julia." The girl gripped the napkins, refusing to let her put them away. "I've thanked you numerous times for bringing me here. It was so kind of you."

"Yes. And it's rankled Constance a good deal. Everyone gets what they want."

"But why hasn't the duke arrived yet? The Season's quite done."

"Ashworth is traveling the Continent. I've told you before, his plans have been fixed for some time. This was our arrangement from the start."

"But you don't want it to be. Do you?"

Sometimes, Susannah could be dreadfully perceptive. Julia elected to forget the napkins and stood with the basket.

"Do bring the blanket, please." She then strode away, resigned to Susannah's ongoing questions. Her stepsister took up the blanket and followed.

"I still don't understand what's happened between the two of you."

"Nothing's happened," Julia said. Nothing and everything all at once. Julia's head was sensible, and she knew it was good that Gregory was absent. That didn't stop her from rising every morning and looking out the bedroom window, trying to see as far down the winding road of their estate as possible. Searching for the sign of a carriage, or Gregory on horseback.

But nothing ever changed.

"Perhaps I'm truly better off never marrying, if this is what awaits me." Susannah sounded cross, which was unusual for her. "It doesn't matter how beautiful your home or grounds are if you have to be alone with them."

"I've you and Felicity and Miss Winslow. That's quite enough company for me."

"But Felicity will grow up, and Miss Winslow will find another position, and I'll leave."

"For where? Beaumont House, for life as a spinster with Constance. Believe me, darling, that's a wretched fate."

"I could take my dowry and live comfortably off it abroad," Susannah muttered. They both knew the truth, though. Susannah's father had it in his will that she would not have control over her finances until she either married or turned thirty-five. If Susannah elected for spinsterhood, she would be relying upon Constance's charity for a long time yet to come.

"There's nothing wrong with a marriage of convenience. You're still young and have romantic ideas about life, but when you reach my age you understand that no one can have everything."

Julia had almost possessed everything she'd ever dreamed of, but in the end she'd run away from it and left a note telling it not to follow her. That was right, though. Wasn't it? To pull away first in order to keep from being wounded? Gregory had taught her that much.

"Oh, stop lying, Julia. You're sitting here utterly miserable, and you won't even admit it to yourself."

Susannah had never been this angry with her before.

"Do whatever you want with your life, my love. I think it best for all women to decide their own happiness. But leave me to mine."

With that, Julia sped up and returned to the house ahead of her stepsister. She remained in the library until supper, which turned out to have been a mistake. She could not pick out a book and read even one page without Gregory's face appearing before her. Besides which, sitting in the library reminded Julia of all the heated trysts they'd enjoyed here.

Would she ever find peace on her own again?

Miss Winslow and Susannah talked amiably throughout dinner, but Julia didn't hear much of it. She was not a naturally quiet or dour person, but she found she'd no energy for discussion or laughter.

Soon after their meal, Susannah retired to the music room by herself. Julia and Miss Winslow sat in the parlor, listening quietly as the sounds of Bach floated toward them from over the halls.

"Miss Fletcher has a great talent," Miss Winslow observed. She sipped a glass of sherry and watched Julia.

"What?" It took Julia a moment to return to herself and comprehend the words. "Oh. Yes, she's a genius at the pianoforte."

"The former duchess was a true proficient, so I've been told."

"By whom?"

"Mrs. Sheffield and other members of staff. Mrs. Sheffield in particular recalls the days when the old duke was still alive. This house was filled with visitors throughout the year. The Duchess of Ashworth's musical salons were considered a great treat by the *ton*."

"Ashworth never mentioned such things," Julia said. Odd, because such events seemed like the thing he'd relish most.

"The current duke would have no memory of them, according to the housekeeper. She told me that His Grace did not spend much time with his parents."

"Well. He would have been at school from a young age," Julia said.

"It's not just that. I'm told that His Grace was on his own quite a bit from the time he was born.

He once went a solid eighteen months without laying eyes upon either his mother or his father."

Miss Winslow explained everything with her customary soft, easy voice, but Julia couldn't help feeling that the governess took great interest in her smallest reaction.

"Typical for the child of a duke, isn't it?" But Julia didn't believe her own words. Even the most elite of parents spent an hour or so a day with their children, usually for tea or directly after dinner. "They had him home for holidays when he was at school. Surely."

"Not according to Mrs. Sheffield."

Good Lord, had Gregory's parents truly been so barbarous? Julia knew for herself how wonderful her husband could be, how brilliant and formidable and joyous. He must have been the same as a child, at least a little. How could any decent mother fail to take interest in such a boy? How could any good father not feel tremendous pride?

What kind of damage could such neglect do to a young child? Come to think of it, why was Miss Winslow going into such detail?

"You're being forthcoming tonight," she said to the governess.

"In truth, Your Grace, the staff asked if I would reveal some of the unsavory details to you." Miss Winslow lowered her eyes in quiet deference.

"Why?"

"Because they care very deeply for their master, as they've come to care for you, Your Grace." Miss Winslow studied her folded hands. "I confess,

I feel the same. We want for the two of you to be happy."

"I don't need to be manipulated by my own servants." Julia winced as soon as the words had passed her lips. She sounded like one of those society dames who believed servants and tradespeople were beneath her. Bloody hell, she sounded like Constance. "Excuse me, Miss Winslow. I apologize. I've been tired."

"You needn't ever apologize to me, Your Grace. Forgive my bluntness. It's only that Mrs. Sheffield and I are quite in agreement that you and His Grace are two of the most exceptional employers in England." A faint smile twisted the governess's lips. "I've known my share, believe me. If people such as yourself and the duke cannot be happy, then I doubt happiness is possible for any of us."

Julia considered again how the usually contained governess became red-cheeked and nervous whenever Huntington came to visit. Yes. Everyone wanted to believe in a fairy tale, didn't they?

"But I still don't fully understand why you've told me these horrid stories about His Grace," she said.

"We're all products of the people who've loved us, ma'am. At least, that's my opinion on the matter. We're also formed by the people who *didn't* love us. Sometimes it makes us hard, or heedless, but I don't believe anyone's ever finished becoming themselves. If that makes any sense."

It did, somehow. Gregory's parents and their

cruelty had scarred the boy. The boy had grown into a man who didn't know how to love, or even worse, did not believe himself capable of being loved.

Such a man would believe only the worst of people.

Such a man would also believe anyone who told him that he was unlovable or too broken.

Which Julia herself had done when she wrote that blasted note. She hadn't given him a chance after the discovered moment in the garden with Campbell. Even if he could never love her the way she loved him, perhaps she could make him trust her again. Perhaps she could assure him that he was more than enough.

"Thank you, Miss Winslow. This has been an illuminating evening." Julia rose to her feet, her stomach fluttering with nerves but an unshakeable lightness inside her as well. For the first time in days, weeks, perhaps her entire life, she knew what she needed to do and exactly what she wanted.

Julia went to her room and rang for a servant. She then gave instructions to prepare a carriage first thing in the morning. They were to make a trip to London.

Hopefully, her husband would still be there.

The next morning, Julia hugged her stepsister and Felicity, bade farewell to Miss Winslow and the servants, and rode in her carriage out of Lynton Park. She clenched and unclenched her gloved fists, already eager for the long journey to be done as they bumped along the road. She wished she could fall asleep right now and awaken as soon as the carriage pulled into Grosvenor Square. Sitting by herself for these long hours would be unbearable.

Would Gregory be waiting for her in London? Would he even listen to her when she tried to explain? Could he forgive her?

Julia's temples throbbed and her breath caught in her throat. Tears burned in the corners of her eyes.

She loved him. That was why she'd been restless and miserable these past few days. She loved her husband more than anything on this earth. She wanted only to find herself in his arms, to feel his lips upon hers, to hear the rumble of his laughter, and if he believed himself too broken to be loved, or her too unfeeling to love him properly, Julia would work however long it took to convince him that they were better together than apart.

If it took the rest of her life, she'd do it.

In the early afternoon, they needed to stop and rest the horses for a bit. There was an inn where Julia could find a meal and a few hours of respite. If the horses and driver hadn't needed a rest, she'd have gladly pushed on. As it was, she hoped the inn did a nice mutton stew. Love and nervousness had left her famished.

The innkeeper was a jovial man, thrilled by Julia's fine carriage and clothes. He showed her to a smaller room, reserved for only the best clientele, he said. There was only one other person in the dining room, a man with his back to her. Julia barely glanced around as she took her seat, hungry as she was.

"Would Her Grace care for something to drink?" the man asked. Julia would be expected to maintain the illusion of feminine delicacy, but she'd never been much good at lying.

"The best ale that you have," she replied. If the innkeeper was shocked by her unladylike taste, he said nothing. The man went about his business, leaving Julia alone at her table. She worried the fingertips of her gloves, rehearsing over and over what she would say when she met with Gregory again. How she'd fall into his arms, urge him to speak with her, ask him to forgive her. She'd also probably scold him for not coming after her himself; Julia would never be fully rid of the combative aspect of her nature.

The innkeeper returned with her ale, and she ordered a bowl of stew.

"Very good, Yer Grace." The man gave another little bow, then looked to the secretive traveler at the back. "Anything else for you, sir?"

"The lady has the right idea," a richly familiar voice drawled. "Ale for me as well."

Julia froze, nearly spilling her ale as Gregory stood up behind her. Her mouth went dry as the innkeeper left and her husband made his way over to her.

"The Duchess of Ashworth. What an unexpected surprise," he said.

Julia looked up into his face, still the most handsome she had ever seen in her life, or ever hoped to see. His gray eyes did not flash now, and his full, sensuous mouth did not lift in any hint of amusement. Her husband regarded her with a close, rather cold level of inspection.

"Gregory," she breathed. "Whatever are you doing here?"

The duke took the seat opposite hers.

"I was making for Lynton Park, but that trip seems unnecessary now," he said. "The fact is, I came to find you."

"Yes." Julia felt dizzy. "And why is that?"

"Because I wished to return this to you."

He reached into his coat pocket and pulled out a shoe.

CHAPTER TWENTY-NINE

Damn everything, she was beautiful. Gregory had mentally prepared himself as he rattled down the road to Lynton Park, making a vow that he'd approach her with sense and subtlety. After reading her note, he'd spent a full day struggling to forget her, but then had realized that he couldn't walk away. He'd seduce her, delight her, pleasure and thrill her until she came to realize that he was serious. He wanted to stay with her, always. He'd been the fool, not Julia.

Now here she was, on the road to London. When he'd heard her musical voice speaking with the innkeeper, Gregory had frozen in his seat. He'd hoped violently that Julia was on the road traveling east for the same reason he was headed west.

But if she weren't coming to see him, if his presence merely bothered her, he knew he wouldn't be able to stand it. So he approached her with cold caution. Gregory had never before given anyone the power to hurt him like this woman could with the slightest word or gesture.

But God, she was beautiful. After being parted from her a mere three days, Gregory became entranced by her lips and eyes all over again. His trousers tightened with the simple thought of the sensuous body that lay hidden beneath her clothes. Even her faint lilac scent was enough to get him hard.

If he couldn't have this woman, life was scarce worth anything. But he would not come on too strong. Fear of rejection had held sway over his life so far, and he would be a master of his fears and himself.

But when she'd asked him why he should come looking for her, Gregory knew he could not play this as carefully as he wished. With Julia, nothing was safe. That was what made her so irresistible.

Gregory pulled out the glass slipper she'd lost at the queen's ball and offered it to her. His wife did not take it.

"Oh. You found it," was all she said.

"You might be a touch more impressed. I've traveled a great distance to return it to you." He could not seem to resist teasing her. The indignant flush upon her cheeks always highlighted her beauty.

"Well. One glass slipper seems like a lavish but pointless gift." She finally took it, though.

"Indeed. One glass slipper would be a most ostentatious and ridiculous object," Gregory replied. "However, I came to reunite it with its mate. I believe *two* such ridiculous objects become something quite wonderful when paired together."

Julia's breath hitched. Her lips parted, and her eyes softened with wonder. Fuck, Gregory could have shouted in triumph. What he read on his wife's face was pure relief.

"I agree that two are better than one." She cleared her throat. "Shoes, that is."

Gregory knew that both he and his wife were the sort of people to hide their feelings out of an instinct for survival. So now he dared, with everything he was or had, as he took her hands into his.

"You'll find people pair together very nicely, too."

"Gregory." That was all she said, only his name, but it was the sweetest sound from human lips he'd heard.

"I came to see you because I've been a damned fool," he growled. "I should have known you would never debase yourself with someone like Campbell. I should have trusted in you."

"I should have been more patient with you," Julia whispered. "Miss Winslow told me about your parents."

He stiffened and wanted on instinct to pull away from her, but his wife held on too tightly.

"The past makes no difference," he said.

"It makes every difference. They allowed you to believe that you were not enough to be loved, but you're so much more than they could possibly imagine. You're brilliant, and wonderfully alive. You're strong, but there's a tenderness in you no one else can match." Damn everything, the woman allowed a few tears to streak down her face and didn't attempt to hide. He'd never seen Julia this open before. "When she told me what you'd endured, all I could think of was that awful note I'd left for you. I had to find you and tell you to forget all that, if you can, and to forgive me."

"Forgive you for what? For putting up with my theatrics and flaws?" Gregory could feel the blood pulsing at every point in his body. He bent his head and pressed his lips to the palm of his wife's hand. Julia gave a soft moan at that slight touch; she wanted him, as he wanted her. How could a man like him have earned this luck? How could he ever let her go again?

The answer was simple: he never would. He would spend his life making this woman so excessively happy she'd never dream of leaving.

"I could have talked with you after the ball." She stroked his cheek with her other hand, her every word and gesture gentle with love. He doubted that Julia had ever allowed another person to see her as open and vulnerable before. She had given him the rarest gift of all: herself, and her love. He would be a bloody fool if he fouled this up.

"I'd refused to speak honestly with you for days. Why should you have tried again after that? I'm afraid you'll have to accept that I'm the fool here, Julia."

That old, mischievous flame seemed to ignite in her, which delighted him. Gregory needed her fire as much as he craved her sweet acceptance. Those contradictions were what made Julia herself, and he desired every bit of her.

"I assure you, sir, that I'm every bit as capable as you are of being foolish."

"Oh, I don't doubt it. In fact, this is the rare circumstance where *I* have acted the greater fool. You must allow me to savor this unusual achievement."

"To think I'd yearned to see you again." But

the corners of her mouth twitched as Julia attempted to suppress all of her glee.

"I yearned to see you, my lady. To touch you." Gregory leaned nearer, becoming lost in the intoxicating closeness of her. "To taste you once more."

The front of his trousers strained against his burgeoning excitement, and Gregory believed he'd lose his damn mind if they didn't procure a room this instant. He could not wait to return to Lynton Park in order to claim her.

"Er. Beggin' your pardon," the innkeeper said. The man stood before their table, a foaming mug of ale in one hand, a bowl of stew in the other. "Would you be needin' anything else, Yer Grace?"

"My wife and I wondered if you'd be so kind as to arrange a room for us?" Gregory said.

The innkeeper set the food down, blustered something between agreement and apology, and hurried out to do just that.

"My lord, you shall scandalize the man," Julia teased. "He must know exactly what we have in mind to do."

"Oh? Then he has an impressive imagination." Gregory smiled. "I have some truly scandalous ideas."

• • •

Moments later, he and Julia were secured in their own room with the door locked and the windows shut tight. Gregory's instinct was to grab the woman and throw her to the bed in his passion, but he wanted to linger. He wanted to drive her wild with anticipation, to need him with the same desperation he needed her.

Julia moaned when he kissed her, and kissed him back with equal strength. He held his wife's wrists when she began to undo his cravat. Gregory's whole body was burning with expectation, but he would take his bloody time.

"I've been in agony for three days," he hissed. He pressed Julia's body to his, allowing her to feel the straining excitement of his manhood. Soft tendrils of her golden hair had already come undone, and she sighed with anticipation as he slid an arm tightly around her waist. Gregory kissed her neck and whispered in her ear. "If I don't fuck you now, I'll die."

"I couldn't have that on my conscience." But Julia's attempt at levity crumbled as her mouth found his once more. Gregory traced his hands from her shoulders to the small of her back to the plump swell of her ass. Julia sounded undone as he unfastened one button, then another.

"I'm afraid you'll have to do without the comforts of a lady's maid this afternoon," he said.

"You've proven yourself very adept at undressing me."

"Hmm. Excellent point. We might fire your maid and save the twenty pounds a year."

"Gregory, my love?" She kissed him with aching sweetness. "Do be quiet."

"I shall be silent, so long as you are quite vocal."

With those words, he let Julia's gown fall from her shoulders to pile on the floor. His wife's chest rose and fell with excitement, her breasts quivering. They were held up beautifully by her stays, and it seemed to Gregory almost a shame to spoil the picture. But then again, she was even more lovely when naked.

A splendid dilemma, indeed.

Julia's whole being shivered as he loosed her stays and removed her petticoats, leaving her in only the slip of her chemise and her stockings. Gregory was so hard by now he might pass out before he had her fully undressed.

As if reading his thoughts, Julia spoke up.

"Don't tease me now. If I don't have you inside of me soon, I shall run mad."

"You've missed me, then?" He slipped one strap of the chemise from her shoulder. The garment hung low, revealing the sumptuous orb of her breast. Gregory cupped her naked breast, eyeing her pink nipple as it hardened beneath his touch. Julia leaned back in his embrace as he put his lips to her body, his tongue circling round and round her areola. "You missed this, Julia."

"I was miserable without this. Without you."

Despite everything, the tumult of their absurd courtship, the uncertain movements of their marriage, she was miserable without him.

"You love me, then?"

He did not mean to speak the words, especially not with that amount of urgent need. Gregory allowed her to lift his face and hold it in her hands.

"I love you beyond words and reason," Julia whispered. "And for me, that is something extraordinary."

"Yes. Well. You yourself are something extraordinary, madam." Gregory could not believe this. Every wish he'd harbored since he first laid eyes upon this woman had been actualized. Beyond words or reason, she loved him. "I love you, Julia. More than I believed I could love anyone or anything."

She said nothing else after that, but the whimpers and moans she gave as he continued to undress her stimulated him all on their own. Soon, she was naked and in his arms.

"Allow me. Please," she murmured as she tugged at his cravat once more.

"Quick, if you like. I want to be inside of you," he growled.

He shed his clothing with Julia's help, and then lay atop her in the vastness of the inn's bed. Julia arched her back, moving beneath him in a silent plea. Gregory couldn't stand it any longer; he'd burst if he didn't take her. He kissed her deeply, savoring the groan she gave when he slid into her. Julia was wet for him already, her body so welcoming to his.

Gregory whispered her name over and over, all other thoughts and words having fled as he moved. Her body melded with his, and her groans of satisfaction sped him to greater heights.

"I can't lose myself so soon," he rasped. Gregory clutched at the headboard, timing his thrusts so that he did not go out of control. Beneath him, Julia writhed in mounting ecstasy as he drove her nearer to her peak.

"We have all the time we need." Her mouth

formed a delectable *O* as her end hastened. "You can lose yourself in me again, my love. And again."

And again, and once more after that if he had the stamina, and he would. Gregory felt her release, the silken ripple of her body around his as Julia came with a great, euphoric cry. He tried to keep up his pace, not wanting their first coupling of this reunion over so swiftly, but he couldn't manage such stoicism. Gregory finished, this time inside of his wife, spilling within her as he unburdened himself fully. He lay atop her then, his lips in her hair, feeling the bird-like patter of her heart as it began to slow.

"We should spend the night here. It will be dark soon," Julia said.

Gregory frowned. "It's barely two o'clock."

"Well. Time flies."

She made an excellent point. Throughout the rest of that afternoon and well into the evening, the time sped by.

EPILOGUE

The Marquess of Kerrick was in the habit of spitting up right after his nap, but Julia knew she couldn't hold it against him. After all, the marquess was a mere year old today and was quite beautifully behaved for someone that age.

Julia held her son as she stood in the back gardens of Lynton Park, watching the other children frolicking. Felicity was overjoyed by Daphne and Joseph, Laura's twin children, and the dear little toddlers loved to caper after the older girl. They fell down in the mud an awful lot, but thankfully the Weatherfords believed that dirt created character.

"You should be walking soon," Julia said to her son. Arthur beamed gummily up at her and gave a happy shriek. He also wriggled in her arms; he was a first-rate wriggler. "You'll be difficult to catch, I can tell."

"I'll have to tie a bell around him," Miss Winslow said, laughing as she approached. "There was a rambunctious cat at my old school who wore one. It helped to keep track of all the mischief he got into."

"Comparing the next Duke of Ashworth to a troublesome feline?" Julia thought about it. "Given his parentage, that's fair."

Miss Winslow took a turn with the infant, gazing at him with sheer delight. Having another child around meant the governess would still be with them for a good while, which Julia appreciated. While her son and heir babbled and blew spit bubbles, Julia went to see to the party.

Laura and her twins had come, as had Susannah, Percy, and the Duke of Huntington. Even Constance was here, seated beneath a tree and watching the festivities with an only slightly judgmental eye. For her, it was a stark improvement. Since the near disaster with Lucas Campbell, Constance had sheepishly acknowledged that Julia had been right. She might even have apologized, at least somewhat. Perhaps Julia and her stepmother would never be the best of friends, but at least the animosity between them had ceased. Mostly. Constance and Laura sat and watched as Susannah, Percy, and Huntington engaged in a spirited game of lawn bowling.

"Who's winning?" Julia asked as she approached.

"I wouldn't have believed it, but Miss Fletcher has stomped all over the pair of us," Percy said.

"I'm not shocked by it at all," Huntington laughed. "Miss Fletcher has an admirable form."

"Oh, it's only because I've had practice." Susannah's cheeks were full of color, and her eyes sparkled as she bowled another excellent point. Julia joined the men in applause.

Susannah had spent much of the past two years at Lynton Park. While Constance would not allow the girl to travel to the Continent for further musical training, Julia had hired a tutor from one of the most esteemed schools in Vienna. The Park had resounded with music daily for much of the last two years, and Susannah had become a true proficient. The tutor, a Herr Gruber, told Julia that Susannah showed a spark of genius.

A spark that, Julia noted, the Duke of Huntington had begun to appreciate. The past few days he'd been at Lynton Park, he'd spent a great deal of time speaking and laughing with Susannah, and appreciating her playing.

Constance would be only too delighted by such a development. Indeed, she seemed to be watching the pair of them with hawklike curiosity now. Hopefully, she wouldn't swoop.

"Do finish up your game soon. The host will be back momentarily, and then the picnic can truly commence," Julia said, fighting back laughter.

Julia left the partygoers and walked over to Miss Winslow in order to collect her son. Who should she find with the governess, Arthur already in hand, but Gregory himself?

"Your timing's impeccable." Julia was secretly glad when Miss Winslow went to fetch Felicity. She craved every moment she could get alone with her husband. The past two years, every day had been a delight, every evening a paradise. Nothing gladdened Julia's heart, though, like the sight of Gregory holding their son.

When she'd become pregnant, the duke had been afraid that he would prove to be a terrible father as his own had been. But he needn't have worried, because her husband was as natural a father as he was a husband. In Julia's eyes, he was damn near perfect.

"Timing is an important skill." Gregory kissed Arthur's head and returned the boy to his mother. The child had fallen into a sound sleep. "A skill this one should learn. To fall asleep at his own birthday party? The height of rudeness."

Gregory's teasing words stopped when her lips met his. Every time Julia kissed or embraced her husband, the world around them seemed to fall silent. Only Arthur's sleepy squirming as he awoke could break the spell.

"He's a good little chap, isn't he?" Gregory pinched the baby's cheek.

"Like his father." Julia smiled.

"Ah, but willful like his mother. I'd have it no other way."

"I believe we make splendid parents, don't you?"

"I'll never miss out on an opportunity to praise myself. Or you." Gregory kissed her once more, causing Julia's toes to curl within her slippers. The man was delectable.

"Then you shouldn't mind doing this all over again?" she asked slyly. It took Gregory a moment to work out her meaning.

"Julia." His eyes seemed to glow with excitement. "Are you…?"

"Three months along. The doctor called yesterday when you were out." Julia knew it was too early to feel the baby kicking or doing anything, but she still took Gregory's hand and placed it upon her stomach. He stared at her like a man caught in a dream. "Which would you prefer? Girl or boy?"

"I'd like to order one of each."

"I'm afraid that much is out of my hands."

"Then a girl. One who'll shake this whole place up a bit, much like her mother."

Arthur blew a raspberry, seeming to happily concur with the idea.

"Most men wouldn't wish for a troublesome female, my love." Julia walked toward the party with her husband and son, Gregory's arm around her waist.

"Most men are idiots," the duke growled. His lips found her neck for one scintillating instant. "A troublesome woman makes for a happy home."

ACKNOWLEDGEMENTS

Major thanks to Liz Pelletier and Lydia Sharp for their brilliant editorial eyes. I'm so lucky to have landed at Entangled and to be publishing my debut here! Thank you for taking a chance on me. Thank you to everyone at Entangled for all their hard work, including Bree Archer, Jessica Turner, Curtis Svehlak, Elizabeth Stokes, Heather Riccio, and Riki Cleveland. You've all made this the most amazing journey!

Thank you to my incredible agent, Rebecca Friedman, who is one of the truest friends I've ever had and who works tirelessly for me and for my books. Thanks also to Abby Schulman and Brandie Coonis for their help and support.

Thank you to my amazing friends and family. Thank you to John, Colleen, Kodiak, and Erika for sticking with me through the good and bad times. Most of all, thank you to the readers and reviewers who make these books possible in the first place! I hope you enjoy.

*London's most successful matchmaker is
about to break the biggest rule of all...*

THE
DUKE'S
RULES OF
ENGAGEMENT

USA TODAY BESTSELLING AUTHOR
JENNIFER HAYMORE

Joanna Porter is in love with love. As one of London's most promising matchmakers, it's her job to ensure her clients are blissfully happy. Now Jo's about to make the match of the season—*if* she secures the "perfect duchess" for the handsome and irritatingly stubborn Duke of Crestmont. Surely it can't be *that* difficult...

If the Duke of Crestmont doesn't produce an heir soon, his dukedom will fall to his loathsome uncle. Step one? Acquire the perfect duchess. Which is where his new matchmaker comes in. If he wasn't so distracted by the opinionated, infuriating, and utterly kissable Jo—who is more carriage saleswoman than duchess—he might be able to focus on the perfectly eligible young ladies Jo parades before him...

Jo is not immune. She needs to match the duke—not fall in love with him. And yet, here she is. But a romance between them would ruin her reputation, her business, and the support she provides her family...not to mention exposing the secret that would push her past ruin straight into pure devastation.

Shakespeare meets Bridgerton *in this witty and lively marriage-of-*inconvenience *romance.*

USA TODAY BESTSELLING AUTHOR
EVA DEVON

As far as William Easton—the Duke of Blackheath—is concerned, love can go to the devil. Why would a man need passion when he has wealth, a stately home, and work to occupy his mind? But no one warned him that a fiery and frustratingly strong-willed activist like Lady Beatrice Haven could find a way to get under his skin...and that he might enjoy it.

Lady Beatrice is determined to never marry. Ever. She would much rather fight for the rights of women and provoke the darkly handsome Duke of Blackheath, even if he does claim to be forward-thinking. After all, dukes—even gorgeous ones—are the enemy. So why does she feel such enjoyment from their heated exchanges?

But everything changes when Beatrice finds herself suddenly without fortune, a husband, or even a home. Now her future depends on the very man who sets her blood boiling. Because in order to protect his esteemed rival, the Duke of Blackheath has asked for Beatrice's hand, inviting his once-enemy into his home...*and* his bed.